WHA
SECRE**IS** OF THE
DEATH SHIP?

Deep in the void it lurked, a mysterious giant of metal, shaped into a vessel so vast it was beyond belief. And the fate of those who saw it? They died! But the fabulous inner treasures and fantastic technological secrets of this massive, dead spaceship were thought to be worth incalculable wealth, and an alliance of space salvagers would take nearly any risk to lay first claim on her—even at the cost of their lives.

This terrific Edmond Hamilton tale is a true forgotten gem, filled with the kind of action and intrigue that made him one of the most beloved science fiction authors of the 20th Century.

FOR A COMPLETE SECOND NOVEL, TURN TO PAGE 73

CAST OF CHARACTERS

ROSS FARREL
He stumbled upon the biggest deep space find of the century—and he would probably end up getting killed because of it.

TOLTI
She was just a kid, a runaway in the Martian wilderness—but without her, Farrel's life wasn't worth a plugged nickel.

VICTOR
He was Farrel's pal and partner in the biggest outer space salvage job in history. But could he be trusted?

WHITMER
Cool, calm, and collected. He knew what he wanted and he went after it—regardless of whose lives he ruined.

OLD CROY
This crusty old space dog was set in his ways, but his experience and outer space savvy were invaluable.

LEACH
Of course he was in it for the money—but this brutish thug's real pleasure came from inflicting punishment and torture.

BENSON
All he really cared about was money. And he wouldn't mind taking a few innocent lives if it meant garnering a fortune.

THE SHIP FROM INFINITY

By
EDMOND HAMILTON

ARMCHAIR FICTION
PO Box 4369, Medford, Oregon   97501-0168

*For more information about Armchair Books and products, visit our
website at…*

www.armchairfiction.com

Or email us at…

armchairfiction@yahoo.com

CHAPTER ONE

IT WAS BLACK where Farrel was, and cold, and there was nothing above him or below him or on either side but stars, infinitely distant. They watched him while he spun slowly on his own axis, waiting for him to fall and die. But he could not fall. There was no place to fall to. Pluto was a black marble lost in the night. Sol was a fleck of fire no bigger than a match-flame. So he hung, and turned, and felt the whole size of the universe pressing against the frail shell of his armor, star upon star, galaxy piled on galaxy, without end.

Suddenly there was a shadow across the stars.

Heyerman's voice burst from his helmet-phone. "Look at the size of it! My God. I never believed—"

And Victor's voice—screaming, hysterical. "Get moving! Get moving, now, or we'll never catch it—"

And it came on. Swift. Silent. Lightless. Rushing without sound, black through blackness, ancient and huge, barnacled with stellar debris. It was true—no hand of man had ever helped build the vastness of this vessel, and no mind of man had ever dreamed its course outward from—where? God knew.

Hurry, screamed Victor. Hurry, hurry. Hit the propulsion unit and be for a moment a tiny comet, trailing flame across the dark. One, two, three little fiery comets converging, and now there was a place to fall to, an iron plain rushing up, up, up beneath his feet, miles long, a mile broad, blotting out the gulf, hiding the stars, and there was a sign on it, a big queer sign that seemed to say, *Stay a while, for I am Death.* Then they were inside the mighty bulk, in dark and sudden glare. Heyerman said, in a faint reproachful voice, "They must have known I was coming." And then Heyerman was in his arms, and Heyerman was dead—

Stay a while, the ripple saith. Stay a while, for I am Death. Far away the ripple sped, ripple, ripple, running red.

Ripple. Rip. Ship.

The Ship.

The Ship.

5

THE SHIP FROM INFINITY

by

Edmond Hamilton

ROSS FARREL SPRANG up on the narrow bunk. He was sweating and shaking violently. His eyes were wide open, but it was several minutes before the black and monstrous dream dispersed and let the flat gray wall of the detention cell come into focus. With trembling hands he found a cigarette and lighted it and sat huddled up over his knees, sucking in the smoke.

The Ship. How often he had dreamed of it. And the remembered reality was still worse than any dream.

Stay a while, for I am Death.

Silly, how that line from Kipling had got bound up with the nightmare. Maybe not, though, when you thought about it. The crocodile lurking under the waters of the ford, The Ship lurking in the fathomless gulf beyond Pluto, both of them unseen and

6

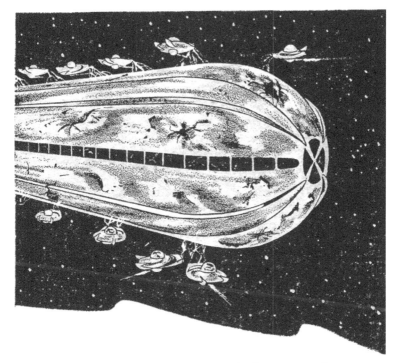

Deep in the void it lurked, a mysterious giant of metal shaped into a vessel so vast it was beyond belief. And those who saw it—died!

insatiable, dragging humans down to death. For more than a century now the legend of The Ship had tempted men out beyond the limits of the Solar System and the capabilities of their craft. Few of them ever came back. The ones that did had either failed to find the dark wanderer, or else had glimpsed it only at a distance, big as a planet almost, they said, but beyond their reach and going fast. Their stories were so fantastic that only other fools believed them.

"But the stories were true," thought Farrel. "And we found The Ship, Heyerman, Victor and me, and old Croy who stayed in our own *Farhope* and hung on tight so the damned Ship wouldn't run away with us."

And it was strange. Unutterably strange. No legend had ever done justice to that huge and enigmatic derelict. They had found their way inside and wandered for a little while in the vast and soundless spaces—whatever sort of air had once been in The Ship it was long gone now—the beams of their torches cutting thin across the enigmatic dark. And it was like walking in a dead city— a city never inhabited by men.

"Where do you suppose it came from?" Victor had said, over and over, and Heyerman had answered:

"From some other star, that's for sure. Something must have happened to it, an accident, maybe a meteor—something like that, and it never got where it started for. It just drifted until our solar system picked it up and it fell into a permanent orbit."

Farrel remembered feeling a warm personal pride through the overwhelming awe and wonder. It had been his calculation of The Ship's orbit, based on a collation of all the sightings since the first one plus some ideas of his own, that had made it possible for them to get within striking distance of it.

And now they had found it they were afraid. Victor kept figuring out loud how much The Ship and what was in it would be worth split four ways—as legal salvage it belonged to them if they could tow it in—but even a healthful greed was not enough to dispel their mounting uneasiness. It was too dark and big and still in there, and the shapes picked out by their torch-beams were too alien and queer. They wanted ground under the hull and a familiar sun overhead, and lots of light before they explored too much.

They were on their way out when they found the big cabin with the curious instruments in it, things like large dark crystalline eggs cushioned in a padded rack. And Victor said, "Hey, let's take a couple of these along for souvenirs."

Rather gingerly Farrel picked one up and put it in his suit pouch. Victor was more choosy. He discarded the first one and picked up another that looked better to him. Heyerman, meanwhile, had looked beyond the rack and said,

"Now, what the devil is that?"

That, Farrel remembered, was a branching crystalline shape, grotesquely formed, gigantic, set in a sort of bracing network of coils so that it hung free like an elephantine spider. Heyerman went toward it. It glittered with a weird magnificence where his torch-beam touched it.

"It might be like—well, a sacred symbol, you know," Victor had said, obviously awed by its shining.

"Sacred or not," said Heyerman, "it looks like the great-granddaddy of all precious stones to me. I wonder if I could get a chip—"

FARREL REMEMBERED that he had opened his mouth to say, "Don't." Now he had said it, but it was too late. Heyerman had already tapped the end of a thin crystal branch with the specimen hammer from his belt. There was a wild blue flare of light, absolutely blinding. Then a moment of chaos, where no effort of memory could bring anything clear. Then Heyerman limp and heavy in his arms, saying, "They must have known I was coming." Heyerman with the air steaming in little icy clouds from the rents in his armor, ripped open by the shock.

Heyerman very quickly dead, in the most familiar and most dreadful way common to spacemen, his unprotected and-unpressured flesh bursting apart from its own internal force. And the crystal hanging in its coiling web, unchanged except that now it was in motion, lurching back and forth in a kind of ponderous dance, as though it was pleased at what it had done.

They had fled in blind panic down the dark immensity of The Ship, leaving the shreds of Heyerman behind, not from callousness but because there was nothing else to do. They had made their way outside again to that broad whale-like back with the lumped and pitted debris on it, and then from there to *Farhope*, riding behind now on a magnetic beam, a ridiculously tiny shape.

Later when they had recovered a little from the awe and shock, they tried the next step—breaking the black monster out of its orbit so they could take it in tow. They might as well have tried towing Pluto.

"*Farhope's* a good salvage tug," Croy had said, "but it'll take her and a dozen like her to bring that brute in."

So they had been forced to leave the richest prize in the System behind. They came back, trying to figure out how to get the equipment they needed without giving away their secret and losing

The Ship to some ruthless and better-outfitted rival. And on Ganymede old Croy had become too engrossed in discussing the problem of salvaging a hypothetical very big ship with another salvage man, and trouble had started almost at once.

Someone was suspicious. Someone was greedy. Someone wanted to find out exactly how much they knew about The Ship.

They had decided to split up and get lost for a while. Croy took the *Farhope* and ran for the Asteroids. Farrel and Victor came by commercial liner to Mars. Victor had some connections there and they figured they could hide out in the backblocks. It had worked fine—for about two Martian weeks. Then men from the Special Police, an auxiliary arm of Earth authority in the Department of Planetary Affairs, whose power had been known to grow in direct ratio to its distance from the watchful eye of its superiors at Earth Central, came and arrested Ross Farrel on suspicion of homicide. When he asked who he was supposed to have killed, they said Heyerman. Later they had extended the charge to cover the missing Croy. Now Victor was missing too. He had been out when the police came. He had not come back.

And Farrel looked bleakly at the pale Martian sunlight that shone through the small window, laying a pattern of steel mesh on the opposite wall. It was morning again, the sixth morning since he had been brought here. He had had his nice comfortable four hours' sleep. In a few minutes the questioning would begin again.

He had managed to hold out so far. But he knew it was only a question of time. It made him mad. It made him so mad that he was determined to let them kill him before he talked. Because he knew that they knew damn well he had never killed Heyerman or anyone else. Nobody had come right out and mentioned The Ship, but they didn't have to.

It was inevitable, Farrel supposed. When you have got your paws even precariously on something worth anywhere from a couple of million bucks on up, somebody is bound to want to take it away from you. It did not make the spot he was in any pleasanter.

The cell door clanked open. The guard—one of three armed guards, so as not to take any chances—nodded to him and said,

"Okay, Farrel, on your feet. Whitmer's waiting."

CHAPTER TWO

AND IT WENT on and on. Only today it was worse. Today they were really opening up on him.

"What happened to Heyerman?"

"I told you."

"Tell us again."

Go carefully now and remember the lie, "We were outside the hull of our tug, making repairs. He tore his suit."

"What kind of repairs?"

Remember now. What the devil kind of repairs, what did I say before? "I—"

The big hard hand ringing off one side of his head and then off the other. That was Leach. Acting Captain Leach of the Earth Special Police force attached to the Sub-Administrator's office for B Sector, Southeast. Leach with the thick muscles and the corded neck and the wind-reddened skin.

"Don't stall, Farrel. What repairs?"

"Detector scope."

"You said aerial before."

"What difference does it make? He—"

Whack. Whack. Stars and darkness, a taste of blood, and anger. There was a man on each side of him, holding his arms. Beyond Leach was Whitmer, sitting quietly on the corner of his desk, smoking. Whitmer was tall and neat and well built. His dark blue Coverall was immaculate. His face was intelligent, interested, and perfectly impersonal. He did not seem to enjoy the beating Farrel was taking. Neither was he upset by it. Whitmer was the Sub-Administrator. He was a civilian official chiefly concerned with government. There was no reason why he should be personally interested in what ought to have been a purely police matter, a routine inquiry about a missing man.

But he was personally interested, and the inquiry was in no way routine. That was how Farrel knew they were lying. They didn't give a damn about Heyerman. They wanted The Ship. Somebody on Ganymede must have contacted Whitmer, and now Whitmer and Leach were framing him for a mythical murder, hoping to force him to talk.

"If it was an accident," Leach was saying, "why didn't you bring his body back?"

"What body?" said Farrel. "Did you ever see what happens to a man when he tears his armor?"

"Where's your accomplice?"

"My what?"

"Victor. He helped you, didn't he? You planned it together, didn't you?"

"I don't know."

"You don't know whether you planned Heyerman's murder together? Come now, Farrel."

"Heyerman wasn't murdered."

"Then why doesn't your pal Victor come in and corroborate your story?"

Farrel looked with heavy hate at Leach and then beyond him to Whitmer.

"I guess," said Farrel, "he knows what he'd get if he did."

Leach's wind-burned face reddened further. He clipped Farrel again, snapping his head back, cutting his lip.

"We'll get him. We'll get Croy, too. Then we'll have the whole story, so you might as well talk. Come on, Farrel. Talk."

Farrel told him where he could go.

Leach sighed and set his shoulders.

"Okay, we'll do it the hard way. What was your course? What was your destination? Did you pick up any salvage? Did you think you were going to? Or were you just roaming around? Come on...answer me. What was your approximate position when you went outside with Heyerman? Did you hear me, Farrel? Did you hear me? Answer!"

It went on for a long time. Part of that time things were pretty vague. Then again they would get very clear. Then he would want to kill Leach. Whitmer, too. The neat, intelligent Whitmer, who sat and smoked, moving from time to time just to ease his backside.

There was once when Farrel came up out of the dark just in time to hear Leach say, "You can let go of him. He's out cold," The hands that had been holding his arms went away. It took a while for that to penetrate Farrel's brain. In the meantime he sat slumped in the chair with his eyes shut. As long as they thought he was out they'd leave him alone.

Leach was talking to Whitmer. "We're going to have to find some other way. This isn't going to work."

Whitmer spoke from a long way off, a man coolly pondering a problem, "Well, we can try the solitary cell for a while. And if that doesn't loosen him up—we'll think of something."

Leach laughed.

FARREL opened his eyes a slit. The first thing he saw was Leach's gun. Leach was standing with his back to him, and the gun holstered low on Leach's stocky hip was almost within his reach.

He didn't stop to think about it.

He lurched forward and grabbed.

And it was as easy as that.

He jammed the blunt muzzle of the high-powered discharge pistol into Leach's spine and told him to stand still, and he stood still. He told the two men who had been holding him and who were now getting a rest and a cigarette to sit still, and they sat still. Whitmer got up, but that was all he did.

"Everybody," said Farrel, breathing hard, "Everybody be careful or I'll kill him."

He jabbed the gun hard into Leach's back, and Leach said, "Yeah. Take it easy."

Farrel began to move toward the door, one step at a time, taking Leach with him.

Whitmer, said, "You won't get away with it. We have all the weight on our side."

Farrel didn't answer him. When he reached the door he put his free hand behind him and opened it and then he planted his foot in the small of Leach's back and kicked him with all the anger he had in him, and it was plenty. Leach flew forward and sprawled on the floor, and Farrel went swiftly through the door and locked it from the outside.

There was nobody in the corridor. Probably they did not want too many witnesses to what they were doing. Farrel ran. The sergeant in charge of the desk was in his cubbyhole office. He stuck his head out and yelled after Farrel had gone by, but it was too late then. Farrel was outside.

Two jeeps and an armored personnel carrier with balloon wheels were in the parking area, and a 'copter drooped like a roosting chicken off to one side. The whole jail and headquarters plant was no more than one small building set against a thousand miles of rust-red nothing, except where the Martian town of Khartach lifted a few ruined towers against the horizon at one end of a line of hills. There were only half a dozen men permanently quartered here. Whitmer and Leach had flown in from New Chicago, the Earth capital of Sector B, Southeast, over two hundred miles away.

Farrel leaped into the nearest jeep, started it, and went roaring away across the desert, trailing a great plume of red dust.

Within not too many minutes, when he looked back, he saw that another plume of dust had been born and was following rapidly after him. The personnel carrier, he thought. It mounted a couple of guns. He estimated the range, the relative speed of the two vehicles, and the distance that still separated him from the hills. He thought he might just make it.

Then he heard the heavy distant roar of the 'copter starting up. Oh, Lord, he thought, that does it. I can't possibly beat a 'copter. He rammed the accelerator in as far as it would go. The jeep flew wildly over the uneven desert, rocking and slipping. Farrel hurt all over. He felt sick and dizzy, but he hung onto the wheel, and behind him the 'copter choked and banged and died. It started again, and died again. This was not an unusual thing on Mars for any machine with a motor. The all-pervading, always blowing, omnipresent dust could filter through the best seals ever made.

"Let there be a lot of dust in her," Farrel prayed. "Let her fuel lines be solid with it." The hills were getting closer. The personnel carrier was not gaining. If the 'copter would just give him a few more minutes—

The motor caught. He could hear the sound, made small by the increasing distance. It ran, but roughly. He glanced back, and they had not tried to take off. He sobbed and hunched his body forward over the wheel, urging the jeep along.

HE ran it half way up a dry canyon before he realized that he was where he wanted to go. The canyon twisted, removing him momentarily from the view of the men in the personnel carrier. He stopped the jeep, took the two canteens from their clips on its side, and jumped out. He saw what looked like a way up the cliff. He began frantically to climb it.

The personnel carrier could not come into the canyon because of its balloon wheels, which did not do well on sharp rock. By the time the men from it found the jeep Farrel was out of sight in the tumbled mass of wind-eroded, time-shattered rock. They hunted for him until dark, but Farrel eluded them easily, lying still in the shadowed pockets or creeping swiftly through holes and tunnels. He did not know the hills intimately, but neither did they. And he wanted more passionately to stay free than they wanted to catch him. The 'copter joined in the search just a little later than the men, buzzing sullenly up and down the ridges, but he was careful and they didn't see him. When the long shadows flowed out over the desert and thickened into night, and the stars came out, Farrel peered from a crevice in the rock and saw the lights of the jeep and the personnel carrier journeying away. The sky was quiet. Then he drank up a large part of his water, and slept.

When he woke again both moons were in the sky and the desert was a great rumpled sheet of tarnished silver. It was cold and very still, so still that you could hear the thin wind rubbing and whining at the rock and making the grains of dust fall down. Farrel descended to the floor of the desert and walked as rapidly as he could toward Khartach.

Whitmer and Leach, of course, would be expecting him in Khartach. There would be men already camping on the doorstep of the Martian house where he and Victor had stayed, and where he had been arrested. But Farrel was not going there. Khartach was a big city. Very few people lived in it any more, or had lived in it for thousands of years, but most of it was still there. Probably tomorrow they would search the ruins for him, but they didn't have enough men to attempt the job at night. He thought it would be safe enough to go there.

Safe or not, he had to go. There was a chance he might find Victor there. But if he didn't, and Victor had not already taken it, there was something in the ruins he wanted. Something he had hidden…

The dark crystal he had brought with him out of the Ship.

Victor had dropped his at the moment of Heyerman's death, so there was only the one. It was during the long haul back to Jupiter, after they had failed to move The Ship, that they found out what the crystal was for.

First Farrel discovered the delicate wires and the very slender platinum rod retracted into the crystalline "egg." Then Victor suggested that the almost microscopic terminals on the wires were intended to be attached to a power source. They modified the terminals to fit one of their tack-sized atomic batteries. The crystal became animated with a spark of light, and it pushed its thin rod out and out, uncannily like a long feeler. But otherwise, nothing happened.

Farhope had been all by herself then in the nowhere beyond Uranus. As she came closer to Jupiter, the last outpost of human habitation, there began to be other shipping. Suddenly, without warning, the steady spark inside the crystal began to pulse. The platinum rod adjusted itself. And they were listening to the crew of a mine-jumper on its way out to Neptune, to spend months in the bitter inhuman darkness searching for some pocket of precious minerals that would make them all rich.

They were listening, not to their radio, nor even to their spoken words, but to their *thoughts*.

The crystal was a sensitive receiver that picked up thought waves beyond a certain distance—they could not hear each other—amplified them, and rebroadcast them in a short-range but powerful form direct to the minds of the listeners.

Old Croy had come up with the most logical explanation.

"The people of The Ship must have planned to stop at a lot of worlds. Maybe they were explorers, or conquerors, or just people looking for a new home, but whatever they were, they would have to have contact with different races, different planets. And what would be the quickest and surest way to explore a strange world? Why, to be able to know what its people were *thinking*."

THAT had made sense to Farrel. There would be no language barrier. Physical differences would be canceled out—you would *know* whether or not a given life form was intelligent. You would know for sure whether it was friendly or hostile, docile or dangerous. With a mental eavesdropper like that, you would eliminate ninety percent of the dangers of landing on a strange world. And the technology that had built The Ship would not have found such an instrument very difficult to design.

They had come to call the crystal by a familiar name—the peeper. But they had not lost their awe of it, and it had made them realize even more the incalculable value of The Ship and the things it contained. When the trouble started on Ganymede, the peeper gave them warning. It enabled them to get away, but it was a hot and dangerous thing to have around. If it was found on them it would be proof positive that they had located The Ship, and then whoever was after them would never give up. And there was always the chance that it might be stolen. The Martian Guild of Thieves is an ancient brotherhood indeed. So before they had come into Khartach proper, Farrel and Victor crept by night into the vast sprawl of ruins and hid the crystal.

Now the situation was changed. Whitmer had said, "We have all the weight on our side." But the peeper might even that up—long enough, anyway, to join forces with Victor again and figure out what they ought to do. With the peeper, he could hope to keep one jump ahead of Whitmer and Leach.

Phobos went racing down the sky and only Deimos gave a stark pale glimmer to the ruins of Khartach, lying in a valley of the worn hills. Once, you could imagine, there had been orchards and gardens, a river winding down to the plain, a spread of verdant fields. Now there was rock and dust, and the bare, naked, scattered bones of a city.

Roofless towers and shattered walls, wide courts choked with fallen stones and broken statues, rooms full of drifted sand, black holes dropping to forgotten cellars where a man would die before he could ever get out again. And the wind, nudging the old stones and saying, "Remember?"

Farrel hated the place. He watched and listened for a time from a place above the valley. Then he set his eyes on a duster of three marble towers about a quarter of a mile in from the edge of the city, and made for them along what had been at one time a broad avenue connecting with a road that came southward through the hills. There was no more road, and the city gate was gone, and Farrel's boots sank deep in the quiet dust. Behind him, the wind smoothed away his tracks almost as soon as he had made them.

He approached the towers. There was not much left of them but three gaunt shells. Their moon shadows stretched darkly across the wide-open space around them that perhaps had been a public square, or perhaps had been crowded with buildings now completely vanished. The wind riffled the dust, and the shadows wavered.

In the darkness under the walls something moved,

CHAPTER THREE

FARREL'S first thought was that Victor had hidden out in the ruins. His second was that somebody had got ahead of him there to steal the crystal. Both thoughts went through his head in the time it took him to pull Leach's gun out of his belt, and meanwhile he was taking no chances. He crouched and sprang forward.

Something caught its breath and dodged under the shelter of a broken wall.

Farrel got himself behind the stump of a pillar, "All right," he said. "Come out of there. I've got a gun."

There was a pause. Then from behind the wall a girl's voice said, "Farrel?"

He straightened up, "Tolti? Is that you?"

She came out into the moonlight, stepping light and quick, a little black-haired, cat-eyed creature with gold in her ears and around her ankles, and a poverty-stricken cloak of mangy fur. She was the oldest daughter of the house where Farrel and Victor had stayed. She was not very old.

She ran to him. "Victor said you would come here if you lived," She spoke his language very badly, but no worse than he spoke hers, "When the police came hunting for you in Khartach I sneaked away and waited here, I have a message from Victor."

"Where is he?"

She made a sweeping gesture. "Gone. He never even returned to the house after you were taken. He hid by the path to the wells, and when I went for water he caught me and had me bring some of his things. And he said if you got away, or they let you go, I was to tell you he had gone to—let me be sure now I have it right."

She paused and then said carefully, "To the place where old Croy fell out the window."

For a minute Farrel's mind was a blank. Then he remembered, first a certain dingy house, and then old Croy with his unreverend gray hairs awry and his hand still clutching a bottle, tumbling backward out of a window while the women laughed. It had been a low window. He remembered the street and then the town and then the planetoid it was on. Ceres, where there was no sky but a plastic dome with the stars glittering through it even at high noon.

"Do you understand?" asked Tolti, watching him.

Farrel said he did. Then he thanked her, "I haven't anything to give you, Tolti—but you wait. One of these days I'll come back and then you shall have gold anklets too heavy to walk in."

"Oh," said Tolti, smiling, "That will not be necessary."

"But I'd like to—"

She hitched her cloak around her and stood beside him, "I am going with you."

"Oh, no," said Farrel. "Oh no you're not." He moved away from her. "You're going straight home."

She shook her head. "I like you, Farrel. I would like you to live. Look out there," She pointed at the desert, glimmering like a sea under the moon, "Look, and look." She pointed to the passes of the gaunt hills and by inference to the deserts that were beyond. "How will you live unless I go with you? How will you escape unless I show you the way?"

"I'll manage," he said. "Victor did."

"They were not hunting so close on his heels. And I happened to know of a caravan that was only a day and a half out from Khartach. I showed him how he should catch up to it." She leaned her back up against the pillar stump and crossed her ankles, "With me you can get away. Without me—" Her hand flashed out and down like the chopping of a knife.

There was much in what she said. The peeper could tell him what Whitmer and Leach were doing, but it could not find him water or food or transportation in this out-back of a strange planet. All the trade and travel routes would be watched now at both ends. He would have to make it by devious ways if he made it at all. When he stopped to think about it, his chances did not look very promising.

But he said, "I can't, Tolti. You're just a kid. You could get hurt, or killed. It wouldn't be right. Your parents—"

She shrugged. "My parents have put my name on the marriage list. The young men of Khartach have already been around to see if I am strong and healthy enough to bear all their burdens and their children too, I would rather marry you, Farrel."

"But—" said Farrel, horrified.

"Or if you do not wish that, then I would rather be your friend. In any case, I shall not go home. My parents will beat me, the police will beat me, and I will be given to some evil young man who will beat me until I catch him asleep and cut his throat. Then they will take me out into the desert and leave me to die. So you see? I must come with you."

"No," said Farrel. "Please, Tolti. Try to understand. You can't—"

"Very well," she sighed. "I'll go alone, then."

SHE returned to the dense patch of shadow where he had first seen her move and began to pick up various things and sling them around herself, ending finally with a bundle, which she hung between her shoulders. He thought she was trying him, and he watched her without speaking. But she didn't look at him again and when she was finished she marched away, not toward the hills as he had expected, but directly into one of the towers.

Then he ran after her and looked through the slim carved arch of the doorway. The moonlight fell dim and greenish through the broken walls. Parts of a marble floor still showed where the sand had not covered it, but in the center was nothing but a great black gaping hole.

Tolti was climbing into it.

He shouted at her to stop. She only looked at him from the black edge as he ran toward her, and made a jeering face.

"These are my ruins, Earthman, I know them. You find your own way."

She disappeared. He heard the thump of her landing on soft sand below.

"Wait!" he called. "Tolti...wait!"

"I have no time," she answered. "I must be beyond the hills by morning."

Farrel didn't stop to ponder that one. He only said, "You win. But you must wait for me a minute. There's something I have to get. Will you wait?"

She said she would.

He rushed out, took his bearings from the middle tower, and paced off the right number of paces to a hump of fallen stone, no different from a thousand other humps. He got down and dug with his hands like a terrier. The peeper was still there.

He put the crystal carefully into his shirt, not stopping to connect the battery, and ran back toward the tower. He was about halfway there when he heard a man's voice calling, "Tolti! Tolti!" There was a sound of someone walking in the ruins. The sand muffled sounds, but he thought there was more than one man. He crouched low and raced for the arched doorway. The calling continued, unchanged, but coming closer.

He slid down into the dark hole in the floor. "Now you see?" he said angrily. "They've found you're missing and they figure you came to meet me somewhere. They're hunting for you."

"Never mind. Come on," She took his hand and led him away from the patch of moon glow under the hole.

Farrel balked. "That's your father calling."

"Let him. He will have the police with him. If you give me away you will be caught too."

She pulled him into a long echoing darkness cushioned underfoot with sand. In a minute she lighted a little lamp that gave a weak glow, just enough to move by. They were in a vaulted tunnel built of massive stone blocks, very ancient but sound.

"In some places the sand has almost filled it," Tolti said, "but the last time I came through I always managed to get by."

"What is it?"

"Nothing, now. It used to be a water-tunnel. There are four of them under Khartach. I think they used to come together in a huge lake in the middle of the city—but it's hard to believe there was ever that much water."

"Are there other ways in and out of the tunnel?" Farrel asked.

"Oh, yes. Many places built over it have their floors caved in like the tower."

"Does your father know about it?"

Tolti shrugged, "Who can say? My father tells me little except that I must find some other man to feed me."

"But others do know?"

"Oh, yes. I should think half the children in Khartach have been through the tunnels at least once."

"Stop," said Farrel. "There's something I have to do."

HER eyes widened as he pulled the crystal out of his shirt and started to connect the tiny battery. "What is that?" she asked, and he told her he would explain later.

"Quiet, now," he said, and put his hand on her.

The crystal pulsed and flickered. Tolti gasped once, sharply, and then she was still.

There were three other men beside Tolti's father up there in the ruins. They were all Earthmen, and all from the police. They were tired, bored, and apprehensive. They disliked the ruins. One of them thought of ghosts. One saw himself falling into a bottomless pit. One remembered a similar walk he had taken through the Valley of the Kings by moonlight and thought vaguely philosophical thoughts about life and death and time and empires.

Tolti's father thought chiefly about what he was going to do to Tolti when he caught her, to pay her back for making him all this trouble. Almost as large in his mind hung the thought of how much reward he could expect to get out of the Earth-bastards if he helped to catch Farrel, and what he would do with that. Behind both was the latently explosive fury of the notion that his salable female property might have run off with Farrel for free.

Tolti did not seem surprised. She only whispered, "You see?"

Farrel nodded. He focused more sharply on the man's mind, and found in it a vague picture of the aqueduct, but more like something told to him than something actually seen. He did not seem to know about the tower and the particular hole in its floor. There were other things in his mind, though. Tolti's father was not a nice man. Farrel shut off the peeper and said, "Let's go." He no longer had any compunctions about taking Tolti with him.

She grinned and led him swiftly away along the tunnel.

It was a curious sort of journey. Several times they crawled over mounds of sand and twice Farrel thought they were not going to get through. The dim light of Tolti's lamp, the featureless length of the tunnel and the darkness contributed a timeless quality so that Farrel was not sure whether the trip was taking them hours or days.

Several times he stopped to listen with the peeper, but the three policemen did not care very passionately whether they caught Farrel or not, and they cared even less about catching a Martian's runaway daughter. They dragged their feet more and more and passed eventually out of range.

The slope of the tunnel became steeper. There were no more openings and the floor was almost free of sand. They climbed and climbed and suddenly there was light. Tolti put out the lamp. They crept blinking and exhausted into a great jagged pit in the hills that had once been a reservoir. It was day and the sun was high in the cold sky.

Farrel listened with the peeper and heard nothing. He and Tolti sat in the mouth of the tunnel and ate and drank sparingly. She had brought with her all the food and water she could carry— probably one reason her absence had been noticed.

"There is a tunnel on the other side," she said, pointing across the dry pit, "that served a city beyond the range. I've never been through that. But we have a story that Khartach and this other city went to war over the water when there was no longer enough for both, and that Khartach won."

"You'd never know it now, would you?" said Farrel.

They crossed the floor of the pit and found the mouth of the other tunnel about the middle of the afternoon. Tolti believed that it was open to the place where the army of Khartach had broken it between the other city and the hills. They entered its dry darkness, and just after they did so, while Tolti was lighting her lamp again, Farrel heard the helicopter come booming and bumbling over the valley outside.

They were still hunting for him. If it had not been for the tunnels he might have found it impossible to keep out of their sight. He smiled and went off hand in hand with Tolti. Here at least they could not follow him.

NEARLY three weeks later Farrel and Tolti were in the overcrowded steerage of a not-too-legal tramp that carried everything from mining machinery and pigs to people. Those three weeks were among the roughest Farrel had ever gone through, and he would not have lasted through the first of them without Tolti to show him where to dig for the meager drops of water that kept them alive after the bottles were emptied, or to guide him to a caravan track far from Khartach.

They had traveled with a caravan for days, and once the 'copter had appeared in the sky and swung low over the line of march while Farrel sweated under his borrowed Martian cloak and made sure his gun was free. But the 'copter went on. Then they had a piece of luck, hitching a ride on a mining company's big double-rotored workhorse that had been delivering parts close to the caravan track.

In ten hours they were in a port city, and Farrel was looking for a way to the Belt. It had been a touchy thing, having to keep out of sight and operate without the proper papers, but the peeper had kept him informed of policeman and it had been an immeasurable help in finding a booking-agent who did not greatly care where his money came from as long as he got it.

They had raised enough by selling everything they had but their clothes, the peeper, and Leach's gun, to pad out the money Farrel had on him when he was arrested and which Leach and Whitmer had not bothered to take away.

They wallowed for weeks among the whirling ports of the Belt, eating bad food and breathing bad air. Tolti was sick, and she must have wished herself back in Khartach many times, but she never once complained. Farrel got very fond of her, and the fonder he got the more he worried about what was going to happen to her.

He worried about what was going to happen to him, too. If Victor had not reached Ceres after all, or had gone on, he was going to be in a mess. He didn't have money enough left to feed them, let alone pay passage anywhere. If Victor failed him, he was sunk.

The tramp docked at last on the flat tableland of bare black rock beside Ceres' clustered domes. Sealed trucks took them from the ship's lock through the airlock of the dome, dumped them, and went on.

Farrel stood for a minute with Tolti beside him, looking around. She was staring up at the plastic dome with black sky on top of it, and the stars, and the sun that was no bigger than a Christmas tree ball and not much warmer. Farrel was used to that. He was looking at people, at the blackrock streets and the dirty plastic houses. Gradually he drew Tolti away from the rest of the group and behind a huge stack of crates close to the dome edge.

He turned on the peeper.

The flood of jangling thoughts it loosed on him was dizzying. He stayed with it, though, winnowing back and forth through the tumult of hunger and ambition, hope and despair, grief and love, fear and defeat. One steady note stood out and he tried to focus on it. It was his name. Victor was thinking his name over and over, and there was a message with it.

The gray building opposite the lock. The top window. Join me. I have news from Croy.

Farrel looked out around the crates. He saw the building, a dingy spaceman's hotel, and he saw the top window, but at this distance he could not see Victor. Victor, though, would be able to see him perfectly well with glasses. Farrel felt a vast relief. He reached out for Tolti's hand. And then Victor's thought came through with sudden sharpness.

Look out, there are two men going toward you—I think they're cops!

CHAPTER FOUR

FARREL caught Tolti and pulled her farther back behind the crates. He had been so intent on clarifying Victor's thought that he had overlooked the less strongly concentrated thoughts of the two men who had come so abruptly into the picture. Now he sought them out.

They were detectives from Ceres Central. They were looking for him. They knew that he might be traveling with a Martian girl, and they had seen him when he moved behind the crates. They were fairly sure he was Ross Farrel. They were on their way to find out.

From their minds he received a composite picture of the square stack of crates perhaps thirty-five feet long and twenty thick and almost as high as the height of the curving dome at its outer edge. One man was approaching the stack from the right, the other from the left.

Farrel picked up Tolti's wiry little person and boosted it toward the top of the stack. He said, "Climb!" She climbed like a monkey and he followed. "Keep down," he said. The men were now on either side of the stack, toward the back where they expected to find him. Farrel crept the other way, over the flat top. He could hear Victor, practically shouting at him with his mind. Hurry, run, go to the left where those big babies are, you've got a clear field there. Jump, damn it, you've only got a minute—

He jumped, with the girl right beside him. He ran where Victor had told him, in among the towering components of a disassembled power plant, all in their flat protective paint and skeleton crating. The areas near the three main locks were used for freight storage and there was a strip perhaps a quarter of a mile long ahead of him that was one crowded jungle of stuff waiting to be used somewhere in the domes or sent on to one of the mining camps.

He might possibly have made it unseen if it had not been for Tolti. Farrel was a spaceman, and for as long as he could remember he had been adjusting himself automatically to heavy gravity, light gravity, and no gravity at all. He didn't even think about it. But Tolti had never been off her home planet. Mars-normal is light compared to Earth-normal. Compared to Ceres-normal it is very heavy. Tolti jumped but she had no chance to run. She flew like a ragged bird through the air, her cloak flapping behind her, and fetched up with a crash against the side of a generator housing. Farrel swore, but he stopped to pick her up. And one of the detectives came around the corner of the stack of crates and shouted, "Hey!"

Holding Tolti in his arms, Farrel fled among the islands of freight. Now he was glad of the fractional gravity and used it for all it was worth. Tolti was frighteningly limp. He kept asking her if she was hurt, but she didn't answer him. She was bleeding from the nose. He became terribly alarmed, but he did not dare stop. Victor projected a desperate thought...

Stay with it, I'm coming!

After that Farrel kept his mind on what the detectives were thinking, between worrying about Tolti.

They were thinking that they could easily catch him. Ceres' gravity was just as light for them as it was for him, and they were not burdened. They spread out and raced after him, sure they could trap him no matter how he turned and dodged. The one thing they did not count on was the peeper. Farrel knew what they were going to do before they were really sure themselves. Three times they missed him because of this, and then Victor had come into the freight area too, Farrel doubled back to join him.

VERY quickly he lost Victor's thought as he entered the peeper's insensitive range. But he picked him up visually. They met behind the temporary shelter of a gigantic blower unit designed for the atmosphere plant of a dome somewhere in the swarming Belt. There was no time for greetings. Farrel put Tolti down. Light gravity or not, he was breathing hard. He loosed the clasp of her ratty cloak, ran back and threw it in front of the blower where the detectives would be sure to see it. Then he spoke very briefly to Victor, listening to the peeper. Victor nodded and darted away to other shelter. Farrel looked at Tolti and then very reluctantly left her where she was and went dodging away on a circuitous route, doubling back toward the detectives.

He lost them, too, in the peeper's blind spot, and crouched quietly behind a row of pumps until he could see them. They came looking baffled and rather angry, and now they had their guns in their hands. Then one of them saw the cloak on the ground. He pointed and they put their heads close together and whispered. They separated and began to advance on the blower unit, using what shelter there was in case Farrel should be armed. The Want that Ceres Central had received on Farrel had not said anything about armed and dangerous. It had only said that he was to be apprehended and held for local authorities on Mars, and "for questioning" was the only charge against him. But they were not taking undue risks.

"All right," one of them said to the blower unit. "Come out of there. We have you pegged."

They moved a little closer, their guns ready.

Victor appeared on the opposite side of the lane along which the men were advancing, behind them and opposite Farrel. He looked unhappy. He was an easy-going type, inclined to be lazy, and he hated trouble and upset. He had in his hand a ten-inch strip of steel he had picked out of the freight. Farrel nodded to him. Then Farrel took Leach's gun out from under his shirt, caught a deep breath, and jumped.

The two detectives never had a chance to fire their guns. One of them got the first part of a yell out of his mouth before he went down, but it was not loud enough to attract any attention. Farrel's clubbed gun and Victor's steel strip took care of them both with great swiftness. They tied and gagged them—in feverish haste—with their own belts and handkerchiefs, and dragged them between crates where they would not be too readily seen if anybody did happen to come by. Then Farrel ran back behind the blower unit.

Tolti was sitting up, swearing viciously in Martian and holding both hands to her face, which was starting to swell over the nose and one eye.

Farrel kneeled beside her. "That's a relief," he said. "I thought you were hurt."

She glared at him. "I've bashed my brains out, that's all—a thing of no matter."

He kissed her and helped her up. Victor was shifting uneasily from one foot to the other, looking around. "We've got to get out of here," he said. "Can she walk?"

Tolti yanked away from Farrel's grasp. "My legs are not broken, only my head." She lifted the skirt of her tunic and wiped carefully at the blood on her face. Farrel took hold of her again.

"Take it easy until you get the feel of the gravity," he said. "Come on."

They hurried off, not talking much, wanting only to put as much distance as possible between themselves and the two men who would presently come to and start making trouble for them again. They left the storage area and plunged into the narrow blackrock streets, crowded with people and crammed with pre-fab plastic, buildings that housed everything in a sort of insane democracy. Churches and bars were cheek-by-jowl, sometimes on different floors of the same building. Bordellos, hospitals, civic offices, a thriving mortuary, mining company offices, assay offices, machinery and supply companies, lawyer's offices, countless cubby-holes full of people, all jammed together in the inflexible circles of the main dome and the three smaller ones it had been forced to sprout in the slightly more than a century since the first ships had landed on this, the largest of the minor worlds.

FARREL had always enjoyed coming here before. It was relaxation and relief after the endless dark months prospecting and hunting for salvage along the far-flung reefs of the Belt or the outer moons. By comparison with the iron walls of *Farhope* or some other rusty tug, the Ceres domes were wide and bright. Now they felt tiny and evil, like a trap.

"They are a trap," he said aloud to Victor. "They know we're here now. How long can we hide out in this fishbowl?"

"Not very long." Victor licked his lips nervously. He was tall and dark-haired and gangling, dressed like Farrel in a nondescript coverall. "I don't know, Ross. I thought everything was figured out, but now it don't look so good."

"You said you had news from Croy?"

"Did I? Oh. Before, you mean. Yes. He's going to pick us up. Or he was going to."

"What do you mean, he was going to?"

"Well, as soon as I got here I contacted Croy—kind of roundabout, you know. We figured to wait a while for you, and anyway he said he was busy. Then we heard definitely that you'd got away from Mars. So I watched every ship that came in, hoping you'd be on it. Two days ago Croy sent me a message. He'd give you till the end of this week and then he couldn't wait any longer. So he'll land *Farhope* out on the Dead Camp Flat and pick up whoever's there. I figured to hire us a couple of suits and walk it."

"End of the week?" said Farrel.

"I've lost track."

"By Solar Arbitrary," Victor said gloomily, "that's four and a half days. Twenty-four hours is about the limit in a suit. And it isn't going to take the cops anything like three and a half days to run us down."

Farrel walked in silence, thinking. Tolti hung close to him now, afraid of getting separated and lost. The surging streams of people carried them along, squeezing between the narrow walls, caught in eddies around the more populous bars and the mine and employment centers.

"How much money have you got?" asked Farrel suddenly.

"About a hundred credits. Why?"

"We might just be able to do it," Farrel said, and quickened his pace. "Come on, start humping, I want to make it to Number Six Lock before our friends back there get loose and send out a general alarm."

"What're you figuring to do?" asked Victor.

"Get out of the domes. If we hire a truck outfit, we can at least keep moving."

"The kind of a truck outfit we can afford," Victor muttered, "won't keep us moving long."

But he hurried beside Farrel. Before they left the main dome for one of the smaller ones, Farrel tried the peeper again. He was able to disentangle the thoughts of the two detectives from the irrelevant chaos that flooded in. They were awake again. Their heads hurt. And they had ideas about what they were going to do as soon as they got free.

Farrel moved even faster toward Number Six Lock.

CHAPTER FIVE

THE AIRLOCKS of the minor domes were exit-ports to the countryside—fields of black rock, humps and jags and hollows of black rock, valleys and mountains of black rock, with a black sky overhead and no air to cloud or soften it. When the sun shone there was a good bit of light but very little warmth. At night it was like riding a floe of black ice in an ocean of stars, with the horizon dropping off short on all sides so that you felt if you walked too far in any direction you would fall over into the naked constellations. Only miners, supply-truck drivers, and fools went out.

The man who rented them the truck counted their money three times to be sure it was all there. "Prospecting, eh?" he said.

Victor said, "Yes."

"Whereabouts?"

"Oh," said Victor, "we got an idea or two." He looked anxiously toward Farrel, who had withdrawn to a little distance and was listening to the peeper. Tolti was sitting cross-legged on the ground, looking remote and very Martian.

"Uh huh," said the man shrewdly. "The old South Polar mine idea, I'll bet. Must be a dozen guys like you every year come through here, looking to pick up that vein again, I wish 'em all luck."

"Thanks," said Victor. "Maybe we'll be the lucky ones," Farrel came hurrying back. "Are we all ready?" he said.

"All set," the man said. "Supplies for a week, four suits, everything in working order, guaranteed. Never lost a party yet." He laughed. As an afterthought he added, "There's an emergency repair kit in the tool locker."

He waved the slender wad of credit notes at them. "This pays for two days use only. Arbitrary Time. It's in the contract. Now if you ain't back by the end of that time I won't send the cops out after you right away. But you'll be held responsible for every extra day, and don't bother trying to sneak back in through one of the other locks. We got a system."

"Oh," said Victor, "we sure wouldn't do anything like that."

Farrel beckoned to Tolti. She joined him and the three of them got into the truck. Little beads of sweat were standing out on Farrel's face, "Somebody just found them," he muttered to Victor. He dogged the hatch into place and climbed into the operator's blister. Victor began chocking the air system. Farrel started the motor and rolled, clanking heavily out of the truck rental yard and down the short street to the lock.

Tolti said, "We will live in this for five days?"

"We *hope* to live in it," Farrel said grimly. "It must have been one of the first they ever brought to Ceres. Find that repair kit, Vic, and keep an eye for leaks."

They passed into the air lock and the great door sealed shut behind them. Pumps bled off the trapped air. As the pressure dropped, Victor went around poking and listening, and Farrel peered out of the blister, from which he could see all the beetle-like truck except its belly and extreme rear, looking for telltale wisps of freezing vapor. He did not see any. He resisted an overwhelming impulse to slam on the power and butt his way through the outer door. Every second he expected the vents to be closed and air to be pumped back again, signifying that the lock would not be opened for them. But after what seemed like years the outer door opened up and he sent the truck grinding through it on its flexible tracks. The great tilted plane of a rock face twenty miles across spread out before him in the thin glare of the setting sun. He turned the truck across it, heading south.

After a while Tolti came up and stood beside him, looking out. The little bright ball of the sun was obscured by the rising up of a jagged crest and it was night as suddenly as though someone had thrown a switch. Tolti gasped and flung up her hand against the stars that seemed to spring by the millions out of the sky.

"See anybody coming after us?" he asked her, and she looked back at the domes shining in the midst of the black plain.

"No," she said. "Not yet."

"If we can just make it off this damn pan before they see us," he said between his teeth, "we might have a chance."

HE POURED on more power, torn between the need for haste and concern for the senile frailty of the truck. He had Victor teach Tolti how to get into a spacesuit in a hurry. The heating system did not work very well and the interior rapidly became cold. The air had an unpleasant chemical smell, as though it had already been used far too many times.

The smooth pan broke up in a series of jumbled ledges. Luminous markers appeared, pointing out a place where a natural pass had been blasted and smoothed into a reasonable road. Farrel turned the truck into it. The domes were now hidden from sight and a last look across the pan had not shown any headlights coming after them. Farrel gave Victor the peeper to see what he could pick up with it, and kept the truck trundling on as fast as it would go, its own headlight beam cutting a hard-edged swathe through the airless dark. They were now heading east.

"Get anything?" he asked Victor.

"Everybody's thinking at once," Victor said. He fiddled with the crystal, his eyes shut in concentration. "I can't get anything clear—no, wait a minute. Somebody—yes, the guy that rented us the truck. There's an alarm out for us and he's heard it. He's thinking—he's calling—no, he's *talking* to the guys we hit. Yeah. Now I get them, too." He paused, "I think we just made it. And I think we better keep going—fast."

The truck jolted and lurched and groaned, creaking at every seam. Farrel said grimly, "I don't dare wreck her too soon. Which way do they think we've gone?"

"The man is telling them south, but they don't believe it. They figure we let him think that to throw them off."

"Okay," said Farrel. "We'll go south. Check that map for me, will you?"

Victor rolled out the plastic strip map, stained and greasy from much use.

"About a mile ahead there's a turn-off and a pass to the southern flats. After that we're on our own. If we keep going right around *here*—he pointed to a spot on the map—we'll be about within reach of Dead Camp Flat at the right time."

Farrel glanced at the map and grunted, "*If* we keep going," he said.

"Yeah."

The hard white beam of the headlights struck on the cold faces of the tumbled rocks where the road bent. On either side the dark walls closed them in, making their miniature peaks against the stars.

At long last there was another luminous marker and Farrel swung south again, toward the South Polar area where a rich find of uranium had lasted all too short a time. As the man who rented them the truck had said, people still hoped to find an extension of that deposit even though the ground had been so thoroughly worked over that a teaspoonful of uranium could not have been missed.

The map showed several small outfits of various sorts dotted around in the South Polar area but the big mine had been abandoned for years. With any luck if the truck kept running, they could stay out of sight of the small camps, dodging around the rock pans, creeping without lights if they had to. Every mining camp had a radio, and the minute they were seen and reported they knew they were through.

The road climbed between jagged walls. The pass opened, narrow and forbidding, and then they were heading down the farther slope with the glimmering expanse of the southern rock-pans spread out before them.

As Victor had said, from here on they were on their own. There were no roads on Ceres except where a pass or a fill had been necessary. Taking turns at driving, the two men pushed the truck farther and farther into the barren Antarctic regions—a South Pole both worse and better than the Earthly one that had cost so many lives and so much agony. Worse because life of any kind was a precarious intrusion on this sterile rock adrift in the void between Mars and Jupiter, existing from minute to minute only by the complicated interdependence of mechanical aids. Better because the rock was sterile and airless, with neither wind nor snow nor ice to trouble it. Such as it was, it was unchanged and unchanging.

The peeper showed no pursuit close behind them. The police-manned trucks were searching east and north for them, depending on the obvious assumption that they would not say they were going south and then actually go there. But all camps on Ceres had been alerted by radio and asked to report any passer-by. So the truck wound and trundled furtively, giving the collapsible plastic domes a wide berth. They passed the abandoned workings of the uranium mine and then began to angle northwest toward Dead Camp Flat. Tolti cooked for them, wretched meals of powdered and dehydrated foods rather badly prepared. Tolti didn't have much experience with such things, and the ancient cooker didn't work right anyway.

THEY SLEPT in shifts on the narrow bunks and developed a gnawing claustrophobia that must have been agonizing for the girl, bred to the wide deserts and open skies of Mars. Farrel and Victor were used to the confines of a ship, but this was different. A ship was larger and they had definite duties connected with it. It was their living, and they knew it was sound. Here in this cramped shell they lived every second on edge for the sudden hiss of escaping air, for the final stuttering out of the uncertain machinery that gave them breath and warmth.

They found what seemed to be a safe hiding place, in an isolated bay between two protruding tongues of rock, and stopped there to wait until it was time to make the last rush to Dead Camp Flat and meet the *Farhope*. They used the peeper at intervals, listening to the minds of the various groups that hunted them. Ceres was not limitless in extent. Inevitably the search was turning back upon the southern area. They waited, judging time and distance, and after a while they were forced to realize that they were not going to be able to wait long enough. They took off again, trying to keep ahead of and equidistant from the two converging lines of search that were closing in on them from the north and east. Victor drove, and Farrel pored over the map.

"We can't outrun them both," he said, "and even if we could we'd only lead them to where they could catch Croy too when he lands. How long is it now till he's due?"

Victor figured, "About fourteen hours,"

"Keep going," Farrel said. And he showed Victor a place on the map. Victor's eyes widened.

"But that's putting us right in a trap," he said. "We can't get through or over."

"Way I see it," said Farrel, "it's our only chance."

The truck went on, groaning and sagging on its frayed tracks, over the naked rock.

Six hours later they reached the place that Farrel had chosen on the map. It was daylight, a raw glare of sun patched and scored with shadows as sharp-edged as though drawn with ink. The level rock broke off abruptly, ending in a crevass that appeared bottomless because no light reached into it. It was deep enough, even in this light gravity, to smash anything heavy that fell into it. Beyond the crevass was a wild and twisted ridge. Beyond the ridge was Dead Camp Flat.

Farrel stopped the truck.

They got into the space suits—the three best-looking ones, with the least worn equipment. They gave each other a last check over, and then Victor and Tolti got out of the truck. Farrel went up into the operator's blister and started the motor again. He put it in gear and then went down and out in a hurry through the open lock. He joined Victor and the girl and they started away, moving in the long agile leaps of men accustomed to asteroid walking. Each of them held one of Tolti's hands, towing her between them like a captive balloon. Behind them the truck moved with, ponderous stupidity toward the brink.

They had barely reached the northern end of the gap when the truck went over. They stopped to watch it. There was no sound at all. Its forward tracks went spinning out into nothingness and the rear tracks pushed it on until the body overbalanced and fell with a certain slow majesty, catching a last glitter of light on its windows and then vanishing into the utter black below. They could not tell when it hit the bottom. They would, Farrel thought, have to pay for the old heap some day.

THE CREVASS here was narrow enough to jump, in this fractional gravity. They jumped it and began to climb the ridge, going carefully because of rotten rock and jagged outcrops that can tear a suit before a man realizes it. The girl hampered them. But she was small and willing, and though her little face peered out through the helmet glass very white and big-eyed, she never whimpered. The quick night overtook them before they reached the top. When they did they stopped to rest, looking back over the plain they had left behind. Lights showed on it, diamond-bright, moving toward them.

Farrel put his helmet against Victor's—they had not turned on the helmet-radios for fear the pursuing trucks would pick them up—and shouted,

"They'll find our heap in the crevass—let's hope it'll take them a long time to find we aren't in it!"

Long enough, he hoped, to let the three of them get out on the Flat, see where *Farhope* landed, and get aboard.

They made the treacherous descent, again slowly and carefully, and began the trek out across the flat that had taken its name from an early-day tragedy of the mining fields. Now they made all the speed they could, but it was far slower than the truck and they had to rest from time to time. Farrel had the peeper at his belt. He knew when the search parties met and found the crashed truck. He knew when they let a man down on a rope to check it, and when they decided that the three people they were looking for must have gone over the ridge on foot. He "watched" four men—the two detectives and two other policemen—climb into suits and come after them. When they reached the top of the ridge and looked out over the flat, Farrel and Victor and Tolti were lying prone in the shadow of a little hump in the rock, offering no moving target to the eye.

They lay there and waited because it was the only thing they could do for the moment. The four police scrambled down the slope of the ridge and spread out, moving slowly forward. And then faint and far off but swiftly gathering, the peeper field picked up the mind of old Croy. Farrel twisted his head inside his helmet and looked at the sky. *Farhope's* rockets made a lovely trail of fire down the blackness, like a shooting star.

The prone figures gathered themselves. The four walking ones paused, stiffened, and began to run.

Farhope dropped down, settling her dumpy shape almost gracefully onto the rock.

The three prone figures rose and moved in giant bounds toward her, the two tall ones taking the small one between them.

The four also bounded mightily, and two of them produced guns.

The three reached *Farhope's* open lock and tumbled in. Silent and flaring, shots came after them, splashing against the dark iron of the hull and the rapidly closing outer door. Almost before the crack was sealed, *Farhope's* tubes burst into full power and the tug lifted, poised herself mockingly on a glorious pillar of flame, and then took flight, kicking the barren rock of Ceres away beneath her, her blunt nose pointed toward the stars.

CHAPTER SIX

OLD CROY was a master hand at the difficult art of flying the Belt. Most salvage skippers are, because there are more wrecks in the Belt than anywhere, and more chances to pick up a few credits prospecting on the side. He took *Farhope* away from Ceres and sent her whirling and dancing through the labyrinth of hurtling world-lets at a speed and with a diabolical recklessness that shook off any pursuit from Ceres before it got close enough to detect.

Neither Farrel nor Victor offered to help him. They crawled out of the airlock and out of their suits, and they helped Tolti out of hers. Then they crawled into the bunks in the crowded cabin just aft of the cockpit and lay there. For the time being, they had had it.

After a while Croy told them that there was a bottle in the galley locker. Farrel mustered up enough strength to go and get it, overcome with a warm surge of love for *Farhope's* grubby, familiar person. He found the bottle and shared it with Victor and Tolti. Presently they stopped gasping and began to breathe again.

Croy said, "From the looks of things, we might just as well have stayed together."

Victor muttered something about eggs in a basket, and Farrel said, "No, they might have caught us all. As it was, the only one they got was me. Vic and I just picked the wrong place to go. Too far back in. We were noticed. Somebody on Ganymede must have tipped off Whitmer to look for us in his sector." Farrel shook his head. "They sure worked me over."

"Didn't tell 'em anything, did you?"

"You know damn well I didn't!"

"Don't get riled," said Croy mildly, "A man can say a lot when he's half conscious, and no blame to him."

"Well," said Farrel, "fortunately it never went that far. They got careless for a minute, and I got away."

He explained how it had happened. "Hadn't been for Tolti, though, I'd never have made it."

"You were lucky," Victor said, shaking his head. "That Leach has got a big reputation for being tough. He might have killed you."

"They didn't want me dead.

They wanted me alive and talking." Farrel turned to Croy, "How did you do?"

Croy answered without turning his head. They could talk back and forth quite easily between cabin and cockpit, the tug's dimensions being considerably less than a liner's. Croy's thick shoulders were hunched over the control bank, his powerful hands moving with the speed and delicacy of a girl's over the firing keys.

"I did real good," he said. "I hunted up some of the boys and formed what you might call an association. We couldn't bring The Ship in alone, we know that. And if we went to one of these big salvage outfits like Benson's or Pett's on Ganymede, they'd take over, graciously give us ten cents apiece, and send us on our way. So I figured if I've got to share with somebody I'd rather it would be with friends, I lined up Schultz, Wallace, Gilson, Carlucci and Friedman. All good guys, and their tugs are in good shape."

"Yeah," said Victor, considering technical problems. "Six of us ought to be able to do it." He sighed, "I hate to think of having to split up that big beautiful jackpot at all, but like you say, 'Oh, well, I guess there'll be plenty to go around'."

"Boy, you can keep yourself in booze and women for three lifetimes on even the smallest amount you could get." Croy grinned at them over his shoulder. "All we have to do is get the six of us there, break The Ship out of its orbit and get it under a legal tow, and then nobody can take it away from us."

"What's the plan?" Farrel asked.

"They're going out separately, from different places all through the Belt. That way, nobody'll notice them. We'll rendezvous well beyond Pluto and then go on together."

"What about supplies?" said Farrel.

"That was a problem. I don't dare bring *Farhope* into port anywhere, so we worked it out like this. The tugs will outfit in different ports, and each one will take on something extra. Then on their way out we calculated the orbits real careful so it'd work out right—they'll drop off the extra stuff in a cache on Umbriel. We'll pick it up. Simple as that."

"Sounds good," Farrel said.

"It is good," Croy said, indignantly. "What's the matter with you?"

"Nothing," said Farrel. "Just beat." He laid back in the bunk and patted *Farhope's* side. "Nice to be home again."

He called to Tolti, but she was already asleep. Farrel said to Croy, "Call me when it's my watch," and went to sleep himself. And a vague uneasiness troubled him even in his dreams.

IT CONTINUED to trouble him in the weeks that followed, while they left the asteroids behind and then the orbit of Jupiter, heading out into the dark void where few ships ever went and from which even fewer ever came back. He could not shake off a feeling that somehow, somewhere, something was wrong.

He could not say in what way, or why he felt it. Croy was sure of his plan, and Croy was smart and shrewd, a long time in the game. He had seen to it that he was not followed in his secret prowlings around the Belt. And he was positive that he could trust every one of the men he had contacted.

Farrel didn't doubt this. None of them could possibly gain as much from selling the secret to someone else as they could get by actually salvaging The Ship. Anyway, Farrel knew all the men himself and knew they were okay.

Nobody had followed them out from Ceres, either. They had got away too fast, and Croy's expert piloting had lost *Farhope* almost immediately in the swirling mazes of the Belt.

Yet the uneasiness itched and tugged at Farrel. It made him constantly get out the peeper to see if he could pick up anything. Croy and Victor both complained that he was giving them the jumps, and finally he took to doing it in secret when he was piloting and the others slept.

They left Saturn, its rings and swarm of moons behind and far to starboard, a spot of cold glittering splendor against the distant stars. *Farhope* plunged sturdily on toward Uranus, running short now on everything, food, fuel, oxygen, water.

Uranus, huge and dimly gleaming, rolled toward them on its orbital path, a dead planet sheathed in ice, forever beyond the reach of warmth and life. They picked up the tiny circling chunk of rock that was Umbriel and began the approach.

Farrel switched on the peeper.

For the first time he heard something.

There were ships in the void behind them, far behind, but following.

He shouted to Croy and Victor and they came to listen. The confused babble of many minds was unclear at first, but then Croy's face became flint-hard and his eyes blazed.

"A salvage fleet," he said, "One of the big outfits. Benson's, I think. We've been sold out—"

"Wait," said Farrel urgently. "Listen," He was trying to focus down on the leading ship. Somebody was talking. The communications man. The clearly directed thought behind the words sprang out from the random background.

Signal coming through, faint but steady. They're heading for one of the moons.

I wonder why? asked another mind, and Farrel stiffened. He looked at Victor, "That's Whitmer," he said. "And Leach is there too. Hear? They were talking with Benson, then. But—"

A third mind, probably the captain's, said, *All we can do is follow the signal. Not too fast, either. We don't want them taking fright and—*

Croy suddenly struck the peeper out of Farrel's hands and smashed it on the iron floor.

"Signal," he said. "Fine. So that's why you've been playing with that thing every five minutes. You had it rigged some way to broadcast a tracer." His hand shot out and gripped Farrel by the throat. "You escaped from them, did you? How much did they pay you to escape, Farrel? How much, you Judas?"

Farrel got white. He rose from the edge of the bunk where he was sitting. He knocked Croy's hand away and hit him in the

THE SHIP FROM INFINITY

stomach, a good, hard angry blow. Croy staggered back and leaned against the opposite bulkhead, bent over.

"You damned old fool," said Farrel. "If I'd sold out to them I wouldn't have had to escape. I'm your navigator, remember? I plotted The Ship's orbit the first time and I'm the one that'll plot it again. I don't need either you or Victor. I could have taken them right on out and you'd never have known it until we brought The Ship in."

HE KICKED the shards of crystal with his toe. "We could have found out how they were following us, but you had to go and smash it. Now how will we ever know?"

"Well," said Victor, his face heavy with suspicion and the fear of losing The Ship, "if you didn't sell out, somebody else sure as hell must have," He looked at Tolti, "She's been with you all the way. Kind of funny wasn't it, she would all of a sudden want to leave home that bad?"

Tolti hunched together like a threatened cat. "You lie," she said. "If it wasn't for me he would never have got away from Mars."

"Maybe," said Victor. "All the same, I want to see what you got in your pockets."

She backed away from him, "You let me alone."

"Yes," said Farrel. "Let her alone." He caught Victor by the shoulder and swung him around. "How about you, when I think of it? How do I know what you've been doing all this time when you were supposed to be waiting for me to join you?"

"That's a fine way to talk," said Victor, "after I saved your neck back there."

He wrenched away from Farrel's grasp. "What's the matter, don't you trust your little Martian friend? Are you scared to have her searched?"

He grabbed again for Tolti, but her thorny Martian pride had been outraged by Victor's accusation. She dodged agilely under his arm, reached Farrel's bunk, and grabbed the gun that Farrel had taken from Leach and which was now hung up on the bulkhead. Before anybody could stop her she had spun around and snapped a shot point-blank at Victor, her face a perfect mask of fury.

And nothing happened.

"Hold it," said Farrel sharply, "Everybody hold it."

They held it, Victor pale and shaken by the realization of what had almost happened to him, Tolti staring at the gun. Farrel took it away from her. Croy, who had gotten his breath back, straightened up against the bulkhead but remained leaning against it, watching them all.

Farrel moved to where there was nothing in front of him but the bare after-bulkhead. He fired the gun.

Again nothing happened.

He fired it two or three times with the same result. Then he took the gun into the tiny machine shop and began in silent and furious haste to tear it apart.

The others stood bunched in the doorway and watched him.

"There," said Farrel. "There you are. Look at that." He pointed to the scattered parts of the gun. "Judas is right. Judas goat, with a little bell around my neck. I should have known, I should have realized that my whole goddamned escape was a phony, just rigged up so I'd lead them to The Ship. There isn't even a power pack in the gun! It's just a dummy with a transmitter in it."

He picked up a hammer and pounded the compact little transmitter into a useless lump of crystal and wire.

"No wonder that 'copter kept brushing us so close on Mars. They knew where we were every minute."

He swore. "If I hadn't been so groggy," he said, "I'd have realized it was too easy. Leach practically asking me to take his gun—oh, hell!"

Victor said, "Those guys on Ceres sure weren't in on it."

"Nobody would be in on it but Whitmer and Leach. Naturally. And they'd have to put out a general alarm or it would look too funny. They had to take some risks. I suppose they figured if I did get caught they could always arrange another escape. Anyway, they didn't have much to lose. They weren't getting anywhere the other way."

Victor looked at Croy, "You believe him?"

Croy said, "Sure I believe him."

"Why?"

"Because there's one thing he said there ain't any doubt about."

"What's that?"

"He don't need either you or me to find The Ship again. Like he said. If he'd sold out, we wouldn't have known about it till it was all over."

"Yeah," said Victor. "I suppose that's so. Well, what do we do now?"

"I don't see how there's any choice about that," Croy said. He gestured toward the bench where the wrecked transmitter lay. "They haven't a signal to follow now. They know we're heading for one of the moons, but they don't know where we'll go afterward. They're a good way behind. If we crack on all the power we've got, we might just out run 'em."

It was on the tip of Farrel's tongue to say, "We might, if Benson's tugs weren't so much newer and faster than ours."

He restrained himself. Croy was right—they did not have any choice of action. They might as well have hope.

CHAPTER SEVEN

URANUS, fourth largest of the system's worlds, hung above their heads so low and massive that it seemed as though the upside-down peaks of its icy ranges would strike them if they straightened up. All of them including Tolti were frantically busy, transferring supplies from the cache left by the outgoing tugs into the nearly-empty bins, holds and tanks of *Farhope*.

In Umbriel's practically nonexistent gravity the task was not hard. It just seemed to go on forever. Farrel caught himself peering anxiously into space every few minutes, thinking to see the flares of Benson's salvage fleet across the stars. It was pretty obvious now what the deal had been. Benson on Ganymede had got wind of the rumored find of The Ship—he was the one who had tried to trap them there. When they got away Benson had been able to trace Victor and himself to Mars and had alerted Whitmer, who as subsector administrator would be able to hunt the two men out and arrest them with a pretense of legality. Benson probably had known Whitmer already. Or it might have been simply that Whitmer was the right man in the right position. Anyway, they had joined forces, and if Benson could bring in The Ship and Whitmer could share in the proceeds, Whitmer would be able to buy and sell Mars itself, let alone B Sector, Southeast.

They did not see the rockets of the salvage fleet. It must still be well behind. But now that they no longer had a signal to follow they would close up as fast as possible in order to track *Farhope* with conventional radar. And Benson's tugs were among the best in space.

There was, as Croy had said, only one thing to do, and they did it. They wrestled in the supplies as fast as possible and then took off again, heading at top speed into the black immensity beyond. They proceeded straight to the rendezvous because there was not fuel enough to spare for any elaborate dodgings or false leads to throw Benson and Whitmer off. They passed the orbit of Neptune, raced on, left Pluto's path behind them, and entered the shallows of the great interstellar ocean that runs for light-years between the stars. Out here there was nothing, no life, no world, no sun.

Nothing but five little tugs hovering on their auxiliaries, all huddled together for comfort in the face of that empty vastness.

Now for the first time *Farhope* broke radio silence to speak briefly to the others, warning them of the need for haste. And one by one the main drives flared to life and the six ships moved off together on the last leg of this journey that had turned into a deadly race. They did not use either radio or radar to learn how close behind them Benson's fleet might be. There was no use in setting up signposts for them to follow. Anyway, there was nothing they could do about it. All they could do was run and hope.

Farrel lived, ate and slept with the old clacking computer, working out the complicated coordinates of juxtaposition with the previously calculated or bit of The Ship.

They reached a point. An imaginary point, marked with an imaginary pencil on millions of miles of nothing.

They waited.

AND IT CAME. Ponderous, silent, and oh God, how incredibly huge and dark. A ship as big as a world and helpless as any dead thing, rushing headlong out of the void in pursuit of its endless and meaningless journey around an alien sun. The starlight burned on its iron flanks, on the humped discolored patches of stellar debris caught by its field of gravity and welded to it by long association.

The Ship. Legend, reality, wealth, danger, death.

They sprang at it, the six little tugs, motes beside a mammoth. But they were strong motes. And they were clever. They had planned their strategy long ago, before they ever left the Belt. Magnetic beams licked out invisible lines of force, concentrating on the exact area of the mighty hull where the most leverage could be applied, using The Ship's own mass and velocity to help shift it on its axis. They did not try to do it all at once. They let The Ship carry them with it, applying their lateral blasts judiciously so that the six tugs began to act as a sort of drogue, gently pulling, gently nudging, wheedling the enormous plunging mass of The Ship into doing what they could not possibly make it do by force. The twenty-two men who manned the tugs worked around the clock. Sleep had ceased to be a regular and accepted thing. When a man fell into his bunk they let him lie there until he got up again, but nobody planned on it. You could always sleep. You could not always, or ever again, be engaged in the greatest and richest salvage operation ever attempted in the history of space flight.

If they had had time they would have succeeded.

They did not have time.

A fleet of nine tugs accompanied by Benson's own fast cruiser came swooping out of the trans-Plutonian darkness and there was no longer any hope that they might possibly have been lost or overlooked. Probably, Farrel thought, the fast cruiser had ranged ahead of the tugs, quartering space until it had located *Farhope* and got a radar fix. Then all they had to do was wait until they caught up.

They had caught up now. They had found Croy's little fleet, and they had found The Ship. Radio silence was not important any more. They broke it.

Croy, as senior captain, sent a call to Benson's ship—the standard warning from one salvage vessel to another to stand off from a job already claimed.

The message was not answered.

It was not even acknowledged. Benson's fleet continued to sweep toward them.

"What the hell are they doing?" said Croy, and then shouted to Victor in the communications room. "Keep trying. Somebody in that bunch has got to answer."

Nobody did.

Croy's other captains—Wallace, Carlucci, Friedman, Gilson, and Schultz—tried, too. They sent out repeated demands for recognition and acknowledgement.

They didn't get it. Benson's fleet came closer and closer, glinting in the starlight.

The tugs of Croy's fleet talked tensely back and forth.

What are they up to? Why don't they answer? They're coming in fast—for crying out loud, are they going to ram us?

How could they do that without killing themselves? They just want to scare us into cutting loose. If we do that The Ship is free to them.

Don't cut loose. I'll slaughter the first man who drops his beam!

Yeah, but what are they going to do?

It became obvious what they were going to do. It was a thing not unknown in the annals of salvage, men being what they are. A tug is not armed in the conventional sense. It does not carry guns. But it possesses all the tools of its trade. It has contained-charges for clearing wreckage, and lateral-blast charges for getting a dead hulk moving. It has magnetic beams to grapple with and thrust-beams to push away with. And it has a demolition beam for sectioning a ship's hull the way a chicken is sliced with a carving knife. Who needs guns?

BENSON'S CRUISER shot ahead and above into a position where it could act as observer and coordinator. The nine tugs separated, six of them coming in separately, each on a target; and the other three hanging back waiting for things to develop so they could see the best place to add their weight.

Things developed fast. In all six of Croy's tugs there was a frantic scramble into space suits and then the men hurried like soldiers to battle-stations. In *Farhope* Croy handled the ship's controls and Victor the thrust beam. Farrel had the demolition beam. The rocket launchers for the contained charges were between them.

Victor had the magnetic beam too, the invisible line of force that held them to The Ship. "Don't cut loose," said Croy, "unless I tell you, no matter what. But if I tell you, don't sit sucking your thumb, but cut fast!"

Benson's tugs closed on them, looking large and sleek and unpleasantly strong. They were the newest thing off the spaceways, heavy-duty craft with the most improved type of tools. Old Croy cursed them. He cursed Benson and Whitmer and Leach and all thieves alike. Farrel knew that part of his rage was the fear that he was going to lose *Farhope*. He did not love *Farhope* like a woman, nor yet like a child. But a man cannot live in and with and by a ship for many years without feeling a certain familiar attachment to it. Anyway, it was his.

Victor was practically crying inside his helmet, a small boy hanging desperately to a balloon when he knows that the bigger boys will inevitably take it from him. A balloon over two miles long and worth more money than all of them could count. Farrel did not blame him.

He glanced out the port and then turned his head to look at Tolti. She was strapped into a deck harness beside the rocket-launchers, supported by webbing so that the wild pitching of the ship should not throw her into a bulkhead. Her too large suit hung limp and dejected around her and her head was lost inside the bulging helmet. He had tried to make her strap in to her bunk to be as safe as possible, but she had refused. So now she was manning the launchers that he had showed her how to handle, and she smiled at him, and there was something in her eyes that got to him with a sudden pang right at the last moment he would have chosen to think about how he felt toward Tolti.

He looked out the port again at the oncoming tugs, braced himself, and waited with a hot and deadly anger for them to come within range.

They didn't quite do that. They didn't have to. Their thrusts and demos and charge launchers were newer and more efficient over long distances. And Croy's tugs were handicapped. They had The Ship and they couldn't let go, and as long as they couldn't let go they couldn't maneuver.

Farhope was hit suddenly by a thrust-beam that laid her on her beam and sent her lurching dangerously toward the great wall of The Ship's hull. During the time that she was exposed and helpless, a rocket-borne charge exploded against her belly. There was a second terrific jar, a rending sound, and then the distant shriek of leaking air from the lower regions. Red lights flared on the control panel. Automatic doors slammed shut, sealing off the breached hold.

Croy said quietly, "Cut loose."

Victor reached out and slammed the switch.

The magnetic beam, the umbilical that bound them to The Ship and held them helpless, was gone. *Farhope* leaped forward, away from the black towering wall, toward a silver tug with a red emblem on it. Farrel had a brief, half stunned vision of other tugs cutting loose from The Ship, rising, scattering. One had smashed into the giant hull and was falling away with part of its bow broken. He wondered who it was and then he didn't have any more time to think because Croy was barreling straight in on the silver tug with every appearance of wanting to ram him. The silver tug dropped hastily out of the way and Croy laughed. "That's the boy," he said. "That's the dirty little so-and-so. Give it to him, Ross."

FARREL HIT the demo-beam controls and *Farhope* became in an instant a mighty cutting torch, projecting a knife of blue flame from the nozzle just below the curve of her bow. Croy took her low over the Benson tug and held her there as long as he could, perhaps three quarters of a minute, practically riding the other ship's back as it twisted and turned wildly to escape. Then he went on and left it to limp away with a big black hole burned through its upper hull and a great plume of air spouting out of it like the breath of a blowing whale.

Farhope whirled and went lumbering back to her own destruction. Friedman's tug was already hulled and caught between two of the Benson ships, which were driving it relentlessly toward collision with The Ship. There were four or five good minutes during which Tolti launched six rockets and saw one hit. Victor knocked one Benson tug loose from Friedman with his own thrust-beam. Farrel was poised and ready with his demo. And then one of three reserve tugs came up from behind and dropped a lateral-thrust charge fairly on top of them, and *Farhope* split open like a burst can, and that was that.

Croy's voice came over the helmet radio, "All here?"

They were. The blast itself had not reached them, shielded by *Farhope's* thick hull, and their seat belts had kept them from being carried out on the rush of air. They were dazed and deafened, but still alive. Farrel released his belt and went over to Tolti and helped her out of the harness. Croy said,

"We're going to crash into The Ship. Let's get the hell out."

They got out, tumbling through the smashed hull. Tolti panicked for the first time since Farrel had known her, at the sight of the black void falling away with no up or down to the outer edges of infinity. She clung to *Farhope* screaming, and Farrel had to drag her away by main force. Then she fainted and that made it easier. The great hull was very close to them. They cut in their propulsion units full force and clawed away from the point of impact where *Farhope* would end her final voyage. There were other little comets in the night around them, men in spacesuits straining toward their last refuge. Only two tugs of Croy's fleet were still operative and six of the Benson tugs were making short work of them. Three of the Benson tugs were wrecked, two of them probably beyond repair.

Croy said, "Where's the hatch you got in through before?"

The broad black metal plain spread out vast and rough as it had in Farrel's dream. He heard Victor catch his breath in a kind of sob and say, "I don't know how could anybody find one little bitty hole in all this? And they'll be after us in a minute."

Perhaps it was because Farrel was in a state of partial shock from the swift violence of *Farhope's* ending, but more and more this approach to The Ship became like the dream, with the same unnatural clarity of detail. It was as though a recorded tape in his memory vault had suddenly started to unreel. "It's this way," he said, and led off on an angle to his left, without stopping to consider whether he really knew or not. *Farhope* had originally, and for the same reason, hitched on to The Ship at approximately the same place as the six tugs. Farrel and Victor had made the first boarding on their own, but when they had left it after Heyerman's death they had come back almost to where they were now. Farrel led them in reverse, too dazed and shaken to quarrel with his subconscious when it picked out some particular guiding roughness of surface and said, *This way.*

Other suited figures joined them, straggling out in a long line. Fourteen, fifteen men. If Farrel was wrong there would be fifteen dead in a very few minutes.

Benson, in his cruiser high up above the flight, must have looked away from the last destruction of Croy's fleet and seen what the men were doing. Perhaps he had not realized that anybody had actually entered The Ship previously and might just do so again.

The cruiser dived toward them and a couple of the silver tugs came after.

Farrel found the hatch. It was large and it was open just as it had been when they found it before, and for millennia before that. It swallowed the fifteen men easily before the spraying flame of the cruiser's jet could touch them. They dodged into the shelter of that mighty hull and somebody said, "Fine, but they'll be down after us soon."

"Oh, no," said Farrel. "There's a control." He hunted for it and found it. There must have been automatic power controls, of course, but the builders of The Ship had provided a manual as a stand-by. He tugged at the great wheel and two or three others joined him. In space there had not been any rust or corrosion. The perfectly machined, simply designed parts had not corroded or jammed. The huge hatch cover slid into place, blotting out the starlight.

They sat in the dark that was slashed by one sharp torch-beam. For a long time nobody spoke.

Then Carlucci said, "They can cut in through the hull anywhere they want to."

"I don't think they will," Farrel said. "They don't know what they might be destroying inside. I'm not even sure they could if they wanted to. This hull is the toughest metal I ever saw. Not just an alloy, either—the builders must have altered the molecular structure of the stuff. Our ordinary torches didn't even scratch it."

"So okay," said Croy wearily. "They can't or won't get in at us, at least right away. So what? Our air won't last long. Not nearly long enough for us to starve or die of thirst. In about twenty-four hours it won't matter to us when, how, or if Benson gets inside The Ship."

Silence fell again, except for two small sobs from Tolti, who had come out of her faint too soon.

CHAPTER EIGHT

IT WAS HARD to think, hard to prod the weary and hopeless organism into life again. It was easier just to sit and wait until the last long sleep came over you.

But you didn't. There was a law against it. An old law, unwritten, unspoken, handed down intact from the first beginnings of life. You got up and went on as long as there was half a breath left in you.

Farrel said, "We might look and see what these people of The Ship used for air. We might even get the atmosphere plant going again."

Faint hope. Several of the men said so.

"Okay," said Farrel. "So I'm crazy, but I'm going to look anyway. We didn't see any signs of extensive damage when we were here before. Maybe there wasn't any. Maybe there was another reason why The Ship's voyage ended up like this. Come on, Tolti." He helped her up. "Victor? Croy?"

They groaned and muttered but they got up. One by one the others did too. They would live longer if they sat perfectly still and conserved their oxygen supply, but when they thought about it there did not seem to be much point in it.

They straggled off across the vast emptiness of the hold they were in, to wide doors standing open on a corridor that stretched fore and aft as far as their torch beams carried.

Farrel pointed forward. "Vic and I went that way before. There are transverse corridors, and a whole bunch of stairways going to other levels. I think they were escalators when The Ship had power. We didn't get too far."

"If we split up," Croy said, "we'd stand a better chance of finding something." He did not quite say "in time."

"Be damned careful what you touch," said Farrel, who then told them what had happened to Heyerman.

Without much hope, but beginning in spite of themselves to feel the awe and astonishment of actually being aboard this giant nameless wanderer from some alien star, they separated and began to move off by twos and threes.

Farrel went aft this time. He had a shrinking aversion to seeing the room of the great crystal again, with the frozen shreds of Heyerman's body still in it. Besides, he wanted to look at the vital organs of The Ship, and they were more likely to be aft and below, linked together by the main power plant. The four of them from *Farhope* traveled together for a time and then Croy and Victor chose a different corridor and Farrel went on with Tolti.

It was eerie going. The darkness and the still dead desolation were bad enough. But it was so damned big.

The corridors went on forever, with hundreds of doors opening into hundreds of unnamed spaces designed for unnamed purposes by builders of an unnameable race.

They gave up trying to look into every one them. Some were crammed with different types of equipment, or were nearly empty of different kinds of supplies, or were entirely empty. A lot of them had obviously been living quarters, and it was equally obvious from the chairs and other furniture that the people of The Ship had been humanoids, perhaps even humans. The rooms were all neat and clean, but with no personal touches, no clothes or books or pictures. It was as though block after block of occupants had moved out, leaving nothing of themselves behind.

"I wonder what they were like," Tolti said, "and where they came from, and where they went."

"God knows," said Farrel and shivered, oppressed by the rows of empty rooms.

They went on deeper into the bowels of The Ship.

THERE WERE very large spaces like ballrooms or gymnasiums or theaters. A couple or them he was pretty sure of. There were mess halls and a gigantic galley. Everything was quite old and well worn, but whoever the people of The Ship had been they were sticklers for keeping things spotless and in good repair. The electronic ranges in the galley looked as though they would still work if there was only power for them. Farrel began to have a totally unreasonable stirring of hope.

Tolti was looking at stacks of plastic dishes in their dispenser-racks. "You know?" she said. "It is as if they expected to comeback and use all this again."

Farrel shook his head. "I don't think so. Nothing changes in space—look around. There isn't a single bit of anything to indicate continuity. They scrubbed up after the last meal and put everything away and left it."

"Scrubbed up for who?" said Tolti. "If it wasn't for themselves, I mean. Maybe they left it all—for us?"

"For us?"

"For whoever found The Ship, sometime. Maybe—" Her voice came quick and eager over the helmet radio, like a child dreaming up a story. "Maybe they were proud of themselves and their Ship. Maybe they didn't want all this to go to wreck and ruin even if they had to die themselves, so that someday people would know—"

Friedman's voice broke in on them, sharp with excitement. "I think we've found the main power plant. And this you've got to see to believe."

A few minutes later Farrel and Tolti were standing with Friedman and four or five others at the very heart of The Ship—a central Core incredibly huge, with marching lines of giant dynamos carrying power aft to the colossal chambers of the main drive and forward to all other parts of The Ship.

Friedman pointed excitedly to the pile that squatted like an emperor among his slaves above the dynamos, "You know what that is?"

He raced on before Farrel could give him an answer, which was no. "It's a cold-fusion furnace. We've been working on it for over a century and never got it out of the laboratory yet, but they mastered it, and it gave them just what our researchers always said it would give—practically unlimited power and faster-than-light speeds."

Farrel remembered that as far back as the middle of the last century the possibility of controlling nuclear fusion at temperatures close to absolute zero had already been under study. He stared hungrily at the mighty face of the pile, with all its dials and gauges inert and all its signal lights dead. Power. Power unlimited. Power enough, if there was still any fuel at all, to—

No. That was crazy.

But it looked so well preserved, the whole complex of furnace-pile and dynamos, as though it had been shut down carefully and laid up like any ship in mothballs—only in the sterile cold of space there was no need of protective coverings against rust. He flashed his torch-beam back and forth over the looming pile and something caught his eye, a painted symbol that glowed when his light touched it. He held the beam on it. It was painted large on a blank area of the wall, and it had a horrid familiarity. He turned suddenly cold and flicked the light away, and Friedman said,

"What was that? It didn't look like part of the board markings—"

"It isn't," Farrel said grimly.

"It's an outline sketch of the big crystal that killed Heyerman." He moved away uneasily. "Let's see if we can locate the atmosphere plant."

CROY AND VICTOR had got there before them. They joined forces there, a handful of tiny mobile figures dwarfed by the giant pumps flanking an enormous cylindrical chamber that must have been half a mile long. Here too was the same look of care, of preserving for future use.

"It's the same way up there," said Croy, pointing forward, "There's a bunch of what seem to be synthesizers for food and water, just like this one is for air. They look as though all you'd have to do is push a button."

"Yeah," said Victor, "but I ain't pushing any. You know what, Ross? Everyone of those synthesizers has got a picture on it, of the crystal—"

"That killed Heyerman," Farrel said, "I know. The main pile has one." He poked around with his torch beam. "See there? Up over that selector panel. There's one there too."

"It's a warning," said Victor, "That's what it is. Hands off. If we try to fool with these things they'll kill us just like that crystal did Heyerman."

"Now wait," said Farrel sharply. "Wait just a minute. That's what I thought, but when you put it in words like that... Listen, suppose we hadn't just happened to find that particular cabin the first time, and Heyerman hadn't tried to chip a hunk off the crystal, how would we know?"

"I don't get you," said Victor, "Well, the people of The Ship went around painting that symbol on all these things. It must have been some message for the people they hoped and expected to see it—that's us. If they meant it as a warning—what good is a warning if people don't know they're being warned? They could have thought up a symbol for danger that wouldn't be so highly specialized that nobody but themselves could understand it."

"Hey," said Croy, "maybe you got something there. Maybe they were trying to tell us something else. But what?"

"I don't know. But the crystal is the only thing in The Ship that's still powered. That was a static discharge that killed Heyerman—the potential must have been building up in the crystal for thousands of years, from the tiny bits of energy it could pick up from cosmic radiation. It must have been designed for the purpose, so it would have power even when The Ship itself was shut down and dead."

"Power," said Croy, "for what?"

"I don't know," said Farrel, "but I'm damned sure it wasn't for killing stray spacemen who might happen on it. If they wanted to booby-trap The Ship they'd have done better than that. Instead, they left the door open."

He started away, spurred by his own swift excitement. "I'm going to have another look at that crystal."

Tolti ran after him immediately, and then Croy said he would come, too. So did Friedman. The rest of them, including Carlucci who had now joined them, decided they would stay and see if they could puzzle out the operation of the power plant, which was the first requisite to getting anything started. Victor said he would stay with them.

"I was in that room once, and once was enough."

"Okay," said Farrel, "but for God's sake take it easy with that reactor. You could blow the whole Ship to pieces on a teaspoonful of fuel."

"He's right," said Croy. "No need to get reckless just because you figure you're dead anyway. Who knows, maybe Farrel's right, and the old people left some kind of a message that would help us."

Somebody, probably Victor, muttered that it was a fat chance. Farrel paid no attention. He was suddenly in a fury of haste to get back to the cabin where the crystal was.

He wasn't exactly sure why. But it was more than a hunch. It was a conviction, a certainty that the people of The Ship had painted that symbol everywhere for a purpose.

He could not find the cabin at once in the labyrinthine gloom of corridors and great rooms full of curved glass screens and massed computer banks and the rigid memories of life, long vanished—paint worn to the bright metal underneath by the passage of many feet or the daily friction of someone's hand or elbow at a table, the million scars and stains of use. The Ship had come a long way before it died.

FINALLY HE CAME across a place that was familiar to him and turned a corner, and the room was there, large and shadowy, with the rack of peepers and beyond it the huge crystal like a grotesque and glittering spider in its web of coils, with the shrunken and twisted thing still on the deck beneath it.

"Okay," said Croy, "You found it. Now what do we look for?"

"I don't know." Farrel walked slowly toward the crystal, keeping his torch-beam on it and his eyes averted from Heyerman's wreckage.

There was the crystal. Probably artificially constructed to a specific design. There were the springy coils, and that was all.

There was no protective device to keep people away. Ergo, the thing was not intended to be lethal or those who had worked with it originally would not have been exposed to too much danger. Ergo, it had built up more potential than it was supposed to, enough to kill a fool who whacked it with a metal hammer.

Probably even so if there had been air, and Heyerman had not depended on a suit for existence, he would only have been shocked or singed a little. The charge itself hadn't killed him. It was the bursting of the suit sleeve that did it.

But the crystal must have waited a lot longer time than its makers had planned for it, loading itself with a slow accretion of energy it had no way to discharge.

For what? For what?

He turned and looked at the peepers, the dark crystal eggs racked in their cushioned pockets. Mind readers, mental eavesdroppers. The people of The Ship had mastered that borderline country of science, too.

Little crystal, big crystal. There must be a connection, a solution—

But the peepers would not receive at short range. That wasn't it.

He moved the light around, a spot of hard brilliance with no refraction, no scatter in this vacuum.

He saw, beyond Heyerman, a slender metal column about four feet high, with a bar of crystal mounted on it. The bar was set parallel to the face of the big crystal. One end of it was longer than the other. The short end was flared and bore a crest of slender filaments.

When he looked closer he saw that the long end was shaped to fit a receptacle in the big crystal, exactly where that end would strike it if the bar were turned on its column until its axis was vertical to the opposed face.

The others had come up behind him. They must have seen the significance of the bar about as soon as he did, but nobody said anything. He would have to make up his own mind, and since he was there first he could have first turn. If he decided not to risk touching the thing he could step down and let the next man decide.

If he did risk it there might not be any further decision.

Sweat ran cold and unpleasant down his face and the air in his suit seemed stifling.

It was that that decided him. He only had a few more hours anyway, so he might as well go now as then, if the same thing happened to him that had happened to Heyerman. If it didn't, and the people of The Ship hadn't played some kind of a cruel joke on them, it might mean life for all of them.

"Stand back," he said, and pushed Tolti firmly out of the way. Then, feeling sick with fright, he reached out and grabbed the bar and swung it into place before he had time to think about it.

CHAPTER NINE

THERE WAS A SHOCK, but it was in his mind. He put up his gauntleted hands quite futilely to the sides of his helmet and reeled back to the farthest end of the cabin, the way he would have from a stunning burst of sound.

The super-charged crystal was pouring out a tremendous volume of *thought*.

We do not know who you are, but we have prepared this record against your coming, so that our name and the knowledge of what we have accomplished may live even though we ourselves must die.

Croy, who had made his own hasty way to the far end of the room, swore in startled surprise. Friedman, beside him, whispered, "Shut up and listen!"

The crystal, shot through now with latent glimmerings that pulsed outward through the rod and lit the filaments with a brightening glow, sent its message roaring into their minds. Tolti, cowering against the wall, reached out and took Farrel's hand.

The languages of men are clumsy and difficult to learn. Perhaps in time you will learn ours, for there is much of value in our library. But we have chosen to speak directly to your minds, for only that way can you really understand the meaning of what we have done—

Thought formulated into the equivalent of speech gave way almost without transition to pictorial images. Not the external and impersonal images of video, but the vivid, proud, poignant memories of a living mind. They entered into Farrel and took him over, so that he forgot who he was and why he had come here and what he had to do. He forgot Tolti and Croy and Whitmer and Leach and Benson. He became another man, from another world far, far away in space and time.

A beautiful world. It had seas and mountains, wide plains and deserts, little villages and great cities. It had good weather and bad, good people and bad, good laws and bad. It circled a blue-white star on the edge of a cluster on the other side of the galaxy. At night the sky was glorious with stars. The world was called Fehar.

Science was far advanced on Fehar. Its ships had been in space for several hundred years, roaming from star to star, charting great sectors of the galaxy. Now the crowning achievement in the field of interstellar flight was about to be attempted.

The Ship was finished.

It had been built in space, where its great size was not unwieldy. It had taken thirty years to build. The great ribs of the primal skeleton had been laid and bolted before Nen-sur was born. Nen-sur was a man now, a junior officer, standing in the ranks of The Ship's company, one thousand and three young men gathered together in the assembly hall.

Beyond the ports a great crowd of public and private craft hung watching in space, and in the assembly hall dignitaries of Fehar were making speeches. Nen-sur did not hear them. He was thinking of home, of his parents and brothers and sisters, and he wanted to cry for them at the same time his heart was swelling and his pulse pounding with pride and dreams of glory.

When the speeches were over and the dignitaries had left, the signal bells rang and the lights flashed and Nen-sur went with the others who were off duty to the ports to watch.

Far beneath his feet the mighty drives of The Ship stirred and roused to life. The decks quivered. Slowly, ponderously, with immense pride, The Ship began to move. And the watching craft all flashed a final salute, and as Nen-sur looked at them they became like tiny flecks and then were gone, and Fehar dwindled behind them. Presently it too was gone.

The Ship had begun its voyage.

And Nen-sur thought...

To travel clear around the galaxy, to circumnavigate the Milky Way—and I will chart the unknown stars!

THE SHIP GATHERED its strength and speed and dropped Fehar's sun and then the whole cluster far astern. It passed into hyper-drive, from which it only emerged into normal space to examine a solar system with habitable planets or map more closely the shores of a nebula.

And Nen-sur charted the stars. In the vast chart-room of The Ship, he and the others of his particular craft sat surrounded by the huge image-conversion screens and all the other intricate apparatus for star-mapping. They created year by year a three-dimensional strip-map of the galaxy and stored it in the banks of the cartograph center, to be brought forth again at will and projected in the stereo tank. Nen-sur changed from a young man to a middle-aged man, and he thought often of his family and friends at home, and mourned them all as dead. Because of the time factor involved in The Ship's tremendous velocity, he would outlive his contemporaries by several of their centuries. The goodbyes they had said had been more than mere words.

But always there were more stars to chart.

As the ship's company aged and the vast circle of the galactic rim began to slope homeward again, they talked more and more of Fehar and their return. Already they knew that many of them would not make it. The time factor had been calculated accurately, but not accurately enough where an infinitesimal error couldn't mean a man's life.

They buried increasing numbers of their company in space, among the alien stars. But still there would be many left to see home again.

They believed this. But it was not so.

A factor they had not known before, because no other voyage of this speed and duration had ever been attempted, became manifest. The retardation of time was canceled eventually by a limitation of living cells, which could not be made to continue living indefinitely.

The death rate accelerated with frightening speed. The ship's company drew together in ever-smaller compass, leaving whole blocks of living quarters vacant. The Ship grew larger and more lonely, more silent, peopled more by memories than by living men. It took on a quality of doom. The mathematicians worked endlessly with their computers, balancing what they knew against what they hoped.

And Nen-sur charted the stars.

Fewer than half of the young men who had been with him in the chart-room were left. They were no longer young. Neither was he. And there were still a billion stars between him and the sight of home.

The mathematicians told them finally what they already knew in their hearts. Fehar was as lost to them as their own youth. Now they had a choice.

They could go on with the voyage until the last one died and The Ship went rushing on untended at its terrible velocity, a potential force great enough to vaporize a star and all its worlds and peoples. Or they could stop here, laying up The Ship and letting it drift with the slow galactic tides until somewhere, sometime, a race of men might find it and find a use for all the vast store of knowledge they had bought at the cost of their thousand and three lives, so that it would not all be lost. So that even, some day, word might be taken back to Fehar of how the voyage had ended.

They chose the latter way.

We have taken care that everything should be preserved. The Ship is ready to live again at a touch, so that wherever she may be found she need not suffer the shame of being taken as a derelict—this ship that would have completed the circle of the galaxy if her weak human crew had not failed her!

We have made this mental record—I, Nen-sur, was chosen to make the actual recording because I am now the senior officer of those few who remain: Vi-shan, the senior engineer, will now instruct you in the operation of The Ship. After that we shall take our places, the last nineteen of us, at the hatch that will be opened to exhaust the air.

It will be a quick death. And we go proudly. We failed, but not through cowardice or faintness of will. What we did accomplish is more than men have ever done before. We are content. And to you, the unknown and unknowable men of an alien star to whom I speak, we bequeath our pride. Do not betray it!

Silence.

THE MIND OF Ross Farrel began feebly to reassert itself. Then he realized that the engineer Vi-shan was speaking, detailing the simple operations by which The Ship's almost entirely automatic machinery could be reactivated. And this was more important than all the glorious panoramas of star-streams and nebulae, all the human implications of splendid defeat. He listened.

Beside him Croy and Friedman were listening too. But Tolti wept.

When the mental record ceased Farrel and the others stood where they were for a moment, still dazed and shaken. Then Croy said hoarsely, "Did you get all that? About starting the pile and the air-plant and all."

"Yeah," said Friedman. "I got it."

So had Farrel.

"Then let's get the hell busy."

Croy and Friedman ran out of the room. Farrel, coming after them with Tolti, picked up one of the peepers from the rack.

Back down in the heart of The Ship, while Croy and Friedman told the others what had happened and then got them to work on the preliminaries, Farrel gave the peeper to Victor and told him to get it going.

"We need to know what those bastards out there are doing," he said, nodding toward where the tugs of Benson's fleet must be outside the hull. "If Whitmer and Benson are figuring some way to louse us up we ought to know it."

Victor grunted and went off to one side where he began the effort of hooking the fine terminals to a spare torch-battery, cursing the clumsiness of his gauntleted hands.

Farrel, still feeling eerily that he was two men in one body, joined the others on the power complex.

The people of The Ship had done well. In what seemed like an incredibly short time the great cold fusion furnace was turning the long-silent dynamos and the atmosphere plant was operating. They waited, panting over the vitiated air in their suits, watching the telltales rise as pressure built up in the vast spaces of The Ship, driven by the monstrous pumps. The engineer Vi-shan had given the chemical content of their normal atmosphere, and it was close enough to Earth's to be safely breathable. The men of Fehar must have been very human in their bodies as well as their emotions.

Farrel watched the gauges, with his lungs laboring and his throat on fire. And finally, when he had to breathe or die, he flung off his helmet and there was air—thin, odd-smelling, still bitterly cold because the heating units had a long way to go, but air.

Just when he was feeling happy about it, dancing around in a kind of feeble jig with the others while their breath steamed and it seemed as though they might be going to survive after all. Victor came up and said,

"I've been listening. The tugs are already hooked on and they'll have The Ship out of her orbit before long, with the start we've already given them. Meantime, they've got to get rid of our bodies. Besides, Whitmer and Benson and Leach just can't wait to see what they've got inside here. They figure we're dead by now so we won't give them any trouble. They're just now coming with a crew to try and cut in through that hatch."

CHAPTER TEN

SOME TWO HOURS LATER, dressed again in their vac-suits but with oxygen cylinders recharged, Farrel and eight other men—all that could be spared—stood in the dark hold through which they had first entered The Ship. The rest of the great craft was lighted now. The men of Fehar had closed all the protective shutters before they took their last step into space, so that no light showed from outside the hull to give warning, and they needed it for what they were planning to do.

In the hold it was pitch dark and the inner door was sealed. The air had been pumped out. Now for almost an hour they had waited, feeling the vibrations of enormous effort around the hatch transmitted faintly through the hull. Several times as they watched the hatch glowed brightly through cherry-red to white, but it did not melt or show any signs of weakening.

Farrel grinned, a bitter and humorless expression that was almost a snarl. He was remembering what Whitmer and Leach had done to him in the hope of this moment, and what they and Benson had done together to a lot of better men.

He switched on his torch and blinked it three times as a signal—their helmet radios were off. Then he swung the beam to center on the huge wheel of the manual hatch control. He walked toward it and Victor walked beside him. The others disposed themselves on the deck here and there and lay still. But each one of them had a weapon in his hand, something hard and heavy.

The torch-beam went out.

Farrel and Victor took hold of the wheel and turned it, a quarter turn.

Instantly the vibrations from above were doubled in strength. Farrel smiled. He turned the wheel a little farther and then left it free. He crouched down beside the wheel, as though he had died trying to open the hatch again. Victor lay down near him.

The crew outside the hull worked like madmen on the hatch, forcing it open. Farrel could sense the slow turning of the wheel and then he could see a glare of bluish light from a work flare and there was an opening in the hull.

Someone leaned in and probed around with the beam of a powerful light. The beam went around two or three times, picking out the inert forms in the hold and making sure there was no reaction. Then the someone came in, half jumping, half floating in the light gravity, to the deck. Others followed. Farrel counted. Seven came down, and then no more. For once the odds were on their side.

He jumped up and sprang at the nearest man and hit him hard on top of the helmet with a heavy iron tool he had brought from one of the machine shops down below.

For quite a while then in the dark, amid the erratic slashing beams of torches that gyrated as the men who held them fought or tried to run, there was an intense and silent confusion.

Farrel's move was the signal. The others rose from the deck and flung themselves on Benson's astounded party. Victor grabbed the wheel and tried to wrestle the hatch cover shut again and another man joined him. Something hit Farrel a crashing blow and knocked him back and he thought for a minute his suit was torn. Then he saw a man leaping frantically upward toward the closing aperture of the hatch. He leaped too and caught the man's boot in mid-air and dragged him down again and they fought in the curious balloon-like fashion of men in low gravity.

Three times he was aware of the flash of a gun going off. But apparently only a few of the party were armed and some of them must have been taken by surprise in that first onslaught when the "dead" men had sprung up and attacked them. Four out of the seven were already down.

FARREL HIT the helmet of the man he was grappling with twice very hard with the iron tool and the man sagged over and fell, knocked out by the concussion. Then the hatch had swung shut again and there was no escape. Farrel saw that the last two of Benson's party were being subdued. One of his own men had been killed by gunfire, but the trap had been completely unexpected, and the fight was over so soon that this had been their only casualty.

Farrel went over and pounded on the sealed door into the Corridor.

The lights came on, recessed tubes set in the curving wall. The pumps began to force air back into the hold. Pretty Soon Farrel could hear the men who had been left outside the hatch battering frantically to get in.

In a few minutes more the door opened and Carlucci signaled that it was all right to take their helmets off. They did, stripping their suits one by one while others stood by with the captured guns, on guard. Then they made the prisoners do the same. Farrel watched, anxious to see what faces emerged from the obscuring helmets.

Whitmer was there. And Leach.

Whitmer looked at Farrel as though he wished now he had killed him when he had the chance, but he shut his jaw tight and said nothing. He was thinking, figuring, waiting until he knew more of this situation.

Leach was less patient. His face was red and ugly, and when he saw Farrel he did not waste any time in speech. He went for him. Farrel let him almost get his hands on him, and then he hit Leach with everything he had. Leach did not quite go down. But he did not make any more attempts to fight when one of the men caught his collar and hauled him back into line again.

"Which one of you is Benson?" Farrel asked.

A broad blocky man with gray hair and a granite face said, "I am."

He was looking at the lights and smelling the air.

Farrel said, "Okay, take the rest of them and lock them up. You and Whitmer come with me."

Carlucci and Victor, with guns, fell in as a guard behind them. Farrel led the way swiftly along corridors and down escalators—which were working now—toward the central part of The Ship, above the power plant and forward of it.

Benson said, "I wouldn't have thought any of it would still be operative."

Farrel did not answer, and Benson shrugged. But he and Whitmer both looked around eagerly at every step, their eyes shining with greed and exasperation. Presently Farrel led the way into a large cabin, handsome in an alien fashion but sober and well worn. Croy sat behind the broad low desk. Friedman was beside him, standing. Here the captain of The Ship had lived.

Tolti, sitting in an attitude of strained anxiety in a corner, jumped up as Farrel came in. He smiled at her and she smiled back and sat down again.

Farrel said to Croy, "We got them," He told their names, and Croy looked at them as though he had found them in a piece of rotten meat.

Benson met his eye without embarrassment. "It seems to be about time for a top-level discussion," he said. "You have us, but we have you. My tugs are hooked on. The Ship is already edging out of her orbit, and it won't be long before we're on our way— whether I get back to my flagship or not. They won't stop because of that. So I'd say we could start thinking about a deal."

He glanced at Whitmer. "What would you say?"

Whitmer said coolly, "I'd say there's enough to go around. In fact, if you people hadn't been so greedy in the first place all this trouble might have been avoided."

"Sure," said Croy. "You could have stolen The Ship all for yourselves and never had to share a nickel of it. What kind of a deal?"

"Double shares against your not bothering the authorities with any of our private quarrels. The salvage business is a rough game. We all know that. People get hurt. You can't help it." He looked around the cabin, "There seems to be more here than I'd figured even. It's promising. You've got light, air, and heat already from The Ship's own power—"

As an apparent afterthought he asked, "What are you going to do for food and water?"

"The synthesizers all work," said Croy. "We don't need any of your supplies."

THE SHIP QUIVERED slightly, shifting and creaking as the strains of countless years were altered. Distant boomings and clatterings echoed faint and hollow down the labyrinthine corridors and through the empty spaces.

Benson smiled, "You see? I told you the work would go on.

And my men will have the whole time before we make Ganymede to find some way to get in through the hull. You can't keep us prisoner forever. And if you kill us you'll have more to explain than we will."

"It's a good deal," said Whitmer. "You'd better take it."

The Ship quivered and creaked again, nudging farther and farther out of her age-old orbit.

Croy said, "Perhaps. Come on in here and we'll talk about it."

He got up and went with Friedman through a door, and the others followed.

They stood now in the bridge, the brain center that controlled the pounding heart below. The lights on the main board glowed. Benson saw them and his face tightened, but he did not say anything. Friedman went and switched on the screens that were all around the circular room. Farrel took his place beside Croy, Carlucci and Victor remained with the guns trained on the prisoners. Tolti came in quietly and went up and stood beside Farrel.

The screens warmed and sprang to life, showing space and stars, the ponderous bulk of The Ship, the sturdy little tugs laboring with a rhythmic flaring of blasts to warp that mighty bow around—the bow that had forged more than half way around the galaxy.

"Now," said Croy, and pushed a lever, and then another. Farrel put his hand on the auxiliary board and waited. His heart was pounding as Nen-sur's hand had and the queer duality was on him again. He thought of a world and a sun he had never seen, and a crowd of ships signaling farewell. Far beneath his feet the mighty drives of The Ship stirred and roused to life. The decks quivered. Slowly, ponderously, with immense pride, The Ship began to move—

Benson and Whitmer cried out furiously, but Farrel hardly heard them. He was speaking across a deep dark gulf to Nen-sur, saying...

It is as you wished.

And the great drives of The Ship beat stronger and stronger, and she moved and flung away the impertinent tugs from her flank and left them far behind as if they had never existed. The great dark bow like an iron mountain swung and pointed toward the distant sun, and The Ship was finishing her voyage.

Once more Tolti's eyes shone with tears. Farrel put his arm around her, knowing that she was thinking of Nen-sur too, and the thousand and three young men who had gone out from Fehar so long ago.

Probably, Farrel thought, The Ship would never see her home world again. But because of the gallantry and forethought of the men who had sailed her on that brave and foredoomed voyage, the children of Sol would reach the stars much sooner and voyage farther than they could ever have done without her. From her they would learn all they needed to know of drives and power and the far-flung starlanes, and from her men they would learn what kind of hearts and minds were needed, to fly the ships they would build.

Someday, Farrel knew, a ship would touch at Fehar, and across a galaxy a proud memory would come home at last.

THE END

NEXT STOP...THE MOON!

Out in the remote California desert Mike Novak was sitting on a powder keg. He was working on the biggest thing since the atom bomb!

Hired by the government to build a mock-up fuel tank for a mock-up spaceship, Mike discovered he was looking at a design that, if done right, could actually work! A design that would soon turn his life upside down.

Here is a wildly exciting story torn from newspaper headlines—the story of man's first triumphant step into outer space. It is an unforgettable, nerve-clenching novel of the first moon-rocket and the men who dared to build it—told by one of the great masters of science fiction...C. M. Kornbluth

CAST OF CHARACTERS

MIKE NOVAK
This disgruntled government employee took a new job working on a moon rocket project—a job that could get him killed!

AMY STUART
Nothing like having a glamorous, high society dame working at your side. What exactly was her interest in a "toy" spaceship?

MR. ANHEIER
Los Angeles based agent-in-charge for the A.E.C. He had said he was only curious, but then people started to die…

AUGUST CLIFTON
It was just a mock-up spaceship he was working on. Or was it? Would he even live long enough to find out the truth?

JOE FRIML
Could he handle the pressure? He was a nervous little man who found himself in way over his head.

JAMES MACILHENY
He was the big cheese behind the moon project, but just naïve enough to not know what was really going on.

LILLY CLIFTON
The poor grieving widow—a dead husband with a bullet hole in his head. Was she really the simple-minded waif she appeared?

TAKEOFF

By
C. M. KORNBLUTH

ARMCHAIR FICTION
PO Box 4369, Medford, Oregon 97504

CHAPTER ONE

MORNING of a bureaucrat.

On the wall behind his desk Daniel Holland, general manager of the U. S. Atomic Energy Commission, had hung the following:

His diploma from Harvard Law, '39;

A photograph of himself shaking hands with his hero, the late David Lilienthal, first A.E.C. chairman;

His certificate of honorable active service in the Army of the United States as a first lieutenant, in the Judge Advocate General's Department, dated February 12, 1945;

A letter of commendation from the general counsel of the T.V.A., which included best wishes for his former assistant's success on the new and challenging field of public administration he was entering;

A diploma declaring in Latin that he was an honorary Doctor of Laws of the University of North Carolina as of June 15, 1956;

A blowup of *The New Republic's* vitriolic paragraph on his "Bureaucracy versus the People" (New York, 1956);

A blowup of *Time* magazine's vitriolic paragraph on his "Red Tape Empires" (New York, 1957);

Signed photographs of heroes (Lilienthal, the late Senator McMahon); industrialists (Henry Kaiser, the late Charles E. Wilson of General Motors, Wilson Stuart of Western Aircraft, the late John B. Watson of International Business Machines); scientists (James B. Conant, J. Robert Oppenheimer) and politicians (Chief Justice Palmer, Senator John Marshall Butler of Maryland, ex-President Truman, ex-President Warren, President Douglas).

An extract from the January 27, 1947, hearings of the Senate half of the joint Senate-House Committee on Atomic Energy—held in connection with confirmation of the President's appointees to the A.E.C., particularly that of Lilienthal—which ran as follows:

Senator McKellar *(to Mr. Lilienthal): Did it not seem to you to be remarkable that in connection with experiments that have been carried on since the days of Alexander the Great, when he had his Macedonian scientists trying to split the atom, the President of the United States would discharge General Groves, the discoverer of the greatest secret that the world has ever known, the greatest discovery, scientific discovery, that has ever been made, to turn the whole matter over to you;*

who never really knew, except from what you saw in the newspapers, that the Government was even thinking about atomic energy?

The Chairman: *Let us have it quiet, please.*

Senator McKellar: *You are willing to admit, are you, that this secret, or the first history of it, dated from the time when Alexander the Great had his Macedonian scientists trying to make this discovery, and then Lucretius wrote a poem about it, about two thousand years ago? And everybody has been trying to discover it, or most scientists have been trying to discuss it, ever since. And do you not really think that General Groves, for having discovered it, is entitled to some little credit for it?*

"Read that," said Holland to his first caller of the morning. "Go on, read it."

James MacIlheny, Los Angeles insurance man and president of the American Society for Space Flight, gave him an inquiring look and slowly read the extract.

"I suppose," MacIlheny said at last, "your point is that you wouldn't be able to justify granting my request if Congress called you to account."

"Exactly. I'm a lawyer myself; I know how they think. Right-wrong, black-white, convicted-acquitted. Exactly why should A.E.C. co-operate and exchange information with the people? If you're any good, we ought to hire you. If you aren't any good, we oughtn't to waste time on you."

"Are those your personal views, Mr. Holland?" asked MacIlheny, flushing.

Holland sighed. "My personal views are on the record in a couple of out-of-print books, a few magazine articles, and far too many congressional-hearing minutes. You didn't come here to discuss my personal views; you came for an answer to a question. The answer has got to be 'no.'"

"I came on your invitation—" MacIlheny began angrily, and then he pulled himself together. "I'm not going to waste time losing my temper. I just want you to consider some facts. American Government rocket research is scattered all over hell—Army, Navy, Air Force, Bureau of Standards, Coast and Geodetic Survey, and God-alone-knows-where-else. You gentlemen don't let much news out, but

obviously we're getting nowhere. We would have had a manned rocket on the moon ten years ago if we were! I'm speaking for some people who know the problem, a lot of them trained, technical men. We've got the drawings. We've had some of them for fifteen years! All that's needed is money and fuel, atomic fuel—"

Holland looked at his watch, and MacIlheny stopped in mid-flight. "I see it's not getting through," he said bitterly. "When the Russian or Argentine lunar guided missiles begin to fall on America you'll have a lot to be proud of, Mr. Holland." He started for the door. Before he was out, Holland's secretary was in, summoned by a buzzer.

"Let's hit the mail, Charlie," Holland said, lighting a cigarette and emptying his overflowing "in" basket on his desk.

Ryan's bid on the Missoula construction job. "Tell him very firmly that I want him to get the contract because of his experience, but that his bid's ridiculously high. Scare him a little."

Damages claim from an ex-A.E.C. employee's lawyer, alleging loss of virility from radiation exposure. "Tell Morton to write this shyster absolutely nothing doing; it's utterly ridiculous. Hint that we'll have him up before his state bar association if he pesters us any more. And follow through if he does!"

Dr. Mornay at Oak Ridge still wanted to publish his article arguing for employment of foreign-born scientific personnel in the A.E.C. "Write him a very nice letter. Say I've seriously considered his arguments but I still think publication would be a grave error on his part. See my previous letter for reasons and ask him just to consider what Senator Hoyt would make of his attitude."

The governor of Nevada wanted him to speak at a dam dedication. "Tell him no, I never speak, sorry."

Personnel report from Missoula Directed Ops. "Greenleaf's lost three more good men, damn it. Acknowledge his letter of transmittal—warm personal regards. And tell Weiss to look over the table of organization for a spot we can switch him to where he'll stay in grade but won't be a boss-man."

Half-year fiscal estimate from Holloway at Chalk River Liaison Group in Canada. "Acknowledge it but don't say yes or no. Make copies for Budget and Comptroller. Tell Weiss to ride them for an opinion but not to give them any idea whether I think it's high, low, or perfect. I want to know what *they* think by tomorrow afternoon."

Messenger query from the A.P. on Hoyt's speech in the Senate. "Tell them I haven't seen the text yet and haven't had a chance to check A.E.C. med records against the Senator's charges. Add that in my own experience I've never met an alcoholic scientist and til I do I'll continue to doubt that there's such an animal. Put some jokes in it."

The retiring Regional Security and Intelligence Office agent in charge at Los Angeles wanted to know Holland's views on who should succeed him. Records of three senior agents attached. "Tell him Anheier looks like the best bet."

The Iranian ambassador, with an air of injured innocence, wanted to know why his country's exchange students had been barred even from nonrestricted A.E.C. facilities. "Tell him it was a State Department decision. Put in some kind of a dig so he'll know I know they started it with our kids. Clear it with State before I see it."

A rambling petition from the Reverend Oliver Townsend Warner, Omaha spellbinder. "I can't make head or tail of this. Tell Weiss to answer it some way or other. I don't want to see any more stuff from Warner; he may have a following but the man's a crank."

Recruiting program report from Personnel Office. "Acknowledge this and tell them I'm not happy about it. Tell them I want on my desk next Monday morning some constructive ideas about roping better junior personnel in, and keeping them with us. Tell them it's perfectly plain that we're getting the third-rate graduates of the third-rate schools and it's got to stop."

Letter from Regional Security and Intelligence office at Chicago; the F.B.I. had turned over a derogatory information against Dr. Oslonski, mathematical physicist. "Hell. Write Oslonski a personal letter and tell him I'm sorry but he's going to be suspended from duty and barred from the grounds again. Tell him we'll get his clearance over with in the minimum possible time and I know it's a lot of foolishness but policy is policy and we've got to think of the papers and Congress. Ask him please to consider the letter a very private communication. And process the S. and I. advisory."

A North Dakota senator wanted a job for his daughter, who had just graduated from Bennington. "Tell Morton to write him that Organization and Personnel hires, not the general manager."

Dr. Redford at Los Angeles wanted to resign; he said he felt he was getting nowhere. "Ask him please, as a personal favor to me, to delay action on his resignation until I've been able to have a talk with him. Put in something about our acute shortage of first-line men. And teletype the director there to rush-reply a report on the trouble."

A red-bordered, courier-transmitted letter from the Secretary of the Department of the Interior, stamped *Secret*. He wanted to know when he would be able to figure on results from A.E.C.'s A.D.M.P.— Atomic Demolition Material Program—in connection with planning for Sierra Reclamation Project. "Tell Interior we haven't got a thing for him and haven't got a date. The feeling among the A.D.M.P. boys is that they've been off on a blind alley for the past year and ought to resurvey their approach to the problem. I'm giving them another month because Scientific Advisory claims the theory is sound. That's secret, by courier."

Hanford's quarterly omnibus report. "Acknowledge it and give it to Weiss to brief for me."

Messenger query from the Bennet newspapers; what about a rumor from Los Angeles that the A.E.C. had launched a great and costly program for a space-rocket atomic fuel. "Tell them A.E.C. did not, does not, and probably will not contemplate a space-rocket fuel program. Say I think I know where the rumor started and that it's absolutely without foundation, impossible to launch such a program without diverting needed weaponeering personnel, et cetera."

Field Investigations wanted to know whether they should tell the Attorney General about a trucking line they caught swindling the A.E.C. "Tell them I don't want prosecution except as a last resort. I do want restitution of the grafted dough, I want the Blue Streak board of directors to fire the president and his cousin in the dispatcher's office, and most of all I want Field Investigations to keep these things from happening instead of catching them *after* they happen."

And so on.

MacIlheny went disconsolately to his room at the Willard and packed. They wouldn't start charging him for another day until 3:00 p.m.; he opened his portable and began tapping out his overdue "President's Message" for *Starward*, monthly bulletin of the American Society for Space Flight. It flowed more easily than usual. MacIlheny was sore.

Fellow Members:

I am writing this shortly after being given a verbal spanking by a high muckamuck of the A.E.C. I was told in effect to pick up my marbles and not bother the older boys; the Government isn't interested in us bumbling amateurs. I can't say I enjoyed this after my hopes had been raised by the exchange of several letters and an invitation to see Mr. Holland about it "the next time I was in Washington." I suppose I mistook routine for genuine interest. But I've learned something out of this disheartening experience.

It's this: we've been wasting a lot of time in the A.S.F.S.F. by romancing about how the Government would some day automatically take cognizance of our sincere and persistent work. My experience today duplicates what happened in 1946, when on campaign for the Government to release unnecessarily classified rocketry art was the flop of the year.

You all know where we stand. Twenty years of theoretical work and math have taken us as far as we can go alone. We now need somebody else's money and somebody else's fuel. A lot of people have money, but under existing circumstances only the A.E.C. can have or ever be likely to have atomic fuel.

The way I feel about it, our next step is fund-raising—lots of it—hat-in-hand begging at the doors of industrial firms and scientific foundations. With that money we can go on from the drawing board to practical experimental work on bits and pieces of space ship, lab-testing our drawing-board gadgets until we know they work and can prove it to anybody—even an A.E.C. general manager.

When we have worked the bugs out of our jato firing circuits, our deadlight gaskets, our manhole seals, our acceleration conches, and the hundred-and-one accessories of space flight, we'll be in a new position. We will be able to go to the A.E.C. and tell them: "Here's a space ship. Give us fuel for it. If you don't, we'll hold you up to the scorn and anger of the country you are blindly refusing to defend."

James MacIlheny
President, A.S.F.S.F.

MacIlheny sat back, breathing hard and feeling more composed. There was no point to hating Holland, but it had been tragic to find him, a key man, afraid of anything new and even afraid to admit it, hiding behind Congress.

He still had some time to kill. He took from his briefcase a report by the A.S.F.S.F. Orbit Computation Committee (two brilliant youngsters from Cal Tech, a Laguna Beach matron to punch the calculating machine and a flow-analysis engineer from Hughes

Aircraft) entitled "Refined Calculations of Grazing Ellipse Braking Trajectories for a Mars Landing After a Flight Near Apposition." Dutifully he tried to read, but at the bottom of its first mimeographed page the report ran into the calculus of variations. MacIlheny knew no mathematics; he was no scientist and he did not pretend to be one. He was a rocket crank, he knew it, and it was twisting his life.

He threw himself into a chair and thought bitterly of the United States moon base that should have been established ten years ago, that should be growing now with the arrival of every monthly rocket. He knew it by heart; the observatory where telescopes—of moderate size, but unhampered by Earth's dense and shimmering atmosphere— would have new stellar mysteries every day; the electronics lab where space-suited engineers would combine and recombine vacuum-tube elements with all outdoors for their vacuum tube; the hydroponics tanks growing green stuff for air and food, fed exhaled carbon dioxide and animal waste, producing oxygen and animal food under the raw sunlight on the Moon.

And he could see a most important area dotted with launchers for small, unmanned rockets with fission-bomb war heads, ready to smash any nation that hit the United States first.

He could see it; why not they? The scattered, uncoordinated, conservative rocketry since World War II had produced what?

Army guided missiles, roaring across arcs of the Pacific every now and then on practice runs.

Air Force altitude jobs squirting up on liquid fuel from the deserts of the Southwest. There was a great, strange, powder-blue city of half a million souls at White Sands, New Mexico, where colonels spoke only to generals and generals spoke only to God. They were "working on" the space-flight problem; they were "getting out the bugs."

The Coast and Geodetic Survey firing its mapping rockets up and over, up and over, eternally, coast to coast, taking strips and strips of pictures.

The Bureau of Standards shooting up its cosmic-ray research rockets; for ten years they "had been developing" a space suit for walking on the Moon. (There were space-suit drawings in the A.S.F.S.F. files—had been for fifteen years.)

The Navy had its rockets, too. You could fire them from submarines, destroyers, cruisers, and special rocket-launching battlewagons that cost maybe sixty-odd what a space ship would stand you.

MacIlheny glumly told himself: might as well get to the airport. No point hanging around here.

He checked out, carrying his light overnight bag and portable. An inconspicuous man followed him to the airport; he had been following MacIlheny for weeks. They both enjoyed the walk; it was a coldly sun-bright January day.

CHAPTER TWO

THERE WAS an immense documentation on Michael Novak, but it was no more extensive than the paper work on any other A.E.C. employee. For everyone—from scrubwoman to Nobel prize physicist—the A.E.C. had one; so-and-so was eighty-seven years old and dribbled when he ate. Their backgrounds were checked to the times of their birth (it had once been suggested, in effect, that their backgrounds be checked to nine months before their birth—this by a congressman who thought illegitimacy should be sufficient reason for denying an applicant employment by the A.E.C.).

The Security and Intelligence Office files could tell you that Michael Novak had been born in New York City, but not that he had played squat tag under and around the pillars of the Canarsie Line elevated shortly before it was torn down. They could tell you that his mother and father had died when he was sixteen, but not that he had loved them. They could tell you that he had begun a brilliant record of scholarship-grabbing in high school, but not that he grabbed out of loneliness and fear.

Rensselaer Polytechnic Institute: aeronautical engineering (but he had been afraid to fly; heights were terrifying) and a junior-year switch to ceramic engineering, inexplicable to the A.E.C. years later.

A ten-month affair with a leggy, tough, young sophomore from the Troy Day College for Women. They interviewed her after ten years as a plump and proper Scarsdale matron; she told the Security men yes, their information was correct; and no, Michael had shown no signs of sexual abnormality.

Summer jobs at Corning Glass and Elpico Pottery, Steubenville, Ohio (but not endless tension: will they do what I tell them, or laugh in my face? Are they laughing at me now? Is that laughter I hear?)

Ten years later they told the Security men sure I remember him, he was a good kid; no, he never talked radical or stuff like that; he worked like hell and he never said much (and maybe I better not tell this guy about the time the kid beat the ears off Wyrostek when he put the white lead in the kid's coverall pocket).

Scholarship graduate study at the University of Illinois, the Hopkins Prize Essay in Ceramic Engineering (with at first much envy of the scatterbrained kids who coasted four years to a B.A., later thin disgust, and last a half-hearted acceptance of things as they were).

The teaching fellowship. The doctoral dissertation on "Fabrication of Tubular Forms from Boron-Based High-Tensile Refractory Pastes by Extrusion." Publication of excerpts from this in the *Journal* of the Society of Ceramic Engineers brought him his bid from the A.E.C. They needed his specialty in N.E.P.A.—Nuclear Energy for the Propulsion of Aircraft.

He had taken it, his records showed, but they did not show the dream world he had thought N.E.P.A. would be, or the dismaying reality it was.

N.E.P.A. turned out to be one hour in the lab and three hours at the desk; bending the knee to seniors and being looked at oddly if you didn't demand that juniors bend the knees to you. It was wangling the high-temperature furnace for your tests and then finding that you'd been bumped out of your allotted time by a section chief or a group director riding a hobby. It was ordering twenty pounds of chemically pure boron and getting fifty-three pounds of commercial grade. It was, too often, getting ahead on an intricate problem and then learning by accident that it had been solved last year by somebody else in some other division. It was trying to search the records before starting your next job and being told that you weren't eligible to see classified material higher than *Confidential*. It was stamping your own results *Restricted* or at most *Confidential* and being told that it was safer, all things considered, to stamp them *Secret* and stay out of trouble.

It was being treated like a spy.

It was, in spite of all this, a chance to work a little at new and exciting problems.

And then, his records showed, in August of his second year, he had been transferred to Argonne National Laboratory, Chicago, as N.E.P.A. Refractories Group Liaison with Neutron Path Prediction Division of the Mathematical Physics Section. The records did not say why a ceramic engineer specializing in high-tensile refractories and with a smattering of aircraft background had been assigned to work in an immensely abstruse field of pure nuclear theory for which he had not the slightest preparation or aptitude.

From August to mid-December, the records said, he bombarded the office of Dr. Hurlbut, director of Argonne Lab, with queries, petitions, and requests for a rectification of his absurd assignment, but the records showed no answers. Finally, the records showed that he resigned from A.E.C. without prior notice—forfeiting all salaries and allowances due or to become due—on a certain day toward the end of the year.

This is what happened on that day:

Novak stopped in the cafeteria downstairs for a second cup of coffee before beginning another baffling day at Neutron Path Prediction—a day he hoped would be his last if Hurlbut had looked into the situation.

"Hi, there," he said to a youngster from Reactor Design. The boy mumbled something and walked past Novak's table to one in the corner.

Oh, fine. Now he was a leper just because he was the victim of some administrative foolishness. It occurred to him that perhaps he had become a bore about his troubles and people didn't want to hear any more about them. Well, he was sick of the mess himself.

A girl computer walked past with coffee and a piece of fudge cake. "Hi, there," he said with less confidence. She had always been good for a big smile, but this time she really gave out.

"Oh, Dr. Novak," she gulped, "I think it's just *rotten.*"

What was this—a gag? "Well, I hope to get it fixed up soon, Grace."

She sat down. "You're filing a grievance? You certainly ought to. A man in your position—"

"*Grievance?* Why, no! I actually saw Hurlbut yesterday, and I just grabbed him in the corridor and told him my troubles. I said that evidently my memos weren't getting through to him. He was very pleasant about it and he said he'd take immediate action."

She looked at him with pity in her eyes and said: "Excuse me." She picked up her tray and fled.

The kid was kidding—or nuts. Hurlbut would straighten things out. He was a notorious scientist-on-the-make, always flying all over the map for speaking dates at small, important gatherings of big people. You saw him often on the front pages and seldom in the laboratory, but he got his paper work cleaned up each month.

Novak finished his coffee and climbed the stairs to the Mathematical Physics Section. He automatically checked the bulletin board in passing and was brought up short by his own name.

FROM THE OFFICE OF THE DIRECTOR

To: Dr. Michael Novak (NPPD) Re: Requested Transfer

Your request is denied. The Director wishes to call your attention to your poor record of production even on the routine tasks it was thought best you be assigned to.

The Director suggests that a more co-operative attitude, harder work, and less griping will get you farther than your recent attempts at office intrigue and buttonholing of busy senior officers.

"The man's crazy," somebody said at his shoulder. "You have a perfect grievance case to take to the—"

Novak ignored him. He ripped the memo from the board and walked unsteadily from the bare white corridors of the Mathematical Physics Section, through endless halls, and into the Administrative Division—carpets, beige walls, mahogany, business suits, pretty secretaries in pretty dresses walking briskly through these wonders.

He pushed open a mahogany door, and a receptionist stopped doing her nails to say: "Who shall I say is—hey! You can't go in there!"

In the carpeted office beyond, a secretary said: "What's this? What do you want?" He pushed on through the door that said: *Dr. Hurlbut's Secretary.*

Dr. Hurlbut's secretary wore a business suit that fitted like a bathing suit, and she said: "Oops! You weren't announced; you startled me. Wait a minute; Dr. Hurlbut is engaged—"

Novak walked right past her into the director's mahogany-furnished, oak-paneled office while she fluttered behind him. Hurlbut, looking like the official pictures of himself, was sitting behind half an acre of desk. A man with him gasped like a fish as Novak burst in.

Novak slapped the memo on the desk, asking, *"Did you write this?"*

The director, impeccably clothed, barbered, and manicured, rose looking faintly amused. He read the notice and said: "You're Novak, aren't you? Yes, I wrote it. And I had it posted instead of slipping it into your box because I thought it would have a favorable effect on morale in general. Some of the section chiefs have been getting sadly lax. No doubt you were wondering."

He had been warned by the "personality card" that accompanied Novak on his transfer to expect such piffling outbursts. However, the man worked like the devil if you just slapped him down and kept hectoring him. One of those essentially guilt-ridden types, the director thought complacently. So pitifully few of us are smooth-running, well oiled, efficient machines…

"Here's my resignation," said Novak. He gave his resignation to Hurlbut on the point of the jaw. The Director turned up the whites of his eyes before he hit the gray broadloom carpeting of his office, and the man with him gaped more fishily than ever. The secretary shrieked, and Novak walked out, rubbing his split skin on his knuckles. It was the first moment of pure satisfaction he had enjoyed since they took him off refractories at N.E.P.A.

Nobody pulled the alarm. It wasn't the kind of thing Hurlbut would want on the front pages. Novak walked, whistling and unmolested, across the lawn in front of Administration to the main gate. He unpinned his badge and gave it to a guard, saying cheerfully: "I won't be back."

"Somebody leave ya a fortune?" the guard kidded.

"Uh, no," said Novak, and the mood of pure satisfaction suddenly evaporated. Nobody had left him a fortune, and he had just put a large, indelible blot on his career.

The first thing he did when he got back to his hotel was phone a situation-wanted ad to *Ceramic Industries*. Luckily he caught the magazine as it was closing its forms on classifieds; subscribers would have his ad in ten days.

CHAPTER THREE

THEY WERE ten bad days.

The local employment agencies had some openings for him, but only one was any good and he was turned down at the interview. It was a scientific supply house that needed a man to take over the crucibles and refractories department; it involved research. The president regretfully explained that they were looking for somebody a little more mature, a little more experienced in handling men, somebody who could take orders—

Novak was sure the crack meant that he knew about his informal resignation from A.E.C. and disapproved heartily.

All the other offers were lousy little jobs; mixing and testing batches in run-down Ohio potteries, with pay to match and research opportunities zero.

Novak went to cheap movies and ate in cheap cafeterias until the answers to his ad started coming in. A spark-plug company in Newark made the best offer in the first batch; the rest were terrible. One desperate owner of a near-bankrupt East Liverpool pottery offered to take him on as full partner in lieu of salary. "I feel certain that with a technical man as well qualified as yourself virtually in charge of production and with me handling design and sales we would weather our present crisis and that the ultimate rewards will be rich. Trusting you will give this proposal your serious—"

Novak held off wiring the Newark outfit to see what the next day would bring. It brought more low-grade offers and a curious letter from Los Angeles.

The letterhead was just an office number and an address. The writer, J. Friml, very formally offered Dr. Novak interesting full-time work in refractories research and development connected with very high-altitude jet aircraft. Adequate laboratory facilities would be made available, as well as trained assistance if required. The salary specified in his advertisement was satisfactory. If the proposition aroused Dr. Novak's interest, would he please wire collect and a telegraphed money order sufficient to cover round-trip expenses to Los Angeles would be forthcoming.

One of the big, coast aircraft outfits? It couldn't be anything else, but why secrecy? The letter was an intriguing trap, with the promised money order for bait. Maybe they wouldn't want him after all, but there was nothing wrong with a free trip to Los Angeles to see what they were up to. That is, if they really sent the money.

He wired J. Friml, collect, at the address on the letterhead:

Interested your offer but appreciate further details if possible.

The next morning a more-than-ample money order was slipped under his door, with the accompanying message:

Full details forthcoming at interview; please call on us at your convenience wiring in advance. our office open daily except sunday nine five. J. Friml, Secretary Treasurer.

Of what?

Novak laughed at the way he was being openly hooked by curiosity and a small cash bribe, and phoned for an airline reservation.

He left his bag at the Los Angeles airport and showered in a pay booth. He had wired that he would appear that morning. Novak gave the address to a cabby and asked: "What part of town's that?"

"Well," said the cabby, "I'll tell you. It's kind of an old-fashioned part of town. Nothing's *wrong* with it."

"Old-fashioned" turned out to be a euphemism for "rundown." They stopped at a very dirty eight-story corner office building with one elevator. The lobby was paved with cracked octagonal tile. The lobby directory of tenants was enormous. It listed upwards of two hundred tenant firms in the building, quadrupled and quintupled up in its fifty-odd offices. Under *f* Novak found J. Friml, Room 714.

"Seven," he bleakly told the unshaved elevator man.

Whatever was upstairs, it wasn't a big, coast plane factory.

Room 712 stopped him dead in the corridor with the audacity of the lettering on its glass door. It claimed to house the Arlington National Cemetery Association, the Lakeside Realty Corporation, the Western Equitable Insurance Agency, the California Veterans League, Farm and Home Publications, and the Kut-Rite Metal Novelties Company in one small office.

But at Room 714 his heart sank like a stone. The lettering said modestly: *American Society for Space Flight.*

I might have known, he thought glumly. Southern California! He braced himself to enter. They would be crackpots, the lab would be somebody's garage, they would try to meet their payroll by selling building lots on Jupiter...but they were paying for his time this morning. He went in.

"Dr. Novak?" said a young man. Nod. "I'm Friml. This is Mr. MacIlheny, president of our organization." MacIlheny was a rawboned, middle-aged man with a determined look. Friml was sharp-faced, eye-glassed, very neat and cold.

"I'm afraid you might think you were brought here under false pretenses, Doctor," said MacIlheny, as if daring him to admit it.

Friml said: "Sit down." And Novak did, and looked around. The place was clean and small with three good desks, a wall banked with good files—including big, shallow blueprint files—and no decorations.

"I asked for research and development work," Novak said cautiously. "You were within your rights replying to my ad if you've got some for me."

MacIlheny cracked his knuckles and said abruptly: "The anonymous offer was my idea. I was afraid you'd dismiss us as a joke. We don't get a very good press."

"Suppose you tell me what you're all about." It was their money he was here on.

"The A.S.F.S.F. is about twenty years old, if you count a predecessor society that was a little on the juvenile side. They 'experimented' with powder rockets and never got anywhere, of course. They just wanted to hear things go bang.

"An older element got in later—engineers from the aircraft plants, science students from Cal Tech and all the other schools—and reorganized the Society. We had a tremendous boom, of course, after the war—the V-2s and the atom bomb. Membership shot up to five thousand around the country. It dropped in a couple of years to fifteen hundred or so, and that's where we stand now."

Friml consulted a card: "One thousand, four hundred, and seventy-eight."

"Thanks. I've been president for ten years, even though I'm not a technical man, just an insurance agent. But they keep re-electing me so I guess everybody's happy.

"What we've been doing is research on paper. Haven't had the money for anything else until recently. Last January I went to Washington to see the A.E.C. about backing, but it was no dice. With the approval of the membership I went the rounds of the industrial firms looking for contributions. Some foresighted outfits came through very handsomely and we were able to go to work.

"There was a big debate about whether we should proceed on a 'bits-and-pieces' basis or whether we should shoot the works on a full-scale steel mock-up of a moon ship. The mockup won, and we've made very satisfactory progress since. We've rented a few acres in the desert south of Barstow and put up shops and—" He couldn't keep the pride out of his voice. He opened his desk drawer and passed Novak an eight-by-ten glossy print. "Here."

He studied it carefully: a glamour photograph of a gleaming, massive, bomb-shaped thing standing on its tail in the desert with prefab huts in the background. It was six times taller than a man who stood beside it, leaning with a studied air against a delta-shaped fin. That was a lot of metal—a *lot* of metal, Novak thought with rising excitement. If the picture wasn't a fake, they had money and the thing made a little more sense.

"Very impressive," he said, returning the picture. "What would my job be?"

"Our engineer in charge, Mr. Clifton, is a remarkable man—you'll like him—but he doesn't know refractories. It seems to be all he doesn't know! And our plans include a ceramic exhaust throat liner and an internal steering vane. We have the shapes, theoretically calculated, but the material has to be developed and the pieces fabricated."

"Internal steering vane. Like the graphite vanes in the various German bombardment rockets?"

"Yes, with some refinements," MacIlheny said. "It's got to be that way, though I don't envy you the job of developing a material that will take the heat and mechanical shock. Side-steering rockets would be much simpler, wouldn't they? But the practical complications you run into—each separate steering jet means a separate electrical system, a separate fuel pump, perforating structural members and losing strength adding weight without a corresponding thrust gain."

"You said you weren't a technical man?" asked Novak.

MacIlheny said impatiently: "Far from it. But I've been in this thing heart and soul for a long time and I've picked up some stuff." He hesitated. "Dr. Novak, do you have a thick hide?"

"I suppose so."

"You'll need it if you go to work for us—crackpots."

Novak didn't say anything and MacIlheny handed him some press clippings:

LOCAL MEN SEE STARS; BUILDING SPACE SHIP

And:

BUCK ROGERS' HEARTS BEAT
BENEATH BUSINESS SUITS.

There were others.

"We never claimed," said MacIlheny a little bitterly, "that the *Prototype's* going to take off for the Moon next week or ever. We down-pedal sensationalism; there are perfectly valid military and scientific reasons for space ship research. We've tried to make it perfectly clear that she's a full-scale model for study purposes, but the damned papers don't care. I know it's scared some good men away from the society and I'd hate to tell you how much it's cut into my business, but my lawyer tells me I'd be a fool to sue." He looked at his watch. "I owed you that much information, Doctor. Now tell me frankly whether you're available."

Novak hesitated.

"Look," said MacIlheny. "Why don't you take a look at the field and the *Prototype?* I have to run, but Friml will be glad to drive you out. You've got to meet Clifton."

When MacIlheny had left, Friml said: "Let's eat first." They went to a businessman's restaurant. Friml had hardly a word to say for himself through the meal, and he kept silence through the drive west to Barstow as the irrigated, roadside land turned arid and then to desert.

"You aren't an enthusiast?" Novak finally asked.

"I'm secretary-treasurer," said Friml.

"Um. Was Mr. MacIlheny deliberately not mentioning the names of the firms that contribute to the A.S.F.S.F.? I thought I caught that."

"You were correct. Contributions are private, by request of the donors. You saw those newspaper clippings."

His tone was vinegar. Friml was a man who didn't think the game was worth the kidding you took for playing it. Then why the devil was he the outfit's secretary-treasurer?

They were driving down a secondary blacktop road when the *Prototype* came into view. It had the only vertical lines in the landscape for as far as the eye could see, and looked sky-piercing. A quadrangle of well-built prefabs surrounded it, and the area was wire-fenced. Signs at intervals forbade trespassing.

There was a youngster reading at a sort of sentry box in the fencing. He glanced at Friml and waved him through. Friml crawled his car to a parking area, where late models were outnumbered by jalopies, and brought it alongside of a monstrous, antique, maroon Rolls Royce. "Mr. Clifton's," he said, vinegar again. "He should be in here." He led Novak to the largest of the prefabs, a twelve-foot Quonset some thirty feet long and mounted on a concrete base. It was a machine shop. Serious-eyed kids were squinting as they filed at bits of bronze. A girl was running a surface grinder that gushed a plume of small, dull red, hot-looking sparks. High-carbon steel, Novak thought automatically. Piece that size costs plenty.

Clifton, Friml's pointed finger said.

The man was in dungaree pants and a dirty undershirt—no, the top of an old-fashioned union suit with buttons. He was bending over a slow-turning engine lathe, boring out a cast-iron fitting. The boring bar chattered suddenly and he snarled at it: "A-a-ah, ya dirty dog ya!" and slapped off the power switch.

"Mr. Clifton," Friml hailed him, "this is Dr. Michael Novak, the ceramics man I told you about yesterday."

"Harya, Jay. Harya, Mike," he said, giving Novak an oil grip. He needed a shave and he needed some dentistry. H didn't look like any engineer in charge that Novak had ever seen before. He was a completely unimpressive Skid Row type, with a hoarse voice to match.

Clifton was staring at him appraisingly. "So ya wanna join the space hounds, hah? Where's ya Buck Rogers pistol?"

There was a pause.

"Conversation-stopper," said Friml with a meager smile. "He's got a million of them. Mr. Clifton, would you show Dr. Novak around if it doesn't interrupt anything important?

Clifton said: "Nah. Bar dug into the finish bore on the flange. I gotta scrap it now; I was crazy to try cast iron. That'll learn me to try and save you guys money; next time I cut the fitting outta nice, expensive, mild steel bar stock. Come on, Mike. Mars or bust, hah?"

He led Novak out of the machine shop and wiped his oily hands on the union suit's top. "You any good?" he asked. "I told the kids I don't want no lid on my hands."

"What would you use for fuel?" Novak demanded.

"Morse-man talk. Fighting word."

"You were a telegrapher?" asked Novak. It seemed to be the only thing to say.

"I been everything! Farmer, seaman, gigolo in B.A., glassblower, tool maker, aero-engineer—bet ya don't believe goddam word I'm saying."

Disgustedly Novak said: "You win." The whole thing was out of the question—crackpot enthusiasts backing this loudmouthed phony.

"Ask me anything, Mike! Go ahead, ask me anything!" Clifton grinned at him like a terrier.

Novak shrugged and said: "Integral of u to the n, log u, d-u."

Clifton fired back: "U to the n-plus-one, bracket, log u over n-plus-one, minus one over n-plus-one-square, unbracket—plus C. Ask me a hard one, Mike!"

It was the right answer. Novak happened to remember it as an examination problem that had stuck in his head. Normally you'd look it up in a table of integrals. "Where'd you go to school?" he asked, baffled.

"School? School? What the hell would I go to school for?" Clifton grinned. "I'm a self-made man, Mike. Look at that rocket, space hound. Look at her."

They had wandered to the *Prototype's* base. Close up, the rocket was a structure of beautifully welded steel plates, with a sewer-pipe opening at the rear and no visible means of propulsion.

"The kids love her," Clifton said softly. "I love her. She's my best girl, the round-heeled old bat."

"What would you use for fuel?" Novak demanded.

He laughed. "How the hell should I know, pal? All I know is we need escape velocity, so I build her to take the mechanical shock of escape velocity. *You* worry about the fuel. The kids tell me it's gotta be atomic so you gotta give 'em a throat-liner material that can really take it from here to Mars and back. Oh, you got a job on your hands when you join the space hounds, Mike!"

"This is the craziest thing I ever heard of," said Novak.

Clifton was suddenly serious. "Maybe it ain't so crazy. We work out everything except fuel and then we go to the A.E.C. and say *give*. Do they hold out on us or do they start work on an atomic fuel? The kids got it all figured out. We do our part, A.E.C. does theirs. Why not?"

Novak laughed shortly, remembering the spy mania he had lived in for two years. "They'll do their part," he said. "They'll start by sending a hundred Security and Intelligence boys to kick you off the premises so they can run it themselves."

Clifton slapped him on the back. *"That's* the spirit!" he yelled. "You'll win your Galactic Cross of Merit yet, pal! You're hired!"

"Don't rush me," said Novak, half angrily. "Are they honestly going to deliver on a real lab for me if I sign up? Maybe they don't realize I'll need heavy stuff—rock crushers, ball mills, arc furnaces— maybe a solar furnace would be good out here on the desert. That kind of equipment costs real money."

"They'll deliver," Clifton said solemnly. "Don't low-rate the kids. I'm working from their blueprints and they're good. Sure, there's bugs—the kids are human. I just had to chuck out their whole system for jettisoning *Proto's* aerodynamic nose. Too gadgety. Now I'm testing a barometer to fire a powder charge that'll blow away the nose when she's out of atmosphere—whole rig's external, no holes in the hull, no gasket problem. And they design on the conservative side— inclined to underestimate strength of materials. But, by and large, a ver-ry ver-ry realistic bunch."

Novak was still finding it impossible to decide whether Clifton was a fake, an ignoramus, or a genius. "Where've you worked?" he asked.

"My last job was project engineer with Western Air. They fired me all right, no fear of that. I wear their letter next to my heart." He hauled a bulging, greasy wallet from the left hip pocket of the dungarees, rummaged through it, and came up with a wad of paper. Unfolded, it said restrainedly that the personnel manager of Western Aircraft regretted that the Company had no option but to terminate Mr. Clifton's employment since Mr. Clifton had categorically declined to apologize to Dr. Holden.

An eighteen-year-old boy with a crew cut came up and demanded: "Cliff, on the nylon ropes the blueprint says they have to test to one-fifty pounds apiece. Does that just mean parting strength of the ropes or the whole rig—ropes whipped to the D-rings and the D-rings anchored in the frame?"

"Be with ya in a minute, Sammy. Go and wait for me." The boy left and Clifton asked: "Think it's a forgery, Mike?"

"Of course not—" began Novak, and then he saw the engineer grinning. He handed back the letter and asked: "Have you been a forger too? Mr. Clifton—"

"Cliff!"

"—Cliff, how did you get hooked up with this? I'm damned if I know what to make of the setup."

"Neither do I. But I don't care. I got hooked up with them when Western canned me. I can't get another aircraft job because of the industrial black list, and I can't get a Government job because I'm a subversive agent or a spy or some goddamned thing like that." Suddenly he sounded bitter.

"How's that?"

"They don't tell you—*you* know that; your ad said you was with the A.E.C.—but I guess it's because I been around the world a couple of times. *Maybe*, they figure, just *maybe*, old Cliff sold out when we wasn't watching him. Also my wife's a foreigner, so better be safe than sorry, says Uncle Sam."

"I know that game," Novak said. "Doesn't matter. You wouldn't have lasted five minutes with A.E.C. even if they did hire you."

"Well, well! So I didn't miss a thing! Look, Mike. I gotta go show my kids how to wipe their noses, so I'll let ya rassle with your conscience and I hope to see you around." He gave Novak the oily grip again and walked cockily from the base of the rocket to the Quonsets.

Friml was at Novak's side instantly, looking impatient. Driving back to Los Angeles, Novak asked bluntly: "Are you people building a moon ship or aren't you?"

"If the A.S.F.S.F. is building a moon ship," said Friml, "I don't want to hear about it. I should tell you that, whatever is being built, they've got a well-kept set of books and a *strictly* controlled audit on the purchasing." He gave Novak little sidelong look. "One man they tried before Clifton made a very common mistake. He thought that because he new technical matters and I didn't, he could pad his purchases by arrangement with the vendors' salesmen and I'd be none the wiser. It took exactly eight days for me to see through his plan."

"I get the hint," said Novak wearily. "But I still don't know whether I want the job. Was Clifton really a project engineer with Western Air?"

"I really don't know. I have absolutely no responsibility for procurement of personnel. I can tell you that he has no local or F.B.I. criminal record. I consider it a part of my job to check that far on employees whose duties include recommending expenditures."

Friml left him at the Los Angeles Airport at his request. Novak said he'd get in touch with him in the morning and let him know one way or the other; then he picked up his bag and took a taxi to a downtown hotel. It was 4:30 when he checked in, and he placed a call at once to the personnel department of Western Aircraft.

"I'd like to inquire," he said, "about the employment record of a Mr. Clifton. He says in his, uh, application to us that he was employed as a project engineer at Western Air last year."

"Yes, sir. Mr. Clifton's first name, sir?"

"Ah, I can't make it out from his signature." If he had been told Clifton's first name, he couldn't remember it.

"One moment, sir...we have a Mr. August Clifton project engineer, employed two years and five months, separated January seventeenth last year—"

"What's the reason for separation?"

"It says 'incompatibility with supervisory personnel.'"

"That's the one. Thanks very much, miss."

"But don't you want efficiency, health, and the rest of it, sir?"

"Thanks, no." He didn't need them. Anybody who hung on for two years and five months at Western as a project man and only got fired after a fight *was* efficient and healthy and the rest of it; otherwise he wouldn't have lasted two hours and five minutes. It wasn't like the A.E.C.; at Western, you produced.

No, he thought, stretching out in his clothes on the bed it wasn't like the A.E.C., and neither was the A.S.F.S.F. He felt a moment of panic at the thought, and knew why he felt it.

Spend enough time in Government and it unmanned you. Each paycheck drawn on the Treasury took that much more of yourself away from yourself. Each one of the stiff, blue-green paper oblongs punched with I.B.M. code slots made you that much more willing to forget you might be running a pointless repeat of a research that had been done, and done, and done, with nobody the wiser, in scattered and classified labs across the country.

Each swig from the public teat had more and more poppy juice in it. Gradually you forgot you had been another kind of person, holding ideas, fighting for them, working until dawn on coffee, falling for women, getting drunk sometimes. You turned gray after enough of the poppy juice—nice gray.

You said: "Well, now, I wouldn't put it that way," and "There's something to be said on both sides, of course," and "It doesn't pay to go overboard; the big thing is to keep your objectivity."

The nice gray people married early and had a child or two right away to demonstrate that they were normal family men. They had hobbies and talked about them to demonstrate that they weren't one-sided cranks. They drank a little, to demonstrate that they weren't puritans, but not much, to demonstrate that they weren't drunks.

Novak wondered if they tasted bile, as he was tasting it now, thinking of what he had almost become.

CHAPTER FOUR

IN THE MORNING he phoned the A.S.F.S.F. office that he wanted the job. Friml's cold voice said: "That's fine, Dr. Novak. Mr. MacIlheny will be here for the next half-hour, and I have a contract ready. If you can make it right over—"

The contract hog-tied Novak for one year with options to conduct refractory research and development under the direction of the Society. The salary was the one he had specified in his ad. Novak raised his eyebrows at one clause: it released the employer from liability claims arising out of radiation damage to the employee.

"You really think the Government's going to let you play with hot stuff?" he asked.

He shouldn't have said "play." MacIlheny was hurt and annoyed. "We expect," he said testily, "that the A.E.C. will co-operate with us as a serious research group when we enter the propulsion stage of the program. They'll be fools if they don't, and we intend to let the country know about it."

Novak shrugged and signed. So did the two Society officers, with the elevator man and the building porter as witnesses. MacIlheny shook Novak's hand ceremoniously after the witnesses were shooed out. "The first thing we want," he said, "is a list of what you'll need and a lab layout. Provisional, of course. There should be some changes after you study the problem in detail?"

"I think not," Novak told him. "A lab's a lab. It's what you do with it that counts. How high can I go?"

Friml looked alarmed. MacIlheny said: "I won't tell you that the sky's the limit. But get what you need, and if you see a chance to save us money without handicapping yourself, take it. Give us the maximum estimated cost and the people you think are the best suppliers for each item."

"*Reputable* firms," said Friml, "The kind of people who'd be prepared to send me a notarized invoice on each purchase."

Novak found the public library and had himself a big morning in the technical reading room, playing with catalogues and trade-magazine ads. After lunch he came back with quadrille paper and a three-cornered scale. The afternoon went like lightning; he spent it drawing up equipment and supplies lists and making dream lay outs for a refractories lab. What he wound up with was an oblong floor plan with a straight-through flow: storage to grinding-and-grading to compounding to firing to cooling to testing. Drunk with power, he threw in a small private office for himself.

Construction costs he knew nothing about, but by combing the used-machinery classifieds he kept equipment and supplies down to thirty-two thousand dollars. He had dinner and returned to the library to read about solar furnaces until they put him out at the ten-o'clock closing.

The next day Friml was up to his neck in page proofs of the A.S.F.S.F. organ *Starward.* Looking mad enough to spit, the secretary-treasurer said: "There's a publications committee, but believe it or not all five of them say they're too rushed right now and will I please do their work for them. Some of the rank and file resent my drawing a salary. I hope you'll bear that in mind when you hear them ripping me up the back—as you surely will."

He shoved the proofs aside and began to tick his way down Novak's lists. "There's a Marchand calculator in Mr. Clifton's laboratory," he said. "Wouldn't that do for both of you, or must you have one of your own?"

"I can use his."

Friml crossed the Marchand off the list. "I see you want a—a continuous distilled-water outfit. Wouldn't it be cheaper and just as good to install a tank, and truck distilled water in from the city? After all, it's for sale."

"I'm afraid not, I have to have it pure—not the stuff you buy for storage batteries and steam irons. The minute you put distilled water into a glass jar it begins to dissolve impurities out of the glass. Mine has to be made fresh and stored in a tin-lined tank."

"I didn't know that," said Friml. He put a light check mark next to the still, and Novak knew this human ferret would investigate it. Maybe he suspected him of planning to bilk the A.S.F.S.F. by making corn liquor on the side.

"Um. This vacuum pump. Mr. Clifton's had a Cenco Hyvac idle since he completed port-gasket tests a month ago. You might check with him as to its present availability…otherwise I see no duplications. This will probably be approved by Mr. MacIlheny in a day or two and then we can let the contract for the construction of your lab. I suggest that you spend the day at the field with Mr. Clifton to clear a location for it and exchange views generally. You can take the bus to Barstow and any taxi from there. If you want to be reimbursed you should save the bus-ticket stub and get a receipt from the taxi driver for my files. And tonight there's the membership meeting. Mr. MacIlheny asked me to tell you that he'd appreciate a brief talk from you—about five minutes and not too technical."

Friml dove back into the page proofs of *Starward,* and Novak left, feeling a little deflated.

The Greyhound got him to Barstow in ninety minutes. A leather-faced man in a Ford with "Taxi" painted on it said sure he knew where the field was: a two-dollar drive. On the road he asked Novak cautiously: "You one of the scientists?"

"No," said Novak. He humbly thought of himself as an engineer.

"Rocket field's been real good for the town," the driver admitted. "But scientists—" He shook his head. "Wouldn't mind some advise from an older man, would you?"

"Why, no."

"Just—watch out. You can't trust them."

"Scientists?"

"Scientists. I don't say they're all like that, but there's drinkers among them and you know how a drinker is when he gets to talking. Fighting Bob proved it. Not just talk."

This was in reference to the Hoyt speech that claimed on a basis of some very wobbly statistics that the A.E.C. was full of alcoholics. "That so?" asked Novak spinelessly.

"Proved it with figures. And you never know what a scientist's up to."

Enough of this nonsense. "Well, out at the field they're up to building a dummy of a moon ship to find out if it can be done."

"You ain't heard?" The driver's surprise was genuine.

"Heard about what? I'm new here."

"Well, that explains it. It's no dummy moon ship. It's camouflage for an oil-drilling rig. They struck oil there. The scientists are experimenting with it to make cheap gasoline. I hear it from the lineman that tends their power line."

"Well, he's wrong," Novak said. "I've been on the grounds and they aren't doing anything but working on the ship."

The driver shook his head. "Nossir," he said positively. "The things a dummy all right, but not for a space ship. Space ships don't work. Nothing there for the rocket to push against. It stands to reason you can't fly where there's no air for it to push against. You could fire a cannon to the Moon if you made one big enough, but no man could stand the shock. I *read* about it."

"In the Bennet newspapers?" asked Novak nastily, exasperated at last.

"Sure," said the driver, not realizing that he was being insulted. "Real American papers. Back up Fighting Bob to the hilt." The driver went on to lavish praise of the Bennet-Hoyt line on foreign policy (go it alone, talk ferociously enough and you won't have to fight); economics (everybody should and must have everything he wants without taking it from anybody else); and military affairs (armed forces second to none and an end to the crushing tax burden for support of the armed forces).

Novak stopped listening quite early in the game and merely interjected an occasional automatic "uh-huh" at the pauses. After a while the *Prototype* appeared ahead and he stopped even that.

The rocket, standing alone in the desert like a monument, was still awe-inspiring. At the sentry box he introduced himself, and the boy on guard shook his hand warmly. "Glad to have you inboard, sir," he said. The word was unmistakably "inboard"—and when Novak had it figured out he had to bite his lip to keep from laughing. The kid was using rocket-ship slang before there were any rocket ships!

The boy never noticed his effort; he was too busy apologizing for stopping him. "You see, Doctor, people don't take our work seriously. Folks used to drive out here the first month and interrupt and even expect us to lend them our drinking water that we trucked out. As if we were here for their entertainment! Finally a gang of little devils broke into one of the Quonsets after dark and smashed everything they could reach. Four thousand dollars' worth of damage in twenty minutes! We were sick. What *makes* people like that? So we had to put up a real fence and mount guard, even if it doesn't look good. But of course we have nothing to hide."

"Of course—" began Novak. But the boy's face had suddenly changed. He was staring, open-mouthed. "What's the matter?" snapped Novak, beginning to inspect himself. "Have I got a scorpion on me?"

"No," said the boy, and looked away embarrassed. "I'm sorry," he said. "Only it suddenly hit me—maybe you'll be one of the people inboard when she—when she goes. But I shouldn't ask."

"The last I heard," Novak said, "*she* is a full-sized mockup and isn't going anywhere."

The boy winked one eye slowly.

"All right," Novak shrugged, amused. "Have it your way and I'll see you on Mars. Where's Mr. Clifton?"

"Back of the machine shop—a new testing rig."

Crossing the quadrangle, Novak passed the *Prototype* and stopped for another look. To the Moon? This colossal pile of steel? It was as easy to visualize the Eiffel Tower picking up its four legs and waddling across Paris. No wonder the taxi driver didn't believe in space fight— and no wonder the kid at the gate did. *Credo quia impossibilis*, or however it went. There were people like that.

He heard Clifton before he saw him. The engineer in charge was yelling: "Harder! *Harder!* Is that all the hard ya can bounce? *Harder!*" And a girl was laughing.

Back of the machine shop, in its shadow, Clifton was standing with a stopwatch over a vaguely coffin-shaped block of molded rubber swung from a framework by rope. Most of the ropes were milky nylon. Six of them were manila and had big tension balances, like laundry scales, hooked into them. Towering over Clifton and the framework was a twelve-foot gas-pipe scaffold, and a pretty girl in shorts was climbing a ladder to the top of it.

As Novak watched, she hurled herself from the scaffold into the coffin. Clifton, blaspheming, snapped his stopwatch and tried to read the jumping needles on the dials of all six balances at the same time.

"Hello," Novak said.

"Harya, Mike. Mike, this is Amy helping out. Like my rig?"

"I thought they worked all this out at the Wright-Patterson A.F.B. Space Medicine School. It *is* an acceleration couch, isn't it?"

"Kindly do not speak to me about Air Force Space Medicine," said Clifton distinctly. "It happens to be mostly bushwah. Ya know what happened? They had this ejector-seat problem, blowing a jet pilot out of a plane because he'd get cut in half if he tried to climb out at 600 m.p.h. So they had an acceleration problem and they licked it fine and dandy. So a publicity-crazy general says acceleration is acceleration, what's good enough for an ejector seat is good enough for a space ship and anyway nobody knows what the hell space flight is like so why worry?"

Clifton folded his arms, puffed out his chest, and assumed the Napoleonic stance, with one foot forward and the knee bent. His hoarse voice became an oily parody of the general's. "My gallant public relations officers! Let us enlighten the taxpaying public on what miracles us air force geniuses pass off daily before breakfast. Let us enlighten them via the metropolitan dailies and wire services with pictures. Let us tell them that we have solved all the medical problems of space flight and have established a school of space medicine to prove it. You may now kiss my hand and proceed to your typewriters at the gallop. To hell with the Navy!"

The girl laughed and said: "Cliff, it *can't* be that bad. And if you keep talking treason they'll lock you up and you'll pine away without your sweetheart there." She meant *Proto*.

"A-a-ah, what do you know about it, ya dumb Vassar broad? What time's Iron Jaw pick you up? Time for any more bounces?"

"Barnard, not Vassar," she said, "and no time for more bounces, because he said he'd be here at noon and Grady is the world's best chauffeur." She took a wrap-around skirt from a lower horizontal of the gas-pipe scaffolding and tied it on. "Are you a new member, Mike?" she asked.

"I'm going to work on the reaction chamber and throat liner."

"Metal or ceramic?"

"Ceramic refractories is my field."

"Yes, but what about strength? I was thinking about tungsten metal as a throat-liner material. It's a little fantastic because it oxidizes in air at red heat, but I have an idea. You install a tungsten liner and then install a concentric ceramic liner to shield it. The ceramic liner takes the heat of the exhaust until the ship is out of atmosphere and then you jettison it, exposing the tungsten. In vacuum, tungsten holds up to better than three thousand centigrade—"

Clifton bulled into it. "Ya crazy as a bunny rabbit, Amy! What about atmosphere on Mars or Venus? What about the return trip to Earth? What about working the tungsten? That stuff crystallizes if ya look at it nasty. What about paying for it? Ya might as well use platinum for cost. And what about limited supply? Ya think America's going to do without tool bits and new light bulbs for a year so ya can have five tons of tungsten to play with? Didn't they teach economics at Miss Twitchell's or wherever it was?"

It was exactly noon by Novak's watch and a black Lincoln rolled through the gate and parked.

"See you at the meeting, Cliff? Glad to have met you, Mike." The girl smiled, and hurried to the car. Novak saw a white-haired man in the back open the door for her, and the car drove off.

"Who was *that?*" Novak asked.

"She's Miss Amelia Earhart Stuart to the society pages," Clifton grinned. "In case you don't read the society pages, she's the daughter of Wilson Stuart—my old boss at Western. She got bit by the space bug and it drives him crazy. The old man's a roughneck like me, but he's in a wheelchair now. Wrecked his heart years ago test-flying. He's been looking backwards ever since; he thinks we're dangerous crackpots. I hear ya got the job okay. Where do you want the lab?"

They left the test rig and walked around the machine-shop Quonset. Clifton stopped for a moment to measure the *Prototype* with his eye. It was habitual.

"How much of a crew does she—would she—hold?" Novak asked.

"Room for three," Clifton said, still looking at her.

"Navigator, engineer—and what?"

"Stowaway, of course!" Clifton roared. "Where ya been all ya life? A girl stowaway in a tin brassiere with maybe a cellophane space suit on. Buckle down, Mike! On the ball or I don't put ya in for the Galactic Cross of Merit!"

Novak wouldn't let himself be kidded. "The youngster at the gate might stowaway," he said. "He thinks the *Prototype* is going to take off some day and we just aren't telling the public about it."

Clifton shook his head—regretfully. "Not without the A.E.C. develops a rocket fuel and gives it to us. The bottom two thirds of her is a hollow shell except for structural members. I wish the kid was right. It'd be quite a trip and they'd have quite a time keeping me off the passenger list. But I built the old bat, and I know."

Novak picked an area for his lab and Clifton okayed it.

They had lunch from a refrigerator in the machine shop, with a dozen kids hanging on their words.

"Give ya an idea of what we're up against, Mike," Clifton said around a pressed-ham sandwich. "The manhole for *Proto*. It's got to open and close, it's got to take direct sunlight in space, it's got to take space-cold when it's in shadow. What gasket material do you use? What sealing pressure do you use? Nobody can begin to guess. Some conditions you can't duplicate in a lab. So what some Stuart cookie in the A.S.F.S.F. figured out ten years ago was a wring fit, like jo-blocks. Ya know what I mean?"

Novak did—super-smooth surfaces, the kind on hundred-dollar gauges. Put two of those surfaces together and they clung as if they were magnetized. The theory was that the molecules of the surfaces interpenetrate and the two pieces become—almost—the same piece. "Ingenious," he said.

"Ingenious," muttered Clifton. "I guess that's the word. Because nobody ever in the history of machine shops put a jo-block finish on pieces that size. I got a friend in South Bend, so I sent him the rough-machined manhole cover and seating. The Studebaker people happen to have a big super-finish boring mill left over from the war, sitting in a corner covered with cosmoline. Maybe my friend can con them into making off the grease and machining a super-finish onto our parts. If not, I'll try to hand-scrape them. If I can't do it on circular pieces—and I probably can't—I'll scrap them and order square forgings. You think *you* got troubles with your throat liner?"

"Generally, what kind of shape is *Proto* in?"

"Generally, damn fine shape. I finish testing the acceleration couch today. If it passes I order two more pads from Akron and install them. Then we're all ready to go except for the manhole problem and a little matter of a fuel and propulsion system that oughtta be cleared up in eight—ten years. A derail."

Clifton picked his teeth and led Novak to a blueprint file. He yanked open one of the big, flat drawers and pulled out a 36-by-48 blueprint. "Here we are," he said. "The chamber, liner, and vane. You're gonna have to make it, you might as well look it over. I'm gonna appoint a volunteer and supervise some more crash dives."

Novak took the print to an empty corner of the shop and spread it out on a workbench. He looked first at the ruled box in the lower right-hand corner for specifications. He noted that the drawing had been made some three months ago by "J. MacI." and checked by him. Material: ceramic refractory; melting point higher than 3,000° C.; coefficient of expansion, less than .000,004; bulk modulus...

Novak laughed incredulously.

It was *all* there—stretch, twist, and bulk moduli, coefficient of elasticity, everything except how to make it. MacIlheny had laid down complete specifications for the not-yet developed liner material. A childish performance! He suspected that the president of the A.S.F.S.F. was simply showing off his technical smattering and was mighty proud of himself. Novak wondered how to tell MacIlheny tactfully that under circumstances it would be Stuarter to lay down specifications in the most general terms.

He studied them again and laughed again. Sure he could probably turn out something like that—one of the boron carbides. But it would be a hell of a note if A.E.C. came up with a 3.750-degree fuel and they had a 3.500-degree liner, or if the A.E.C. came up with a hydroxide fuel that would dissolve a liner, which was only acid-proof. What MacIlheny should have said was something simpler and humbler, like "Give us the best compromise you can between strength and thermal-shock resistance. And, please, as much immunity to all forms of chemical attack as you can manage."

Well, he'd tell him nicely—somehow.

Novak looked from the specifications to the drawings themselves and thought at first that there had been some mistake—the right drawings on the wrong sheet, the wrong drawings on the right sheet—but after a puzzled moment he recognized them vaguely as a reaction chamber and throat liner.

They were all wrong; all wrong.

He knew quite well from N.E.P.A. what reaction chambers and throat liners for jet craft looked like. He knew standard design doctrine for flow, turbulence, Venturi effect, and the rest of it. There were tricks that had been declassified when newer, better tricks came along. This—this *thing*—blithely by-passed the published tricks and went in for odd notions of its own. The ratio of combustion volume to throat volume was unheard of. The taper was unheard of. The cross section was an ellipse of carefully defined eccentricity instead of the circle it should be. There was only one hole for fuel injection— only one hole! Ridiculous.

While the shop was filled with the noise of a youngster expertly hacksawing sheet metal in a corner, Novak slowly realized that it was not ridiculous at all. It wasn't MacIlheny showing off; no, not at all. Anybody who could read a popular science magazine knew enough not to design a chamber and throat like that.

But MacIlheny knew better.

He walked slowly out to the back of the shop where Clifton was clocking dives into the acceleration couch. "Cliff," he said, "can I see you for a minute?"

"Sure, Mike. As long as ya don't expect any help from me."

Together they looked down at the spread blueprint, and Novak said: "The kid at the gate was right. They are going to take off some day and they just aren't telling the public about it."

"What ya talking?" demanded Clifton. "All I see there is lines on paper. Don't try to kid a kidder, Mike."

Novak said: "The specs are for me to develop a material to handle a certain particular fuel with known heat, thrust, and chemical properties. The drawings are the wrong shape. Very wrong. I know conventional jet theory and I have never seen anything like the shapes they want for the chamber and throat of that—thing—out there."

"Maybe it's a mistake," Clifton said uncertainly.

Then he cursed himself. "Mistake! Mistake! Why don't I act my age? Mistakes like this them boys don't make. The acceleration couch. They designed it eight years ago on paper. It works better than them things the Air Force been designing and building and field testing for fifteen years now."

Novak said: "People who can do that aren't going to get the throat and chamber so wrong they don't look like any throat and chamber ever used before. *They've got a fuel and they know its performance.*"

Clifton was looking at the data. "MacIlheny designed it—it says here. An insurance man three months ago sat down to design a chamber and throat, did it, checked it, and turned it over to you to develop the material and fabricate the pieces. I wonder where he got it, Mike. Russia? Argentina? China?"

"Twenty countries have atomic energy programs," Novak said. "And one year ago the A.S.F.S.F. suddenly got a lot of money—a hell of a lot of money. I ordered thirty-two thousand dollars' worth of gear and Friml didn't turn a hair."

Clifton muttered: "A couple of million bucks so far, I figure it. Gray-market steel. Rush construction—overtime never bothered them as long as the work got done. Stringing the power line, drilling the well. A couple of million bucks and nobody tells ya where it came from." He turned to Novak and gripped his arm earnestly. "Nah, Mike," he said softly. *"It's crazy.* Why should a country do research on foreign soil through stooges. It just ain't possible."

"Oh, God!" said Novak. His stomach turned over.

"What's the matter, kid?"

"I just thought of a swell reason," he said slowly. "What if a small country like the Netherlands, or a densely populated country like India, stumbled on a rocket fuel? And what if the fuel was terribly dangerous? Maybe it could go off by accident and take a couple of hundred miles of terrain with it. Maybe it's radiologically bad and poisons everybody for a hundred miles around if it escapes. Wouldn't they want the proving ground to be outside their own country in that case?"

There was a long pause.

Clifton said: "Yeah. I think they might. If it blows up on their own ground they lose all their space-ship talent and don't get a space ship. If it blows up on our ground they also don't get a space ship, but they do deprive Uncle Sam of a lot of space-ship talent. But how—*if* the fuel don't blow up California—do they take over the space ship?"

"I don't know, Cliff. Maybe MacIlheny flies it to Leningrad and the Red Army takes it from there. Maybe Friml flies it to Buenos Aires and the Guardia Peronista."

"Maybe," said Cliff. "Say, Mike, I understand in these cloak-and-dagger things they kill ya if ya find out too much."

"Yeah, I've heard of that, Cliff. Maybe we'll get the Galactic Cross of Merit posthumously. Cliff, *why* would anybody want to get to the Moon bad enough to do it in a crazy way like this?"

The engineer took a gnawed hunk of tobacco from his hip pocket and bit off a cud. "I can tell ya what MacIlheny told me. Our president, I used to think, was just a space hound and used the military-necessity argument to cover it up. Now, I don't know. Maybe the military argument was foremost in his mind all the time.

"MacIlheny says the first country to the Moon has got it *made*. First rocket ship establishes a feeble little pressure dome with one man left in it. If he's lucky he lives until the second trip, which brings him a buddy, more food and oxygen, and a stronger outer shell for his pressure dome. After about ten trips you got a corporal's squad on the Moon nicely dug in and you can start bringing them radar gear and launchers for bombardment rockets homing on earth points.

"Nobody can reach ya there, get it? *Nobody*. The first trip has always gotta bring enough stuff to keep one man alive—if he's lucky—until the next trip. It takes a lotta stuff when ya figure air and water. The first country to get there has the bulge because when country two lands their moon pioneer the corporal's squad men hike on over in their space suits and stick a pin in his pressure dome and— he dies. Second country can complain to the U.N., and what can they prove? The U.N. don't have observers on the Moon. And if the second country jumps the first country with an A-bomb attack, they're gonna *die*. Because they can't jump the retaliation base on the Moon."

He squirted tobacco juice between his teeth. "That's simplified for the kiddies," he said, "but that's about the way MacIlheny tells it."

"Sounds reasonable," Novak said. "Personally I am going right now to the nearest regional A.E.C. Security and Intelligence Office. You want to come along?" He hoped he had put the question casually. It had occurred to him that, for all his apparent surprise, Clifton was a logical candidate for Spy Number One.

"Sure," said Clifton. "I'll drive you. There's bound to be one in L.A."

CHAPTER FIVE

THERE WAS, in the Federal Building.

Anheier, the agent in charge, was a tall, calm man. "Just one minute, gentlemen," he said, and spoke into his intercom. "The file on the American Society for Space Flight, Los Angeles," he said, and smiled at their surprise. "We're not a Gestapo," he said, "but we have a job to do. It's the investigation of possible threats to national security as they may involve atomic energy. Naturally the space-flight group would be of interest to us. If the people of this country only knew the patience and thoroughness—here we are."

The file was bulky. Anheier studied it in silence for minutes. "It seems to be a very clean organization," he said at last. "During the past fifteen years derogatory informations have been filed from time to time, first with the F.B.I. and later with us. The investigations that followed did not produce evidence of any law violations. Since that's the case I can tell you that the most recent investigation followed a complaint from a certain rank-and-file member that Mr. Joe Friml, your secretary-treasurer, was a foreign agent. We found Mr. Friml's background spotless and broke down the complainant. It was a simple case of jealousy. There seems to be a certain amount of, say, spite work and politics in an organization as—as visionary as yours."

"Are you suggesting that we're cranks?" Novak demanded stiffly. "I'm a Doctor of Philosophy of the University of Illinois and I've held a responsible position with the A.E.C. And Mr. Clifton has been a project engineer with Western Aircraft."

"By no means, by no means!" Anheier said hastily. "I know your backgrounds, gentlemen." There was something on his face that was the next thing to a smile. Novak was suddenly, sickeningly sure that Anheier, with patience and thoroughness, had learned how he had socked his A.E.C. director in the jaw and how Clifton had been fired after a fight with his boss. A couple of congenital hotheads, Anheier would calmly decide; unemployables who can't get along with people; crank denouncers and accusers.

Anheier was saying, poker-faced: "Of course we want complete depositions from you on your, your information." He buzzed and a stenographer came in with a small, black, court machine. "And if investigation seems in order, of course we'll get along with no lost time. First give your facts, if you please." He leaned back calmly, and the stenographer zipped out the paper box of his machine and poised his fingers. He looked bored.

"My name is Michael Novak," Novak said, fighting to keep his voice calm and clear. The stenographer's fingers bumped the keys and the paper tape moved up an inch. "I live at the Revere Hotel in Los Angeles. I am a ceramic engineer with the B.Sc. from Rensselaer Polytechnic Institute and M.Sc. and PhD. from the University of Illinois. I was employed after getting my doctorate by the U.S. Atomic Energy Commission in various grades, the last and highest being A.E.C 18. I—I left the A.E.C. last month and took employment with an organization called the American Society for Space Flight at its Los Angeles headquarters.

"I had no previous knowledge of this organization. I was told by officers that it is now making a full-scale metal mock-up of a moon ship to study structural and engineering problems. Purportedly it has no space-ship fuel in mind and intends to ask the co-operation of the A.E.C in solving this problem after it has solved all the other problems connected with the design of a space ship.

"I believe, however, that this is a cover story. I believe that about one year ago the organization was supplied with funds to build an actual space ship by a foreign power which has developed a space-ship fuel.

"My reasons for believing this are that the organization has liberal funds behind it which are supposed to be private contributions from industry, but there are no signs of outside interests in the project; further, I was ordered to execute an extremely unorthodox design for a reaction chamber and throat liner, which strongly suggests that the organization has an atomic space-ship fuel and knows its characteristics.

"I want to emphasize that the unorthodox design which aroused my suspicions was purportedly drawn and checked by James MacIlheny, president of the organization, an insurance man who disclaims any special technical training. In other, nonvital details of the space ship, designing was done mostly by technical men employed in the aircraft industry and by local college students and teachers following space flight as a hobby of a technical nature. It is my belief that the reaction chamber and throat liner were designed by a foreign power to fit their atomic fuel and were furnished to MacIlheny.

"I do not know why a foreign power should erect a space ship off its own territory. One possibility that occurs to me is that their fuel might be extremely dangerous from a radiological or explosive standpoint or both, and that the foreign power may be unwilling to risk a catastrophic explosion on its own ground or radiation sickness to large numbers of its own valued personnel."

He stopped and thought—but that was all there was to say.

Anheier said calmly: "Thank you, Dr. Novak. And now Mr. Clifton, please."

The engineer cleared his throat and said aggressively: "I'm August Clifton. I been a self-educated aero engineer for nine years. For Douglas I designed the B-108 airframe and I rode production line at their Omaha plant. Then I worked for Western Air, specializing in control systems for multijet aircraft. Last year I left Western and went to work for the A.S.F.S.F.

"My ideas about the A.S.F.S.F.'s backing and what they're up to are the same as Novak's. I've been around the Society longer, so I can say better than him that there's not a sign of any business or industry having any stake in what's going on out at the field. That's all."

"Thanks, Mr. Clifton. They'll be typed in a moment." The stenographer left. "I understand there's one prominent industrialist who shows some interest in the Society? Mr. Stuart?" There was a ponderously roguish note in Anheier's voice.

"Ya crazy, Anheier," Clifton said disgustedly. "He's just looking after his daughter. *You* think we're nuts? You should hear Iron Jaw take off on us?"

"I know," smiled Anheier hastily. "I was only joking."

"What about MacIlheny?" asked Novak. "Have you investigated him?"

Anheier leafed through the A.S.F.S.F. file. "Thoroughly," he said. "Mr. MacIlheny is a typical spy—"

"*What?*"

"—I mean to say, he's the kind of fellow who's in a good position to spy, but he isn't and doesn't. He has no foreign contacts and none of the known foreign spys on our soil have gone anywhere near him."

"What ya talking?" demanded Clifton. "You mean there's spies running around and you don't pick them up?"

"I said foreign agents—news-service men, exchange students, businessmen, duly registered propaganda people, diplomatic and consular personnel—there's no end to them. *They* don't break any laws, but they recruit people who do. God knows *how* they recruit them. Every American knows that since the Rosenberg cases the penalty for espionage by a citizen is, in effect, death. That's the way the country wanted it, and that's the way it is."

"Why do you say MacIlheny's typical?" asked Novak. He had a slight hope that this human iceberg might give them some practical words on technique, even if he refused to get excited about their news.

"Mata Hari's out," said Anheier comfortably. "You've seen spies in the papers, Dr. Novak." To be sure, he had—ordinary faces, bewildered, ashamed, cowering from the flash bulbs. "I came up via the accountancy route myself so I didn't see a great deal of the espionage side," Anheier confessed a bit wistfully. "But I can tell you that your modern spy in America is a part-timer earning a legitimate living at some legitimate line. Import-export used to be a favorite, but it was too obvious."

"Hell, I should think so," grinned Clifton.

Anheier went on: "Now they recruit whatever they can, and get technical people whenever possible. This is because your typical state secret nowadays is not a map or code or military agreement but an industrial process.

"The Manhattan District under General Groves and the British wartime atomic establishment were veritable sieves. The Russians learned free of charge that calutron separation of U-235 from U-238 was impractical and had to be abandoned. They learned, apparently, that gaseous diffusion is *the* way to get the fissionable isotope. They learned that implosion with shaped charges is a practical way to assemble a critical mass of fissionable material. They were saved millions of dead-ended man-hours by this information.

"Security's taken a nice little upswing since then, but we still have secrets and there still are spies, even though the penalty is death. Some do it for money, some are fanatics—some, I suppose, just don't realize the seriousness of it. Here are your depositions, gentlemen."

They read them and signed them.

Anheier shook their hands and said. "I want to thank you both for doing your patriotic duty as you saw it. I assure you that your information will be carefully studied and appropriate action will be taken. If you learn of anything else affecting national security in the atomic area in your opinion, I hope you won't hesitate to let us know about it." Clearly it was a speech he had made hundreds of times—or thousands. The brush-off.

"Mr. Anheier," Novak said, "what if we take this to the F.B.I.? They might regard it more seriously than you seem to."

The calm man put his palms out protestingly. "Please, Dr. Novak, he said. "I assure you that your information will be thoroughly processed. As to the F.B.I., you're perfectly free to go to them if you wish, but it would be wasted motion. Cases in the atomic area that come to the F.B.I. are automatically bucked to us—a basic policy decision, and a wise one in my opinion. Technical factors and classified information are so often involved—"

In the street Novak said disgustedly: "He didn't ask us any questions. He didn't ask us whether we were going to quit or not."

"Well—are we?"

"I guess I am—I don't know, Cliff. Maybe I'm wrong about the whole business. Maybe I'm as crazy as Anheier thinks I am."

"Let's go to my place," Clifton said. "We oughtta go to the A.S.F.S.F. membership meeting tonight after we eat."

"Cripes, I'm supposed to make a speech!"

"Just tell 'em hello."

They got into Clifton's car, the long, tall, 1930 Rolls with the lovingly maintained power plant, and roared through Los Angeles. Clifton drove like a maniac, glaring down from his height on underslung late models below and passing them with muttered fusillades of curses. "Me, I like a car with *character*," he growled, barreling the Rolls around a '56 Buick.

His home was in a pretty, wooded canyon dotted with houses. Gravel flew as he spun into the driveway.

"Come and meet Lilly," he said.

Outside, the Clifton house was an ordinary five-room bungalow. Inside it was the dope-dream of a hobbyist run amuck. Like geologic strata, tools and supplies overlaid the furniture. Novak recognized plasticene, clay, glazes, modeling tools and hooks, easels, sketch boxes, cameras, projectors, enlargers, gold-leaf burnishers, leather tools, jewelers' tools and the gear of carpenters, machinists, plumbers, electricians and radio hams. Lilly was placidly reading an astrology magazine in the middle of the debris. She was about thirty-five; a plump, gray-eyed blonde in halter and shorts. The sight of her seemed to pick Clifton up like a shot of brandy.

"Mama!" he yelled, kissing her loudly. "I'm sick of you. I brought you this here young man for you to run away with. Kindly leave without making no unnecessary disturbance. His name is Mike."

"Hallo," she said calmly. "Don't pay him no attention; he alvays yokes. Excuse how I talk; I am Danish. How many letters you got in you full complete name?"

"Uh—twelve."

"Good," she dimpled. "I'm twelve, too. We'll be pals, it means."

"I'm very glad," Novak said faintly.

"Mike, you been factored?"

"I don't think I understand—"

"It's biomat'ematics. You know? You go to a biomat'ematicist and he finds the mat'ematical for-moola of you subconscious and he factors out the traumas. It's simple." Her face fell a little. "Only I get a Danish-speaking subconscious of course, so vit' me it goes a liddle slow. Funny"—she shook her head—"same t'ing happened to me years ago vit' di'netics. Cliff, you gonna give Mike a drink or is he like the other feller you had here last month? Feller that broke the mirror and you nineteen-inch cat'ode-ray tube and my Svedish pitcher—"

"How the hell was I supposed to know?" he roared. In an aside: "That was Friml, Mike. He got pretty bad."

"Friml?" asked Novak incredulously. The ice-water kid?

"He should go to a biomat'ematicist," sighed Lilly. "If ever a boy needed factoring, it's him. Make me only a liddle one please; I don't eat yet today."

She had a little martini and Clifton and Novak had big ones.

"We all go to the meeting tonight I guess? First I want *biftek aux pommes de terre* someplace."

"What the hell, Mama!" Clifton objected. "This time yesterday you was a vegetarian for life."

"I change my mind," she said. "Go get shaved up and dress you'self and we go someplace for *biftek.*"

When Clifton appeared—shaved, dressed, and subdued—Lilly was still in the bedroom, putting on finishing touches. The two men had another martini apiece.

"What about the contracts?" Novak asked.

Clifton understood. "If they try to hold us to them we could just lie down on the job and let them pay us. Hate to work it like that, though. It'd be dull."

"It's still the craziest business I ever heard of."

Lilly appeared, looking sexy in a black dinner dress with a coronet of blond hair swept up from her creamy neck.

Clifton let out a long, loud wolf-howl and said: "The hell with the beefsteaks and the meeting. Let's—"

"Later," said Lilly firmly.

As the maroon Rolls thundered down the canyon, Clifton said casually: "I may quit the space hounds, Mama."

"So what you gonna do for a job?"

"Buy you a red dress and turn mack, I guess. Nah, ya too old and ugly. Maybe I'll open a radio shop or ship out again for an electrician; I guess I still got my card. I kinda hate to leave my best girl out there in the desert, but the whole thing's a joke. She's pretty, but she'll never amount to a damn."

Novak knew why he was lying about the reason. *I understand in these cloak-and-dagger things they kill ya if ya find out too much.*

CHAPTER SIX

THEY HAD dinner at a downtown cafe and were at the A.S.F.S.F. meeting hall by 8:30. Novak was alarmed when the building turned out to be the Los Angeles Slovak Sokol Hall, rented for the occasion.

"Foreigners!" he exclaimed. "Does the A.S.F.S.F. go around *looking* for jams to get into?"

"Relax, Mike," Clifton told him. "The Sokol's strictly American by now. They got a long anti-Communist record."

Still, fretted Novak, foreigners—Slavic foreigners. The building was in the same run-down area that housed the Society's business office. It was liberally hung with American flags and patriotic sentiments. Inconspicuous on the lobby walls were a few photographs of group calisthenics and marchers in Czech national costumes, from decades ago.

A well-worn placard on an easel said that the A.S.F.S.F. meeting was being held at 8:30 in the main hall, straight ahead and up the stairs.

About a score of people in the lobby were having final smokes and talking. Novak could divide them easily into two types; juvenile space hounds and employed hobbyists. The hobbyists were what you'd see at any engineers' convention: pipe-smokers, smiling men, neat, tanned. The space hounds were any collection of juvenile enthusiasts anywhere—more mature than an equal number of hot-rod addicts, perhaps, but still given to nervous laughter, horseplay, and catchwords.

Their entrance had been the signal for the younger element to surround Clifton and bombard him with questions.

"Cliff, how she coming?"

"Mr. Clifton, need a good carpenter at the field?"

"How's the acceleration couch coming, Cliff?"

"Could we get that boring mill at South Bend?"

"Shaddap!" said Clifton. "Leave a man breath, will ya!" They loved him for it. "What's the movie tonight?"

"A stinker," one girl told him. "*Pirates of the Void*, with Marsha Denny and Lawrence Malone. Strictly for yocks."

"They show a space-flight movie," Clifton explained to Novak. "There ain't enough business to kill the time and send everybody home in the proper state of exhaustion." He towed his wife and Novak up the stairs, where a youngster at a card table challenged their membership. They were clamorously identified by a dozen youngsters and went in. The hall seated about four hundred and had a stage with a movie screen and more American flags.

"Better sit in the back—" began Clifton, and then: "For God's sake!" It was Anheier, smiling nervously.

"Hello," said the Security man. "I thought I'd combine business with pleasure. Marsha Denny's a great favorite of mine and I understand there's going to be a preview tonight."

"Well, enjoy yourself," Clifton said coldly. He took Lilly and Novak to the left rear corner of the auditorium and they sat down. He told his wife: "An A.E.C. guy we met. A creep."

MacIlheny climbed to the stage and called to stragglers in the back of the hall: "Okay, men. Let's go." They found seats.

Crack went the gavel. "The-meeting-is-called-to-order. The-chair-will-entertain-a-motion-to-adopt-the-standard-agenda-as-laid-down-in-the-organization-by-laws."

"So move," said somebody, and there was a ragged chorus of seconds.

"All-in-favor-signify-by-raising-one-hand-any-opposed? The-motion-seems-to-be-and-is-carried. First-on-the-agenda-is-the-reading-of-previous-meetings-minutes."

Somebody stuck his hand up, was recognized, and moved that the minutes be accepted as read. The motion was seconded and carried without excitement. So were motions to accept and adopt reports of the membership, orbit computation, publications, finance, structural problems and control mechanisms committees.

"Making good time," Clifton commented.

Under "good and welfare" a belligerent-looking youngster got recognized and demanded the ouster of the secretary-treasurer. There was a very mild, mixed demonstration: some applause and some yells of "Sit down!" and "Shuddup!" MacIlheny rapped for order.

"The motion is in order," he wearily announced. "Is there a second?" There was—another belligerent kid.

"In seconding this motion," he said loudly, "I just want to go over some ground that's probably familiar to us all. With due respect to the majority's decision, I still feel that there's no place for salaried employees in the A.S.F.S.F. But if there *has* to be a paid secretary-treasurer, I'm damned if I see why an outsider with no special interest in space flight—"

Friml was on his feet in the front now, clamoring for recognition on a point of personal privilege.

"Damn it, Friml, I wasn't insulting you—"

"That's for the chair to decide, Mr. Grady! I suggest you pipe down and let him."

"Who're you telling to—"

MacIlheny hammered for silence. "Chair recognizes Mr. Friml."

"I simply want a ruling on the propriety of Mr. Grady's language. Thank you."

"The chair rules that Mr. Grady's remarks were improper and cautions him to moderate his language."

Breathing hard, the youngster tried again. "In seconding this motion to impeach, I want to point out that there are members with *much* more seniority in the organization than Mr. Friml and with it long-demonstrated record of interest in space flight which he cannot match."

MacIlheny called for debate and recognized one of the engineer-types.

"It should be evident to all of us," the engineer said soothingly, "that the criterion for the secretary-treasurer's office ought to be *competence.* We're not playing with marbles any more—I'm happy to say. And I for one am very much relieved that we have the services of a man with a B.B.A., and M.B.A., and a C.P.A. after his name.

"Now, I may have more organizational experience than Mr. Grady, since I've been somewhat active in the A.S.M.E. and the aeronautical societies. I name no names—but in one of those groups we were unwise enough to elect a treasurer who, with all the good will in the world, simply didn't know how to handle the job. We were rooked blind before we knew what hit us, and it took a year to straighten the records out. I don't want that to happen to the A.S.F.S.F., and I seriously urge that the members here vote against the impeachment. Let's not monkey with a smooth-running machine. Which is what we've got now."

There was a lot of applause.

A thin, dark girl, rather plain, was recognized. Her voice was shrill with neurotic hatred. "I don't know what's become of the A.S.F.S.F. In one year I've seen a decent, democratic organization turned into a little despotism with half a dozen people—if that!—running the works while the plain members are left in the dark. Who is this Friml? How do we know he's so good if we don't know the amount and nature of the contributions he handles? And *Mr.* August Clifton, whom everybody is so proud of, I happen to know he was fired from Western Aircraft! The fact is, MacIlheny's got some cash donors in his hip pocket and we're all afraid to whisper because he might—"

MacIlheny pounded for silence. "The chair rules Miss Gingrich out of order," he said. "This is debate on a motion to impeach Mr. Friml and not to reconsider a policy of accepting contributions in confidence, which was approved by the membership as the minutes show. Miss Stuart, you're recognized."

Amy Stuart got up looking grim. "I want to make two statements. First, on a point of personal privilege, that Mr. Clifton was fired from Western because he was too high-spirited to get along in a rather conservative outfit and not for incompetence. More than once I've heard my father say that Mr. Clifton was—or almost was—the best man he had working for him.

"Second, I move to close debate."

"Second the motion," somebody called from the floor.

Miss Gingrich was on her feet shrilling: "Gag rule! Nobody can open his mouth around here except the Holy Three and their stooges! We were doing all right before MacIlheny—" The rest was lost in shouts of disapproval and the whacking of the gavel. The girl stood silently for a moment and then sat down, trembling.

"Motion to close debate has been made and seconded. This motion takes precedence and is unamendable. All in favor raise one hand." A forest of hands went up. "Any opposed?" Maybe twenty. "The motion is carried. We now have before us a motion to impeach Mr. Friml, our secretary-treasurer. All in favor." The same twenty hands. "Opposed?" The forest of hands rose again, and a few kids cried: "No, no!"

"The motion is defeated. Unless there are further matters under good and welfare"—he was refusing to let his eye be caught, and half a dozen members were trying to catch it—"we will proceed to the introduction of a new A.S.F.S.F. full-time scientific worker. Dr. Michael Novak comes to us from two years with the United States Atomic Energy Commission. He has been working with high-tensile, refractory ceramic materials—a vital field in rocketry; I'm sure the application to our work is obvious to all. Dr. Novak."

He was on his feet and starting down the aisle to a polite burst of applause. They might be spies or they might not; he might be working for them tomorrow or he might not, but meanwhile there was a certain rigmarole you went through at these things, and he knew it well.

"Mr. President, members, and guests, thank you." Now the joke. "My field of work stems from very early times. It was a cave man who founded ceramic engineering when he accidentally let a mud-daubed wicker basket fall into his campfire and pulled out, after the fire died down, the first earthenware pot. I presume he did not realize that he was also a very important pioneer of space flight." A satisfactory chuckle.

Now the erudition. "Basically, my problem is to develop a material which is strong, workable, and heat-resistant. For some years the way to tackle such a job has been to hunt the material among the so-called 'solid solutions.' An alloy is a familiar example of a solid solution—the kind in which both the solvent and the solute are metals.

"Tungsten-carbide is known to you with machine-shop savvy. It's a solid solution with one nonmetallic constituent, and its qualities have revolutionized industrial production. Dies and tool bits of this very hard stuff have surely increased our national output by several percent with no other changes being put into effect. Idle time of machine tools has been reduced because tungsten-carbide bits go on and on without resharpening. Idle time on presses of all sorts has been reduced because tungsten-carbide dies go on without replacement.

"This is only one example of the way Mother Nature comes up with the answer to your particular problem if you ask her in the right way. She also offers among the solid solutions the chromium and cobalt carbides, which top tungsten-carbide for refractory qualities, and the boron carbides with which I intend to work.

"In the solid solutions there is a situation that rules out dramatic, abrupt crystallizations of one's problem. An organic chemist trying to synthesize a particular molecule may leap up with a shriek of 'I've got it!' And so he may, for an organic molecule either is there or it isn't: a yes-or-no situation. But working with solutions instead of compounds, there is continuous variation of solvent to solute. Theoretically, it takes an infinite amount of time to explore the properties of *every* boron carbide, even if their properties varied simply and continuously with the ratio of constituents alone. But it is more complicated than that.

"Actually the properties you seek in your carbides do not appear when you turn out a batch fresh from your crucible. There is the complicated business of aging, in which the carbide spends a certain time at a certain temperature. Two more variables. And in some cases the aging should be conducted in a special atmosphere—perhaps helium or argon. Another variable! And secondary properties must be considered. For example, the standard ceramic bond to metal is obtained by heating both parts to red heat and plunging them into liquid air. There are carbides that may have every ocher desirable property but which cannot take such a drastic thermal shock."

MacIlheny, in the front row, was looking at his watch. Time for the windup. "I hope I've given you an idea of what we're up against. But I hope I haven't given you an idea that the problem's uncrackable in a less-than-infinite amount of time, because it isn't. Experiments in some number must be made, but mathematics comes to the aid of the researcher to tell him when he's on the right track and when he's going astray. With the aid of the theory of least squares, plenty of sweat, and a little dumb luck I hope before long to be able to report to you that I've developed a material which can take the heat and thrust of any escape-velocity fuel which may some day come along."

The applause was generous.

Back in his seat, Clifton said: "It sounded swell, Mike. Did it mean anything?" And Lilly said: "Don't be so foolish, Cliff. Was a byoo-tiful speech."

"We have the privilege tonight," MacIlheny was saying, "of being the first audience in this area to see the new space-flight film *Pirates of the Void*—" There were a few ironical cheers. "—through the kindness of Mr. Riefenstahl of United Productions' promotion staff. Audience comment cards will be available on the way out. I think it would be only fair and courteous if all of us made it a point to get one and fill it out, giving our—*serious*—opinion of the movie. And I'd like to add that Sokol Hall has made two projection machines available to us, so that this time there will be no interruption for changing between reels." The cheers at that were not ironical.

"I'm gonna the men's room," Clifton announced, and left. "Cliff don' like movies much," Lilly announced proudly. "He'll be back."

The lights went out and *Pirates of the Void* went on with a fanfare and the United Productions monogram.

The movie, thought Novak as he watched, was another case of the public's faith that space flight is an impossibility. It was a fable in which the actors wore old garments: the men, shiny coveralls; and the women, shiny shorts and bras. The time was far in the future—far enough for there to be pirates of space and a Space Navy of the United World to battle them. Space flight tomorrow, but never space flight today. *But MacIlheny had a fuel and knew its performance.*

He leaned back, wishing he could smoke, and saw Marsha Denny's problem unfold. Marsha was a nurse in the Space Navy and she had a brother (but there was a plant indicating that he wasn't really her brother, though she didn't yet know that) in the Pirate Fleet, high up. She was in love with Lawrence Malone, who took the part of the muscular G-2 of the Space Navy and had assigned himself the mission of penetrating the Pirate Fleet in the guise of a deserter from the regulars.

Somehow fifteen minutes of it passed, and Lilly leaned across the seat between them. "Mike," she asked worriedly, "you mind doing something for me? You go and find Cliff? He's gone an awful long time."

"Why sure," he whispered. "Glad to get out of here."

He slipped from the dark auditorium and promptly lit a cigarette. *Men's Room*, said a sign with an arrow. He followed it to a big, empty washroom with six booths. One of the doors was closed.

"Cliff?" he called, embarrassed. There was no answer.

Cliff must be in the corridor somewhere. His eye was caught by the shine of gold on the corner of a washstand. A wedding band— Cliff's wedding band? Slipped it off before he washed his hands? There was no engraving in it and he didn't remember what Cliff's ring looked like; just that he wore one.

Maybe—

"Mister," he said to the closed door, "I found a gold ring on the washstand. You lose it?"

There was no answer. A thread of crimson blood snaked from under the closed door, slowly over the tiled floor, seeking a bright brass drain.

I understand in these cloak-and-dagger things they kill ya if ya find out too much.

Novak fell on his hands and knees to peer through the six-inch gap between the bottom of the door and the floor. He saw two shod feet, oddly lax, a dangling hand, a little pool of blood, and a small pistol.

He went to pieces and pounded on the door, shouting. It was latched. Novak darted from the washroom to the main hall; Anheier was there, who didn't believe there was anything to their story. He blundered into the darkness where, on the screen, two silvery space ships of the impossible future were slashing at each other with many-colored rays that cracked and roared on the sound track.

"Anheier!" Novak yelled hysterically. "Where are you?" Dark heads turned to stare at him. Somebody stumbled his way across a row of knees and hurried to him.

"Dr. Novak?" asked the Security man. "What's the matter?" People shushed them loudly, and Anheier took Novak's arm, drawing him into the corridor.

Novak said: "There's somebody in a booth in the washroom. I saw blood. And a gun. I'm afraid it's Clifton."

Anheier hurried down the corridor without a word. In the washroom he went into an adjoining booth and climbed up on its bowl to peer over the partition.

"Bad," he said flatly, hopping down. He took a long nail file from his pocket, inserted it between the door edge and jamb and flipped up the latch. The door swung open outwards. "Don't touch anything," Anheier said.

Clifton was in the booth. His clothes were arranged. He was sprawled on the seat with his head down on his chest and his shoulders against the rear wall. There was a great hole in the back of his head, below the crown.

"Get to a phone," Anheier said. "Call the city police and report a homicide here."

Novak remembered a pay phone in the lobby downstairs and ran. Just like a magazine cartoon he crazily thought, when he found a woman talking in it on the other side of the folding glass door. He rapped on the glass imperatively and the woman turned. It was Amy Stuart. She smiled recognition, spoke another few words into the phone, and decisively hung up.

"I'm sorry to be such a gossip," she said, "but that bloody movie—"

"Thanks," he said hastily, and ducked into the phone booth. He saw Lilly coming down the stairs, looking more than a little worried.

The police switchboard took his call with glacial calm and said not to do anything, there would be a car there in less than five minutes.

Lilly and the Stuart girl were waiting outside. "Mike," Lilly burst out, "what's wrong? I sent you out to look for Cliff, you come back and holler for that A.E.C. feller and you run to the phone. You talk straight vit' me please, Mike."

"Lilly," he said, "Cliff's dead. Shot to death. I'm—I'm sorry—"

She said something in a foreign language and fainted on his arm. Amy Stuart said sharply: "Here. Into this chair." He lugged her clumsily into a deep, leather club chair.

"Was what you said true?" she demanded angrily, doing things to Lilly's clothes.

"Quite true," he said. "There's an A.E.C. Security man there now. I was calling the police. Do you know Mrs. Clifton?"

"Fairly well. How horrible for her. They loved each other. What could have happened? *What could have happened?*" Her voice was shrill.

"Take it easy," he told her flatly. "I think you're getting hysterical and that won't do any good."

She swallowed. "Yes—I suppose I was." She fussed efficiently over Lilly for a moment or two. "That's all," she said. "Nothing else you can do for a faint. God, how horrible for her! God, how I hate killers and killing. That bloody movie. World of tomorrow. Death rays flash the life out of five hundred people aboard a ship—call them Space Pirates and it's all right. Call them Space Navy and it's all right, too, as long as you kill Space Pirates to match. They're sitting up there laughing at it. What'll they think when they come out and find somebody's really dead? Who could have done it, Dr. Novak? It's unbelievable."

"I believe it. Miss Stuart, what'll we do with Mrs. Clifton? She and Cliff live alone—lived alone. Could you get a nurse—"

"I'll take her to my place. Father has a resident doctor. I think perhaps I'd better start now. The police would want to question her. It'd be inhuman."

"I think you'd better wait, Miss Stuart. It's—homicide, after all."

"That's absurd. All they could do is badger her out of her wits with questions, and what could she have to tell them about it?"

"Look—poor little rich girl," Novak snarled, angry, nasty, and scared. "Cliff was killed and I may be killed, too, if the cops don't figure this thing out. I'm not going to handicap them by letting witnesses disappear. You just stay put, will you?"

"Coward!" she flared.

The argument was broken up by the arrival of four policemen from a radio car.

Novak said to the one with stripes on his sleeve: "I'm Dr. Michael Novak, I found a man named August Clifton in the washroom, dead. An A.E.C. Security man I know was here, so I put it in his hands. He's upstairs with Clifton now. This is Clifton's wife."

"All right," said the sergeant. "Homicide cars'll be here any minute. Wykoff, you and Martinez keep people from leaving. Don't let 'em use that phone. Sam, come with me." He stumped up the stairs with a patrolman.

It must have been Martinez, small and flat-faced, who asked Novak: "What's going on here anyway, Doc? Ain't this the Cheskies' place? We never have any trouble with the Cheskies."

"It's rented for the night. By the American Society for Space Flight."

"Uh," said Martinez doubtfully. "Borderline cases. Did the guy kill himself?"

"He did not!"

"Aw-*right*, Doc! You don't have to get nasty just because I asked." And Martinez, offended, joined Wykoff at the door. Novak knew he had sounded nasty, and wondered how close he was to hysteria himself.

Anheier came down the stairs slowly, preoccupied. "What's this?" he asked.

"Clifton's wife. I told her. And Miss Stuart. Mr. Anheier from the A.E.C Security and Intelligence Office."

"Los Angeles regional agent in charge," Anheier said automatically.

"Mr. Anheier," said the girl, "can't I take Mrs. Clifton out of this? Before the other police and the reporters get here?"

"I'm not in charge," he said mildly, "but if you ask me it wouldn't be a good idea at all. Best to take our medicine and get it over with. What do you two think of Clifton's emotional stability?"

"He was brilliant, but—" Amy Stuart began, and then shut her mouth with a snap. "Are you suggesting that he took his own life?" she asked coldly. "That's quite incredible."

Anheier shrugged. "The sergeant thought so. It's for the coroner to say finally, of course."

"Look," said Novak, laboring to keep his voice reasonable. "You and I know damned well—"

"*Novak,*" said Anheier. "Can I talk to you for a minute?"

Novak stared at him and they went to the foot of the stairs. The Security man said quietly: "I know what you think. You think Clifton was murdered in connection with the—stuff—you told me this afternoon."

"I think there's an espionage angle," Novak said. "And I know you had your mind made up that Clifton and I were cranks. Man, doesn't this change anything? He's *dead!*"

Anheier considered. "I'll meet you halfway," he said. "When you tell your story to the cops, keep it straight. Don't babble to reporters about your suspicions. Just leave out your opinion that Clifton was murdered. *If* there's an espionage angle, this is no time to give it to the papers."

"How does that add up to meeting me halfway?" Novak asked bitterly.

"I want to see you after tonight's fuss is over. I'll fill you in on the big picture. Meanwhile, don't prejudice our position with loose talk. Here's Homicide now. Watch yourself."

Homicide was three sedans full of photographers, detectives, and uniformed police. Reporters and press photographers were at their heels. A Lieutenant Kahn was the big wheel. Novak watched Anheier brief Kahn calmly and competently and felt a charge of resentment.

The big picture—what was it? Perhaps smoothly meshing crews of agents were preparing tonight to seize members of a conspiracy ramified far beyond his small glimpse—

The lieutenant was firing orders. "Nobody, but nobody, leaves the building until I say so. You, yank that press guy out of the phone booth; that line's for us. Sergeant, make an announcement to the movie audience upstairs. Doc, bring Mrs. Clifton to and let her cry it out. I'll want to talk to her later. No reporters past the stairs for now. Where's this Novak? Come on, let's view the remains."

Now there were two white-faced A.S.F.S.F. kids in the washroom as well as the radio-car sergeant and patrolman. The sergeant saluted and said: "They came in a minute ago, lieutenant. I hold them. Didn't want a stampede."

"Good. Take them down to the lobby with a bull to watch them. Start taking your pictures, Ivy. Let's *go*, you f.p. men! Where's Kelly? Dr. Novak, you found the body, didn't you? Tell us just what happened while it's still fresh in your mind." An uniformed policeman stood at Novak's elbow with an open stenographic pad.

Don't prejudice our position. Fine words; did they mean anything? Fumblingly, Novak went over it all, from Lilly's first worried request to the end. Halfway through he remembered about the ring, went through his pockets, and produced it. Through it all, Anheier's calm eyes were on him. In deference to the big picture and the unprejudiced position he said nothing about foreign powers, space-ship fuel, or espionage—and wondered if he was a fool.

The scene blended into a slow nightmare that dragged on until 1:00 a.m. Parts of the nightmare were: glaring lights from the Homicide photographers' power packs, Lilly conscious again and hysterical, Amy Stuart yelling at the police to leave her alone, Friml clutching him to ask shakily whether he thought Clifton had been embezzling, sly-eyed reporters hinting about him and Lilly, MacIlheny groaning that this would set back the A.S.F.S.F. ten years and telling his story to the police again and again and again.

Finally there was quiet. The names of A.S.F.S.F. members present had been taken and they had been sent home, kids and engineers. Amy had taken Lilly home. The police had folded their tripods, packed their fingerprint gear and gone. Last of all an ambulance whined away from the door with a canvas bag in its belly.

Left in the lobby of Slovak Sokol Hall were Novak, Anheier, and a stooped janitor grumbling to himself and turning out the building lights.

"You said you wanted to talk to me," Novak said wearily. Anheier hesitated. "Let's have a drink. I know a bar up the street." Novak, wrung out like a dishrag, followed him from the hall. The waiting janitor pointedly clicked off the last light.

The bar was dim and quiet. Half a dozen moody beer-sippers were ranged on its stools. Anheier glanced at them and said: "Table okay? I have a reason."

"Sure." The Security man picked one well to the rear. "Watch the bartender," he said softly.

"Eh?" Novak asked, startled, and got no answer. He watched. The bartender, old and fat, deliberately mopped at his bar. At last he trudged to the end of the bar, lifted the flap, plodded to their table, and said: "Yuh?"

"You got double shot glasses?" Anheier asked. The bartender glared at him. "Yuh."

"I want a double scotch. You got Poland Water?"

The bartender compressed his mouth and shook his head. "I want soda with it then. Novak?"

"Same for me," Novak said.

The bartender turned and plodded back to the bar, limping a little. Novak watched him as he slowly went through the ritual of pouring. "What's all this about?" he asked.

"Watch him," Anheier said, and laughed. The bartender's head immediately swiveled up and at their table. His glare was frightening. It was murderous.

He brought them their drinks and Novak noticed that his limp had grown more marked. His fingers trembled when he set the tray down and picked up Anheier's bill.

"Keep the change," Anheier said easily, and the bartender's hand tremor grew worse. Wordlessly the man trudged from the table, rang up the sale, and resumed mopping.

"Would you mind telling me—" Novak began, picking up his double-shot glass.

"Don't drink that," Anheier said. "It may be poison."

Novak's heart bounded. This, by God, was it! Poison, spies, the papers, and Anheier was admitting he'd been right all along!

"Let's get out of here," the Security man said. He got up, leaving his own glass untouched, and they left. Novak's back crawled as he walked out behind Anheier. A thrown stiletto—a bullet—

They made it to the street, alive, and Novak waited to be filled in on the big picture while they walked: he apprehensively and Anheier with icy calm.

"I noticed that old boy came on duty while I was having a beer before the meeting," the Security man said. "He made me think of you. Paranoia. A beautifully developed persecution complex; one of these days he's going to kill somebody."

Novak stopped walking. "He's not a spy?" he asked stupidly.

"No," Anheier said with surprise. "He's a clinical exhibit, and a hell of a man to hire for a bartender. While I was finishing my beer, somebody complained about the weather and he took it as a personal insult. Two lushes were lying about how much money they made. He told them to cut out the roundabout remarks; how much money he made was his business and no cheap jerks could horn in on it. You noticed the limp? We were picking on him by making him walk to the table. I laughed and he *knew* I was laughing at him. Knew I was one of his enemies plotting against him right under his nose."

"You're telling me that I have a persecution complex, Anheier? That I'm crazy?" Novak asked hoarsely.

The Security man said: "Don't put words in my mouth. I am saying you've got a fixed idea about espionage, which makes no sense at all to me—and I'm a pro about espionage; you're a grass-green amateur.

"What have you *got?* A drawing that doesn't look right to you. Why the devil should it? Mysterious financial backing of the rocket club. All corporate financing is mysterious. The big boys divulge exactly as much as the law forces them to—and a lot of them try to get away with less. Every S.E.C. order issued means somebody tried just that. And Clifton got shot through the head; that's supposed to be the clincher that should convince even me. Do you think suicides don't occur?"

Automatically they were walking again and the Security man's reasonable, logical voice went on. "I didn't go to that meeting tonight to investigate your allegations; I went for laughs and to see the movie. Novak, it's always tragic to see a person acquiring a fixed idea. They never realize what's happening to them. If you try to set them right, you only succeed in giving them more 'evidence.' You know the job I have. Lord, the people I have to see! A week doesn't go by without some poor old duffer turning up and asking me to make the A.E.C. stop sending death rays through him. If they get violent we call the city police…"

"That sounds like a threat, Anheier."

"It wasn't meant to. But I'm not surprised that you thought it did. Frankly, Novak, have you considered what your record for the past year is like? I looked you up."

Novak considered, in a cold fury. A transfer—an idiotic transfer. Unsuitable work. Hurlbut's vicious memorandum.

The blowup. Affiliating with a bunch of space hounds. Superficially Anheier might look right. Inside himself he knew better.

"It won't wash," he said evenly. "You're not talking me out of anything. There's going to be an inquest on Clifton and I'm going to speak my piece."

"Better not. And this time it is a threat."

It was exhilarating. "So it's out in the open now. Good. You'll do what?"

"I want very badly to talk you out of your mistaken notion," Anheier said broodingly. "But if I can't, I've got to warn you that you're monkeying with the buzz saw. If the opposition papers get hold of your allegations, there will be hell to pay in the A.E.C. We'll have a spy scare. Security and Intelligence will look bad. Research and Development will look bad because the headlines say another country has beaten us to the punch on rocket fuel. We'll be judged by millions not on the strength of what we do for the nation's security but on what the headlines say we don't do. And all because one Dr. Michael Novak spoke his piece. Novak, do you think we won't counter-punch?"

Novak snorted. "What could you do? I happen to be right."

The Security man gave him a pitying look and muttered: "If you smear us, we'll smear you."

Novak suddenly no longer felt exhilarated. It was a frightening word. "That's blackmail," he said angrily, but his knees had gone weak.

"Please don't put it that way." The Security man sounded genuinely pained. "You think you're right and I think you're wrong.

If you want to talk to me and give me your side, okay. I'll talk to you and give you my side.

"But if you speak up at the inquest or go to the papers in any other way—we'll have to fight you in the papers. It's your choice of weapons. You can damage A.E.C. terribly with an unfounded spy scare. Naturally we'll hit back. And what can we do except try and impeach your credibility by spreading unfavorable facts about you on the record?"

In a low, embarrassed voice he went on: "Everybody's done things he's ashamed of. I know I have. I know you have. Boyhood indiscretions—adventures. Girls, traffic summonses. Friends of friends of friends who were Communists. And there were imaginative or inaccurate people who knew you slightly, maybe disliked you, and told our interviewers anything they pleased. We have a deposition in your file from a fellow you beat out on a scholarship exam. He says he saw you cheating in the examination room. Our evaluators disregard it, but will the headline-readers? What about your inefficiency at Argonne? Your fight with Dr. Hurlbut?"

Novak was feeling ill. "If you people libel me," he said, "I can sue. And I will."

Anheier slowly shook his head. "What with?" he asked. "Who would hire the man whom the headlines called a lunatic, a pervert, a cheat, a drunkard, a radical, and heaven-knows-what-else? None of it *proved*, but—'where there's smoke there's fire,' and the 'Indefinable Something behind the Mysterious All This.'" Anheier's voice became strangely compassionate. "I mean it about the buzz saw," he said. "Surely you know of people who fought a smear and wound up in jail for perjury…"

He did.

"All right, Anheier," Novak said softly and bitterly. "You've made up my mind for me. I was going to speak my piece at the inquest and get out of town. Now it seems I've got to do your work for you.

"A foreign power's operating under your nose and they've just murdered an American as a minor detail of a plan to bring America to its knees. So I'll keep my mouth shut and stick with the A.S.F.S.F. If I live, I'll blow this thing open. And then God help you, Anheier; I'm going to throw you to the wolves."

He walked unsteadily down a side street away from the Security man. Anheier stared after him, poker-faced.

CHAPTER SEVEN

AFTERNOON of a bureaucrat.

Daniel Holland wished he were in the privacy of his office where he could swallow some soda and burp. He was lunching with the commissioners, four trenchermen, and had taken aboard too much duck with wild rice. And the commissioners were giving him hell, in a nice, extroverted way, for the slow—in fact, almost negligible— progress of A.D.M.P., the Atomic Demolition Material Program. A.D.M.P. was scheduled to provide very shortly atomic explosives that would move mountains in the American Southwest, sculpture watersheds into improved irrigation patterns, and demonstrate to a politically shaky area which elected six senators that the current Administration was the dry-farmer's guide, philosopher, and friend. In actual fact, A.D.M.P. had provided only a vast amount of dubious paper work, and some experimental results, which only an insanely optimistic evaluator would describe with even so cautious, a word as "promising."

The chairman of the Commission, a paunchy, battered veteran of thirty years in county, state, and national politics, told Holland gently: "Interior's pushing us hard, Dan—very hard. You know he's got the Chief's ear, of course. And it's our opinion that he's not being unreasonable. All he wants is a definite date—give or take a month— that they can start blasting in the Sierras with our stuff. He doesn't care whether the date's a month from now or a year from now, but he needs it for planning and publicity. Of course the work's got to get going before the nominating conventions, but that's absolutely the only restriction on the program. Now, what are we going to tell him?"

"I don't just know offhand, Bill," Holland grumbled. "No doubt about it, A.D.M.P.'s bogged down. I have some suggestions about getting it out of the mud, but they involve basic policy."

The first commissioner was a handsome, muscular man who had gracefully lived down the tag of "wonder boy" pinned on him when he became a university president at the age of thirty-six. He was currently on leave from the executive directorship of a great foundation dedicated to the proposition that visual education is on the beam and all else is dross. He roared jovially at the general manager:

"Well, spill your guts, Dan. That's our little old job, you know. Let's canvass your suggestions informally right now. If they click we can program them for an on-the-record session."

"You asked for it, Cap," Holland said. "First, we need—I mean *need*—about a dozen good men who happen to be teaching or working in industry around the country right now. One's a Yugoslav refugee with relations left in the old country. Another was a Young Communist League member, fairly active, in 1937 and '38. Another was once tried and acquitted on a morals charge—some little girl got mad at him and told lies. Another—well, I won't bother listing them all. You get the idea."

The second commissioner was a spare, white-headed ex-newspaperman: Pulitzer Prize, *Times* Washington Bureau chief, author, diplomatic correspondent, journalism-school dean, intimate of the great, recipient of very many honorary degrees. He shook his head more—to use a cliché that never would have appeared in his copy—in sorrow than in anger. "Now, Dan," he said, "this is no time to tinker with the machinery. If there's one thing about A.E.C. that's smooth-running now, it's clearance. Congress is mostly happy—except for Hoyt's gang; the papers are happy—except for the opposition rags; and the public's got confidence in the personnel of their A.E.C. We simply can't start *that* fight all over again. What else did you have in mind?"

"Second," Holland said impassively, "we're being slowed down by declassification and down-classification, I've drummed into the boys that most material should be merely *Restricted*, *Confidential* covers most of what's left, and the *Secret* classification should be sparingly used. But they're scared, or conservative, or only human, or taking the safest way or whatever you want to blame it on. Every time I give them hell there's a little flurry of *Confidential and Restricted* and then the *Secret* begins to mount up again and we're back in the same old rut: boys in Los Alamos doing work that's been done in Hanford and not knowing about it. Maybe because of the limited distribution of *Secret* material. Maybe because the Los Alamos boys aren't in high enough grade for access to it. Gentlemen, I think something basic is required to correct this condition."

The third commissioner was a New York investment banker who had doubled his family fortune in ten legendary years on Wall Street and served his country for the next ten as a diplomatic troubleshooter

in the Near East. He was still a formidable welterweight boxer and—
to the dismay of the first commissioner—could speak Arabic, Turkish,
and Court Persian. Alone on the current Commission, he had thought
it his duty to master what he could of nuclear physics and its
mathematical tools. Diffidently he said: "That's a tough one, Dan.
But I don't see what choice we had or have. Our policy, arrived at in
the best interests of the national security, is to 'classify all A.E.C. data
to the extent required to prevent it from being of use to potential
enemies of the United States.' It's broad, I grant you. But the
demands of national security won't be satisfied with anything
narrower."

"Neither will Congress," said the second commissioner.

"Neither will the voters," grunted the chairman. "Dan, we'll just
have to leave that one in your lap for you to lick as an administrative
problem—*within the limits of our policy*. Just a suggestion: what about
setting up a special classifications-review unit charged with checking
the point-of-origin classifications on new data under a directive to
declassify or down-classify whenever possible? You'd be able to keep
a single unit here in Washington under your thumb easier than the
assorted managers and directors out in the field. About how much
would an outfit like that cost?"

Embarrassing moment. How to tell them that Weiss had worked
on such a plan for three months and found it impracticable? "Well,
Bill, it would stand us maybe two million a year in salaries and
overhead. But I see a lot of complications. The personnel in the new
unit would have to be scientists or they wouldn't know what they were
doing. God knows where we'd get enough of them to keep up with all
the data A.E.C. grinds out—you know the scientific manpower picture.
And you'd have a hell of a turnover because scientists like to do
science and not paper work. And *quis custodiet?* The safest thing for
them to do would still be to stamp everything *Secret*; they'll never get in
trouble that way even if it does slow A.E.C. down to a crawl. I'll
explore the idea and give you a report, bit I think it's a policy matter."

The second commissioner said flatly: "We can't change the
classifications policy, Dan. There hasn't been a spy scare worth
mentioning in three years. The public's on our side. We've built up a
favorable press and congressional attitude slowly and painfully and
we're not going to wreck it now. Sure, we'd make a short-term gain if
we published all data. But come the appropriations bill debate!

Congress would cut our funds fifty percent across the board—nail us to the cross to show us who's boss. You've got to do the best you can with what you've got, and never forget the political climate. What else did you have up your sleeve?"

Holland glanced at the chairman and looked away. Then he said slowly: "Third, something I don't understand at all has come up. A.D.M.P. was set up personnel-wise and equipment-wise to handle one ton of thorium metal a month." The chairman coughed nervously. "I learned yesterday," Holland went on, "that for two months they've been getting only .75 tons a month from Raw Materials. They thought the reduction came from me. I checked with R.M. and found that the office of the chairman ordered a monthly quota of .25 tons of thorium to the Air Force Experimental Station with priority overriding A.D.M.P. So R.M. quite correctly diverted the A.F.E.S quota from A.D.M.P.'s quota. I haven't checked so far on what the Air Force has been doing with our thorium." He didn't mention his anger at being by-passed, or his weary disgust at realizing that some fifteen hundred A.D.M.P. personnel had been idle as far as their primary mission was concerned for one sixth of a year because they lacked material to work with.

"Dan," said the chairman slowly, "I owe you an apology on that one. You recall how General McGovern came to bat for us at the last joint Committee hearings. Praised us to the skies for our grand co-operation, said we were all patriots, gentlemen, and scholars he was proud to work with? Half the Committee members at least are red-hot Air Force fans, so it did us a lot of good. Well, McGovern's price for that was the thorium allotment. His boys at A.F.E.S. think they can use thorium warheads in air-to-air guided missiles. The Weaponeering Advisory Committee tells me it's a lot of nonsense and furthermore A.F.E.S. hasn't got anybody who could do the work even if it were possible, so Air's not really fishing in our lake."

"Can we get their thorium quota back to A.D.M.P.?" Holland asked.

"No. I'd be afraid to try it. McGovern's been talking about a bigger quota, to serve notice on me that he's not going to be whittled down. And I live in fear that the Navy will find out about it and demand a thorium allotment of their own. That's why I was so damned secretive about it—the fewer people know about these deals, the better. Maybe we ought to have Raw Materials set up a new group to expedite thorium-ore procurement and refining—but my point was, no; the Air Force has got it and they won't let go. We've got to get along with the military, Dan. You know that. They can make us look awful bad if they've a mind to."

"Well," said Holland, "that's that. I'll get you a report you can show Interior by tomorrow morning. Were there any other points for me?"

"Gentlemen?" asked the chairman, looking around the table. There were no other points, and the general manager left them.

The third commissioner said: "I'm a little worried about Holland. He seems to be going cynical on us."

The chairman said: "He's a little stale from overwork. He refuses to take a vacation."

"Like an embezzler," said the ex-banker, and they laughed.

"He doesn't see the big picture," said the second commissioner, and they nodded thoughtfully and got up to go their various ways:

The chairman to weigh the claims of two areas pleading to be the site of the next big A.E.C. plant;

The first commissioner to polish a magazine article on "Some Lessons of Aquinas for the Atomic Age";

The second commissioner to lobby three congressmen in connection with the appropriations bill coming up in eight months;

The third commissioner to confer with the Secretary of State on the line that State's overseas propaganda broadcasts should take concerning A.D.M.P. as proof of America's peace-loving nature.

Holland, in the privacy of his office, took four soda-mint tablets and burped luxuriously. He phoned his assistant Weiss, and passed him the job of drafting tomorrow morning's report for the Secretary of the Interior.

His "While You Were Out" pad said:

"12:15—Senator Hoyt's office called for an appointment 'as soon as possible.' Said I would call back.

"12:20—Mr. Wilson Stuart called from Los Angeles and asked you to call back today on the private number:

"12:45—Senator Hoyt's office called again. Said I would call back.

"12:48—the Associated Press called asking for an interview at your convenience. I said you were occupied for the coming week and referred them to the P.&T.I. Office.

"1:15—Senator Hoyt's office called again. Said I would call back."

He sighed and knocked down an intercom button. "Charlie, tell Hoyt's people he can come right over. Get me Stuart on—no, I'll place it."

"Yes, Mr. Holland."

The general manager didn't have a phone on his desk, but he did have one in a drawer. It had a curiously thickened base, the result of some wire-pulling in A.T.&T. The curiously thickened base housed a "scrambler" of the English type, which matched one in Wilson Stuart's bedroom phone. It was a fairly effective measure against wiretaps. He pulled out the phone and placed the call.

His old friend must have been waiting by his own phone in the big white Beverly Hills house. "Hello?" said the voice of Wilson Stuart.

"Hello, Wilson. How is everything?"

"Let's scramble."

"All right." Holland pushed a button on the phone. "Can you hear me all right?"

"I hear you." The quality of the transmission had taken an abrupt drop—the result of Wilson Stuart's voice being torn into shreds by his scrambler, hurled in that unintelligible form across the continent, and reassembled by Holland's device. "Dan, things are going sour out here. They're trying to take Western Air away from me—a nice little phony stockholders' revolt. One of my rats in the Oklahoma Oil crowd tipped me today. I don't know how far they've got in lining up their proxies, but it could be bad."

"What's the squawk?"

"I stand accused of running the board of directors like a railroad—which, God knows, I do, and a good thing for Western. Also, and this is the part that scares me, I'm supposed to be squandering the company's resources."

"Um, it isn't a real rank-and-file thing, is it?"

"Act your age, Dan! It's the old Bank of California program: kick Stuart out of Western Air and integrate it with their other holdings. This time they've met Oklahoma Oil's terms."

"Who's fronting?"

"That's the only cheerful part. They've got some squirt Air Force two-star general named Reeves. He commands Great Falls A.F.B. in Montana. They've sounded him out and he's supposed to be willing to take over as board chairman after I get the boot. Such patriotism."

"I can do something about that. Know Austin?"

"I was thinking of him—he'd put the screws on the flyboy. Will you get in touch with him?"

"Sure. Fast."

"Another thing...I'll be in a lot stronger position for the showdown if I can pull a big, big A.E.C. contract out of my hat. What have you got?"

Holland thought for a moment. "Well, Reactor Program's got some big orders coming up. Die-cast one-inch rods, aluminum cans, and some complicated structural members. It might all come to twenty-five million dollars. You set up for die-casting?"

"Hell no, but what's the difference? We can subcontract it to anybody who *is* set up. All I want is the money to show those monkeys on the board."

"You'll get it. How's Amy?"

"No complaints. She brought Clifton's widow home. Too bad about that. You never knew the guy, but he used to work for me—a real character."

"That so! Tell Amy to drop in and say hello next time she's East. I haven't seen her for months."

"I sure will, Dan. Take care of yourself. *And* the fly-boy. *And* the contract. Good-by."

Holland hung up and put the phone back in its drawer. He said over his intercom: "Tell Fallon from Reactor Program Procurement that I want to see him. And get me Undersecretary Austin on the phone—the Air Force Austin."

The Air Force Austin was only an acquaintance, but he had a low boiling point, and handles that stuck out a yard. There were many things that he hated, and one of them was military men who used their service careers as springboards to high-pay civilian jobs.

"Naturally I don't want to meddle in your area, Austin," Holland was telling him a minute later, "but we're all working for the same boss. Can you tell me anything about a major General Reeves—Great Falls A.F.B.?"

Austin's suspicious New England voice said: "Supposed to be a brilliant young man. I don't know him personally. What about him?"

"I hear he's getting involved in a big-business crowd. If you want me to stop talking and forget about it, just say so."

Austin snapped: "Not at all. I'm glad you called me. What exactly did you hear?"

"The people are supposed to be Oklahoma Oil and Bank of California. The way the story went, they want to hire him as a front for the reorganization of some aircraft company or other."

"Nothing illegal? No hint of cumshaw?"

"None whatsoever. Just the usual big-salary bait."

"Glad of *that*. Thanks, Holland. If Reeves thinks he can use the Air Force, he's got a great deal to learn. I'll have this investigated very thoroughly. If you're right, he'll be A.F. Liaison officer in Guam before he knows what hit him."

Holland grimaced at the thought. It was punishing a man for exercising his freedom of contract; as a lawyer he couldn't be happy about it. Unfortunately, Austin was right too. Industry cheerfully fished the armed-forces and civil-service pond for able and underpaid executives; it had to be discouraged. Carry the process far enough and industry would hire away the best military and Government brains, leaving the nation—and itself—defended by an army of knuckleheads and administered by a bureaucracy of nincompoops…

And of course there were other reasons for lowering the boom on Reeves.

"Mr. Fallon to see you," said his secretary.

"Send him in." Fallon was in his early thirties, but there was something about him that made him look younger to Holland. The general manager thought he could guess what it was. "Is this your first public-service job, Fallon?"

"Yes, Mr. Holland."

"What did you do before this?"

"I was with General Motors. Up in Detroit Purchasing, assistant to the department head."

"That was a good job. Why'd you leave it for us?"

He knew why. The itch you can only scratch with service, the uncomfortable feeling that they needed you, the half-conscious guilt that you owed more than your taxes. He knew why. It had ridden him all his life. Fallon tried to put it into words, and didn't succeed. There were glib hacks who could talk your ear off about it, and there were sincere guys like this who couldn't make themselves a case. "I guess I just thought I'd be happier here, Mr. Holland."

"Well. I wanted to talk to you about the upcoming contracts for breeder cans, moderator rods, and retaining-wall members. Five-nineteen, twenty, and twenty-one, I believe. Are you going to invite Western Aircraft to bid?"

Fallon was puzzled. "I'd swear they haven't got die-casting facilities on that scale, Mr. Holland. I wasn't figuring on it, but of course I'll include them if they can swing it."

"They can handle part of it as prime contractor and subcontract the rest."

"But the procurement policy is—"

"This is a special case. I want you to understand that their bid may seem high, but that they deserve very serious consideration. It's essential that we have no holdup on these castings, and I've practically decided that Western Air can do a better job of seeing them through to delivery than any other outfit that's likely to bid. They're a very able, deadline-minded outfit, and the over-all picture at this time indicates that we need their talent."

Fallon was getting upset. "But we've never had any trouble with Inland Steel or G.E., to name just two fabricators who might bid, Mr. Holland. They come through like clockwork, they know our procedure, we know the people there, they know us—it greases the ways."

"Really, Fallon, I think my suggestion was clear enough. I can't be expected to fill you in on the reasons for it. Some of them are military secrets, others are policy matters, and none of them is any particular business of yours."

Fallon looked at him, no longer wide-eyed. "Sure," he said woodenly. "How is Mr. Stuart? I hear he's a good friend of yours."

Well, this was it. The cat was clawing at the bag; the beans were about to spill. Coldly Holland channeled the fear that was exploding through him into artificial rage. He was on his feet, and his chair crashed to the floor behind him. In one stride he was towering over Fallon in the desk-side chair. Holland thrust his face almost into the face of the man from Purchasing. His voice was a low, intense growl.

Watch your language, son. I've been taking a beating for twenty-eight years in public service." *Talk.* Keep him off balance, make him feel young and raw, make him ashamed, make him unhappy. "They've called me a Communist and a fascist and a bureaucrat and a bungler but they've never called me a crook. My worst enemies admit that if I wanted money I've got the brains to get it honestly. If I wanted money, I could quit A.E.C. today, open a law office tomorrow and have a half a million dollars in retainers by next month."

Fallon was beginning to squirm, "I didn't—"

"Shut up. If you think you've turned up evidence of dishonesty, I'll tell you what to do. Pick up your hat and run right over to the Senate Office Building. There's a crowd there that's been trying to nail my hide to the wall ever since you were in knee pants. Maybe you've succeeded where they failed."

"I meant—"

"Shut up, Fallon. You told me what you meant. You meant that I've got nothing to show for twenty-eight years of trying to help run the purest democracy left in the world. That was news to me. I've known for a long time that I wasn't going to get rich out of the Government service. I decided long ago that I couldn't marry, because either the marriage or the work would suffer. I know I haven't got any pride left; I stand ready at any hour of the day or night to get my teeth kicked in by those county-ring Solons up on the Hill. But I thought I had the loyalty of my own kind of people. It seems I was wrong."

"Mr. Holland—"

He didn't interrupt, but the youngster didn't go on. Holland stared him down and then straightened to sit on the edge of his desk. "Go on over to the Senate Office Building, Fallon," he said quietly. "Get your name in the paper. I can stand one more kicking-around and you can use the publicity. Maybe they'll ghostwrite a series of articles for you in the Bennet rags."

But Fallon was almost blubbering. "That's not fair!" he wailed. "I tried to tell you I was sorry. I can't help it if have an Irish temper and a big mouth. I know what your record is, Mr. Holland. It's a—it's a wonderful record." He pulled himself together and got up. "Mr. Holland," he said formally and mournfully, "I feel I should submit my resignation."

Holland slugged him on the biceps and said gruffly: "Not accepted. I could use a hundred more like you. I've got thick hide— usually. Just that crack…but don't let it worry you. Clear about that bid?"

"Clear at last, Mr. Holland," Fallon said with a melancholy smile. "I'll try not to make a damned fool of myself again. You have troubles enough."

When he was alone, the general manager set up the kicked-over chair, leaned back, and lit a cigarette with fingers that shook. It had been a very near thing. Lord, how long could a man be expected to keep this up? The perpetual sweat about wire tappers, loose talkers, shrewd newsmen who might put two and two together, the political opposition relentlessly stalking every hint of irregularity.

Once in T.V.A. he had turned in a friend and classmate for trying to recruit him into a footling little Communist industrial-espionage apparatus. The revelation had been shattering; his duty had seemed clear. But that had been a long time ago...

His intercom said: "Senator Hoyt is here, Mr. Holland."

"Send him in, Charlie." He sprang from behind his desk to shake the senator's hand. "Good to see you again, Bob," he burbled cheerfully.

The senator's meaty face broke into an actor's smile. "Mighty nice of you to find time for us, Dan," he said. It was a reminder that he'd had to wait on Holland's convenience to make the appointment and a threat that some day Holland would sweat for it. The senator did not forget slights, real or imaginary.

"How're you, Mary?" asked Holland, a little dampened.

"So-so," Mary Tyrrel, the senator's secretary, said vaguely. It was odd that she was Hoyt's five-thousand-per secretary, because until last year she had been a twenty-thousand-per Washington by-liner for the Bennet newspapers. But lots of odd things happen in Washington.

"Well, Bob, what can I do for you?"

"I'm collecting a little information, Dan. Normally my investigating staff would handle it. But out of respect for your high position I thought I ought to ask you straight out myself."

Cat and mouse, thought Holland. What's he got?

The senator lit a cigar deliberately. "I like to consider myself a member of the loyal opposition," he said. "Our democracy has kept its vigor because of constant, intransigent criticism and pressure by reformers—realistic, practical reformers—against the abuses of an entrenched bureaucracy. I've been in some good scraps, Dan, and I've loved them. I fought the A.E.C. when it tried to give jobs to foreigners of doubtful loyalty. I've fought when you people tried to give moral lepers and degenerates control of our most precious military secrets. I've fought to root out close-tongued drunkards from the A.E.C."

"It hasn't done you any harm, Bob," Holland said.

The senator wasn't thrown off his stride. "No," he said. "It hasn't. I've enjoyed the rewards of good citizenship. I have the respect of my constituents, and on a national scale I have the backing of a great chain of patriotic newspapers. But Dan, I'm on the track of something that—God willing—will lead to the highest office in the land."

"Dewey didn't make it," Holland said.

The senator waved his cigar expansively in various directions. "He got to be governor at least. If he didn't have the imagination to make the jump to the presidency, it was his fault. Of course in his day the techniques weren't as developed as they are now. I know you take the old-fashioned, strict-construction view of politicking: work hard, improve yourself in knowledge and skill, one day you'll get the nomination on a silver platter. With all respect to you as a student of government, Dan, that theory is as dead as the Lincoln-Douglas debates.

"This is an era of high-level energy in science, industry— government. The nervous tensions under which we all live and work rules out leisurely reflection on the claims of this candidate or that. You've got to electrify people. Make them know who you are. Keep dinning your name at them so it drowns out any other candidate's name. Immerse them in your personality. Have it drummed at them twenty-four hours a day, inescapably. The standing machinery of the press and broadcasting will do it for you if you just give them a news peg to hang it on."

The senator—and his secretary—were watching him narrowly.

Holland said, "You figure you've got a news peg?"

The senator tapped cigar ash to the floor. "I might come up with one," he said. "A scandal and an investigation—the biggest ever, Dan. A blowup that will be on every tongue for a solid month. Housewives, factory hands, professional people, children—there'll be something in it for everybody. Dan! What would you think of a public servant who ignored a great discovery instead of promulgating it for the use of the people of the United States? Wouldn't it be—treason?"

"I thought you used to be a lawyer, Bob," Holland said. "It sounds like malfeasance to me."

"What if every indication was that this public servant behaved in no way different from an enemy agent, Dan?"

"Look," said Holland. "If you're going to denounce any of my A.E.C. boys for incompetence or malfeasance or mopery with intent to gawk, go ahead and do it. We've screened and processed our people to the utmost limit of practicability. You're hinting that a spy got through in spite of it. So all I can say is, that's too bad. Tell me who he is and I'll have Security and Intelligence grab him. Is that what you came to see me about?"

"Oh," the senator said mildly, "we just wanted your general reaction to the situation. Thanks for hearing me out so patiently. If anything else turns up I'll let you know."

He smiled and gave Holland a manly handshake. The general manager saw them to the door of his office, closed the door and latched it. He leaned against the oak panels with sweat popping from his brow. Somebody at Hanford had been talking to a Bennet reporter.

They didn't seem to have anything yet on the fiscal or personnel angles.

Time was getting very short.

CHAPTER EIGHT

THE STORY on page four of Novak's morning paper said:

SPACE SHIP ENGINEER FOUND SHOT
TO DEATH AT ROCKET CLUB MEET

The soaring interplanetary dreams of 146 rocket-club members turned to nightmare at Slovak Sokol Hall last night when the body of engineer August Clifton, trusted employee of the American Society of Space Flight, was found in a washroom of the hall as a meeting of the society was in full swing on the same floor. Assistant medical examiner Harry Morales said death apparently was caused by a head wound from a single .25-caliber bullet. A Belgian automatic of that caliber was found lying near Clifton's right hand, with one shot fired according to Homicide Bureau Lieutenant C. F. Kahn.

The victim's attractive wife Lilly, 35, was taken in a state of collapse to the Beverly Hills home of aircraft manufacturer Wilson Stuart by his daughter Amelia Stuart, a friend of the Cliftons and a member of the rocket club.

The club secretary, Joel Friml, 26, said Clifton had been authorized to spend "sizable" sums of club money in the course of his work, which was to build a pioneer spaceship that club members hoped would go to the Moon. Friml said he did not know of any irregularities in Clifton's accounts but added that he will immediately audit club financial records for the past year with an eye to any bearing they may have on the death.

Other friends of Clifton said he was in good health but "moody" and "eccentric."

Lieutenant Kahn said he will not comment until police fingerprint and ballistics experts have analyzed the evidence. An inquest will be held Wednesday morning.

The body was discovered by Dr. Michael Novak, 30, an engineer also employed by the club, when he slipped out of the meeting room during the showing of a movie. Novak immediately called in the aid of A.E.C. security agent J. W. Anheier, who was attending the meeting as a visitor. Anheier stood guard in the washroom to prevent evidence from being disturbed until police arrived. He later told reporters: "There is no security angle involved. It was just a coincidence that I happened to be there and Dr. Novak called on me."

Two one-column photographs flanked the story. One was of Amy Stuart, very society-page looking captioned: "Socialite shelters stricken wife." The other was a view of the *Prototype*: "Dead engineer's unfinished 'moon rocket.'"

All tied up in a neat little package with a bow, Novak thought bitterly. Without saying it, the newspaper told you that Clifton had blown his brains out, probably after embezzling A.S.F.S.F. money. If you didn't know Clifton, you'd believe it of course. Why not? "They wouldn't print it if it wasn't true."

He went from the lobby newsstand to the hotel coffee shop and ordered more breakfast than he thought he could eat. But he was a detective now; he'd have to act unconcerned and unsuspicious while he was slowly gathering evidence—

Oh, what the hell.

It wasn't real. None of it had been real, for months. Assignment to Neutron Path Prediction, when he didn't know whether neutrons should take paths or four-lane super-highways. Slugging his boss, quitting his job under a cloud—research and development men didn't *act* like that. Going to work for the A.S.F.S.F., an organization as screwball as Clifton himself.

He wanted to laugh incredulously at the whole fable, finish his coffee, get up and walk into the job he should be holding at N.E.P.A.: a tidy salary, a tidy lab, and tidy prospects for advancement. But the climax had eclipsed even the lunacy of the past months. Somehow he had talked himself into pretending he was a detective. Detectives were hard-eyed, snap-brimmed, trench-coated, heroic. On all counts he fell down badly, Novak thought.

But a man was dead, and he thought he knew why.

And he had been threatened cold-bloodedly with a smear backed up by all A.E.C.'s prestige, and perhaps with a perjury frame-up, if he tried to get help. Novak looked helplessly at his scrambled eggs, gulped his coffee, and got up to call on the A.S.F.S.F. business office. There was a disagreeable, uncontrollable quiver in his knees.

Friml and MacIlheny were there. It was incredible that they might be spies or killers—until he remembered the bewildered, ashamed, ordinary faces of spies on the front pages of tabloid newspapers.

"Hello, Dr. Novak," the president of the A.S.F.S.F. said. "Friml and I were discussing the possibility of you taking over Clifton's job as engineer in charge."

There was no time to stop and think of what it might mean. Friml and MacIlheny might be innocent. Or they might be guilty but not suspicious of him. There was no time. He forced surprise: "Me? Oh, I don't think so; I'll be busy enough on my own. And I don't think I could handle it anyway."

"I see you had some years of aeronautical engineering."

"Well, yes—undergraduate stuff. Still, Clifton did say there wasn't a lot of work left."

"He did that much for us," MacIlheny said bitterly. "The damned fool."

"Mr. MacIlheny!" said Friml, with every appearance of outrage.

"*Yes,* Mr. Friml," said the insurance man sardonically. "*De mortuis nil nisi bonum,* as you B.B.A.s and C.P.A.s put it. If he was so nuts he had to kill himself why didn't he resign first? And if he didn't have time to resign, *why* did he have to do it at a meeting? Everything happens to the poor old A.S.F.S.F. Clifton's death is going to set us back ten years in getting public recognition. And our industrial sponsors—" MacIlheny buried his head in his hands.

"I never thought he was a very stable person—" Friml began smugly.

"Oh, shut up!" MacIlheny snarled. "Just stick to your knitting. If I want your learned opinion I'll ask for it."

Novak was appalled at the naked enmity that had flared between the two men. Or the pretense of enmity? Nothing would hold still long enough to be examined. You had to keep talking, pretending. "Could I see," he asked conciliatingly, "just where we stand with respect to structural work on *Proto?*"

"Show him the cumulatives, Friml," said the president, not looking up. With his lips compressed, Friml pulled a folder from the files and handed it to Novak. It was lettered: "Engineering Cumulative Progress Reports."

Novak sat down and forced himself to concentrate on the drawings and text. After a few minutes he no longer had to force it. The papers told what was to a technical man the greatest story in the world: research and development; cool, accurate, thoughtful; bucking the cussedness of inanimate nature, bucking the inertia of industrial firms; bucking the conservatism, ignorance, and stupidity of hired hands—and getting things done. It was the story of *Prototype's* building told by the man who could tell it best, Clifton.

It started about one year ago. "Contacted Mr. Laughlin of the American Bridge Company. I don't think he believed a word I said until Friml took out the A.S.F.S.F. passbook and showed him our balance. After that, smooth sailing."

Sketches and text showed how the American Bridge Company, under Clifton's anxious, jealous eyes, executed ten-year-old A.S.F.S.F. blueprints for the skeleton of *Prototype*. The tower of steel girders rose in the desert to six times the height of a man, guyed down against the wind. There was a twelve-foot skeleton tetrahedron, base down, for its foot. From the apex of the tetrahedron rose the king post, a specially fabricated compound member exactly analogous to the backbone of a vertebrate animal. It bore the main stresses of *Proto's* dead weight; it was calculated to bear the strains of *Proto* in motion; and it was hollow: through its insulated core would run the cables of *Proto's* control systems. Structural members radiated laterally from the

TAKEOFF

king post to carry the weight of *Proto*'s skin, and from its top sprouted
girders over which the nose would be built.

Reports from Detroit: "I been going the rounds for a solid week
and still no dice. If a plant's got the forming presses, its tool room
stinks. If its tool room is okay, the superintendent won't let me barge
in to stand over their die-makers and tell them what to do. But that's
the way it's going to be; those hull plates are too tricky to order on an
inspect-or-reject basis."

Later: "I found a good little outfit named Allen Body Company
that does custom-built jobs. They got one Swedish-built forming
press 40x40 (very good), a great tool room with a wonderful old kraut
named Eichenberg heading it up who's willing to work closely with me,
and a good reputation in the trade. Told them to submit bid to Friml
fast and suggest he fires back certified check without haggling. These
guys are real craftsmen."

Later: "Oskar and me finished the forming and trimming dies for
first tier of plates today. Twenty-four tiers of plates to go, plus
actually stamping and machining them. I guess ninety days tops."

Eighty-five days later: "Mr. Gowan of the Union Pacific says he'll
have a sealable freight car at the Allen siding tomorrow, but that it's
out of the question for me to ride aboard with the plates. That's what
he thinks. I bought my folding cot, Sterno stove and beans already."

Sketches showed what "the plates" were like: mirror-finished steel
boxes, formed and machined to exact curvature. The basic size was
36"x36"x6", with some larger or smaller to fit. The outer, convex wall
of the box was of three-quarter-inch steel; the inner, concave wall was
one-inch armor plate. Each box was open along one of its narrow
6"x36" faces, and each was stuffed with compressed steel wool—the
best shock absorber A.S.F.S.F. brains had devised to slow down and
stop a pebble-sized meteorite if one should punch through the outer
shell. There were six hundred and twenty-five of the plates, each
numbered and wrapped in cotton wool like the jewel it was.

Three days later Clifton arrived aboard his freight car in the
Barstow yards. When a twenty-four-hour guard of A.S.F.S.F.
volunteers was mounted over the freight car, he located a trucking
company that specialized in fine furniture removals. "Not a scratch
and not a hitch. We got them stocked in order under the tarps at the
field. I think it will be okay to use some volunteers on the welding. I
checked with the Structural Ironworkers, the Shipbuilders, and the

Regional C.I.O. people. It seems nobody has union jurisdiction on building space ships, so Regional said we could use unpaid helpers so long as they don't touch the welding torches while they're hot. Tomorrow I go down to the shipyards to get myself the six best damn master welders on the Coast. I figure on letting them practice two—three days at beadless welding on scrap before I let them start tacking *Proto's* hide on. Meanwhile I rent a gantry crane. It'll make a better platform for the welders than scaffolding and cut down your chance of spoilage. Also we'll need one later when we come to installing heavy equipment."

He got his master welders and his gantry crane. Two of the welders grinned behind their hands, refusing to follow his rigid specifications on the practice work; he fired them and got two more. The fired welders put in a beef with the union and the others had to down their torches. Clifton lost a day. "I went down to the hall and gave the pie cards hell. I brought some of the junk those two bums did and I threw it on their desks and they said they'd kill the beef and let them know if there's any more trouble, which I don't think there will be with the new boys."

There wasn't. The first tier of plates went on, and fitted to a thousandth of an inch. Volunteer kids working at the field were horrified to see the latticework skeleton of the *Prototype* sag under their weight, and Clifton told them it was all provided for down to the last hairsbreadth of sag.

As the shining skin of *Proto* rose from the ground in yard-high tiers, the designers of the A.S.F.S.F. passed through the acid test and came out pure gold. Nameless aero-engineers, some long gone from the Society and some still with it, engineering professors and students at U.C.L.A., Cal Tech and Stanford, girl volunteers punching calculators in batteries, had done their job. The great equation balanced. Strength of materials, form of members, distributed stresses and strains, elasticities and compressibilities added and equaled one complete hull: a shiningly perfect bomb shape that could take escape velocity. Six plates equally spaced around the eleventh tier and one plate in the eighth tier were not welded in. The six were to be fitted with deadlights and the one with a manhole.

The welders crawled through the eighth-tier hole for their last job: two bulkheads, which would cut the ship into three sections. The first cut off *Proto's* nose at the ninth tier. It was the floor of her combined living quarters and control room—a cramped, pointed dome some ten feet in diameter and twelve feet high at the peak. From this floor protruded the top of the king post, like a sawed-off tree stump sprouting girders that supported the nose. The second bulkhead cut *Proto* at the seventh tier. It made a cylindrical compartment aft of the control room that could store five hundred cubic feet of food, water, and oxygen. This compartment also doubled as the air lock. The outside manhole would open into it, and from it a second manhole would open into the control room above.

Aft of the bulkhead was two thirds of the ship—an empty shell except for structural members radiating from the king post. It was reserved territory: reserved for a power plant. The stiff paper rattled in Novak's hands for a moment before he could manage them. He had almost been lost in cool, adult satisfaction, as he followed the great engineering story, when fear struck through. This triumph—whose? MacIlheny and Friml glanced briefly at him, and he sank into the reports again.

"Sorry to say...repeated twelve times...seems conclusive...obviously a bonehead play...some of the new silicones may...deadlight gaskets..." Novak's heart beat slower and calmer, and the words began to arrange themselves into sense. Clifton's report on the six planned deadlights was negative. Vacuum-chamber tests of the proposed gasketing system showed that air leakage would be prohibitive. There simply wasn't a good enough glass-to-metal seal. The ring of deadlights was *out*, but a single deadlight in the nose was indispensable. Air leakage from the nose deadlight was cut to an almost bearable minimum by redesigning the assembly with great, ungainly silicone gaskets.

This meant blind uncertainty for any theoretical occupants of *Proto* during a theoretical ascent. The nose deadlight, an eighteen-inch optical flat at the very tip of the craft, was to be covered during the ascent by an "aerodynamic nose" of sheet metal. In space the false nose would be jettisoned by a power charge.

The next series of reports showed Clifton in his glory—control devices, his specialty.

In one month, working sometimes within A.S.F.S.F. specifications and quite often cheerfully overstepping them, he installed: an electric generator, manhole motors, lighting and heating systems, oxygen control, aerodynamic nose jettison, jato igniters, jato jettison, throat vane servos (manual), throat vane servos, (automatic, regulated by a battery of fluid-damped plumb bobs). Controls for these systems were sunk into the head of the king post that jutted from the control-room floor. There was nothing resembling a driver's seat with a console of instruments and controls.

And there were two other control systems indicated in the drawings. At the input end they had provisions for continuos variation of voltage from zero to six, the power plant's maximum. At the output end there was—nothing. The two systems came to dead ends in *Proto's* backbone, one at the third tier and one at the fifth.

Novak had a short struggle with himself. Play dumb, or ask about it? They say they think you're smart enough to take over… He asked.

"Fuel-metering systems," MacIlheny said. "We assumed of course that something of the sort would be needed eventually, so we had Clifton put in dead-end circuits."

"I see."

He was nearing the end of the sheets. The last report said acceleration-couch tests were proceeding satisfactorily with no modifications yet indicated. And then the folder came to an end.

"I think," Novak said slowly, "that I can handle it after all. He's just about finished the job—as far as any private outfit can take it."

MacIlheny looked up and said evenly: "There's some more construction work to be done—on the same basis as the dead-end control systems. Naturally there's got to be a fuel tank, so we're going to put one in. Here's the drawings—" He had them ready in a blueprint file.

It was another of the "J. MacI" jobs, with the same date as the too-specific drawings for the throat liner and chamber. Novak wondered crazily whether MacIlheny or Friml had a gun in his pocket, whether the wrong reaction meant he'd be shot down on the spot. He studied the sheet and decided on his role. The "fuel tank" was a fantastic thing. It filled almost the rear two thirds of the *Prototype* and made no sense whatever.

There was one section forward that consisted of stainless steel. A section aft, much smaller, was quartz-lined lead, with a concrete jacket. Atomic. There was a lead wall indicated between the stainless-steel tank and the *Proto's* aft bulkhead. Atomic. This was a tank for a fuel that burned with atomic fire.

He told them, businesslike: "It's going to cost a hell of a lot of money, but that's your business. I can install it. Just don't blame me if it has to be ripped out again when A.E.C. comes out with an atomic fuel that doesn't fit it."

MacIlheny said into the air, slowly and with burning emphasis: "*Can't* people understand that *Proto's* not a moon ship? Can't they get it through their heads that she's just a dummy to study construction problems? What the hell difference does it make if the fuel A.E.C. comes up with doesn't fit her system? All we're after is the experience we'll need to build a system that does fit."

Novak said hastily: "Of course you're right." Lord, but MacIlheny was convincing! "But it gets a grip on you. Half the kids think it's a moon ship—"

"All right for kids," said MacIlheny grimly. "But we're all adults here. I'm sick of being ribbed for doing something I'm not doing at all. Good-and-sick." He stared at the engineer challengingly, and then his grimness vanished as he added: "I wish it *was* a moon ship, Novak. I wish it very much. But—" He shrugged.

"Well," said Novak uncertainly, "maybe I'll feel that way about it after a year or so of the ribbing. By the way, can you tell me where Miss Stuart lives? I ought to go and see Mrs. Clifton if I can be spared today, and I suppose things are still in a state of flux."

"Thirty-seven twenty-four Rochedale," said Friml, and he jotted it down.

"I suppose it's all right," said MacIlheny. "God, what a headache. Just when things were going smoothly. Suppose you check in tomorrow morning and we may have some plans made for you."

"Won't the membership have to—"

"The membership," said MacIlheny impatiently, "will do as it's told."

CHAPTER NINE

NOVAK THOUGHT he should phone the Wilson Stuart residence before he tried to pay a call. He couldn't find the number in the book and naively asked Information. Information sharply told him that the number was unlisted.

Well, he tried.

He got a downtown cab and enjoyed a long ride into the rolling country lying north of Los Angeles. "Pretty classy," he said.

"*I* should know?" asked the cabby blandly, and added in a mutter something that sounded like: "Stinking rich."

A mile farther on, the cab stopped. "Check point," the driver said. Novak saw a roadside booth, all chrome and with two cops in beautifully fitting uniforms. One of them came out to the car, the driver gave him the address and they rolled on.

"What was that about?" Novak asked.

"A trifling violation of our civil liberties," the cabby said. "Nothing to get upset about. At night, now, they take your name, and phone on ahead if they don't know you."

"California!"

"All over," the cabby corrected him. "Grosse Pointe, Mobile, Sun Valley—all over. I guess this is it."

Thirty-seven twenty-four Rochedale was extreme California modern: a great white albatross of a house that spread its wings over a hilltop. "Well, go on up the driveway," Novak said.

"Nope. If you had any business with folks like that you'd have your own limousine. *You* go in and get arrested for trespassing. These people don't fool around." He turned down the meter flag and Novak paid him.

"I hope you're wrong," the engineer said, adding a half-dollar. He started up the driveway.

It was a confusing house. He couldn't seem to find a place where it began, or a doorbell to ring. Before he knew it, he seemed to be inside the Stuart home, unannounced, after walking through a row of pylons into a patio—or was it a living room? They didn't build like that in Brooklyn or Urbana.

A shock-haired old man rolled into the living room—or patio—in a wheel chair pushed by a burly, Irish-looking fellow in a chauffeur's dark uniform. "I'm sorry," Novak exploded jumpily. "I couldn't find—"

"Who the devil are you?" demanded the old man, and the chauffeur took his hands from the chair, standing exactly like a boxer about to put up his fists.

"My name's Novak. I'm a friend of Mrs. Clifton's. I understand she's here—if this is the Wilson Stuart residence."

"I'm Wilson Stuart. Do you know my daughter?"

156

"We've met."

"I suppose that means she didn't invite you. Did she give you the address?"

"No—she's a member of the A.S.F.S.F., the space-flight society. I got it from the secretary."

The old man swore. "Keep it to yourself. A person has no damned privacy in one of these places and I can't build a wall because of the zoning laws or covenants or whatever they are. Grady, get Miss Amelia." The chauffeur gave Novak a no-funny-business look and left.

"Uh, how is Mrs. Clifton?" Novak asked.

"I don't know; I haven't seen her. I'm not surprised by any of this, though. I thought Clifton's mind was giving way when he took that job with the rocket cranks. Not that I'd keep him on my pay roll. He told my V.P. for Engineering that he didn't know enough to build an outhouse on wheels. That tore it." The old man chuckled. "He could really ram things through, though. Didn't give a damn whose floor space he muscled in on, whose men he gave orders to, whose material he swiped for his own projects. Where are they going to find another lunatic like that to build their rocket?"

"I'm taking it over, Mr. Stuart." What a callous old beast he was!

"You are? Well, be sure you have nothing to lose, Novak. What are they paying you?"

"Rather not say."

It made Wilson Stuart angry. "Well, isn't that too bad! I can tell you one thing. Whatever it is, you're putting a blot on your record that no responsible firm can afford to ignore." He spun the chair to present his back to Novak and scowled through the pylons that formed one wall of the ambiguous room.

Novak was startled by the burst of rage, and resentful. But you didn't tell off a cardiac patient at will—or a multimillionaire.

The chauffeur and Amy Stuart came in. "Hello, Dr. Novak," she said. The old man silently beckoned over his shoulder to the chauffeur and was wheeled out.

"How's Mrs. Clifton?" Novak asked.

"Father's doctor says she should rest for a day or two. He's given her some sedatives. After that—I don't know. She's talking about going back to her family in Denmark."

"May I see her?"

"I think so. Dr. Morris didn't say anything about it, but it should do her good. Come this way."

Crossing large, glass-walled rooms he said: "I don't think I should have come at all. Your father was upset by my knowing the address. Mr. Friml gave it to me."

"Mr. Friml should have known better," she said coolly. "My father has no reserves of energy for anything beyond his business and necessary recreation. It's cruel discipline for him...he's held speed and altitude records, you know."

Novak uttered a respectful mumble.

The girl asked: "What are they going to do about a replacement for Cliff?"

"I think I get the job. I've done some aero-engineering and there's very little structural work left to be done. I suppose if there's anything I simply can't handle, they'll hire a consultant. But I can probably swing the load."

"You can if you're checked out by MacIlheny. The man's a—" She started to say "fanatic" and then interrupted herself. "That's the wrong word. I admire him, really. He's like—not Columbus. Prince Henry the Navigator of Portugal. Henry stuck close to his desk and never went to sea, but he raised the money and did the paperwork."

"Um. Yes. Has Lilly—Mrs. Clifton—been asking for a biomathematicist, I wonder? She has such faith in them that it might do her good at a time like this, when it's a matter of psychological strain."

The girl looked startled. "That's very odd," she said. "As a matter of fact she hasn't. I suppose recreations like that show up in their true light when the pressure is on. Not that it would do her any good to ask for one. Dr. Morris would break the neck of any biomathematicist who showed up here."

She pushed open a flush door of blond wood and Novak saw Clifton's widow in the middle of a great modern bed with sickroom paraphernalia on a side table. "Visitor, Lilly," Amy Stuart said.

"Hallo, Mike. It was good of you to come. Amy, you mind if I speak alone vit' Mike?"

"Not at all."

"Sit down," she said with an unhappy smile as the girl closed the door. "Mike, what's gonna happen now? You don't think Cliff kill himself, do you?" She was fighting back tears with a heartbreaking effort. "He act cra-a-azy. But that was yust because he enjoy life and didn't give a damn for nobody. He wasn't no crazy man to kill himself, was he, Mike?"

"No, Lilly," Novak said. "I don't think he killed himself." And he bit his lip for saying it. The woman was under sedation, she might babble anything to anybody—

"Mike," she said, "I'm glad you say so." She sniffed and dried her brimming eyes, as a child would do, on the hem of her bed sheet.

"How're you fixed for money, Lilly?" he asked. "I thought you might need a little ready cash for—expenses and things."

"Tanks, Mike, no need. We had a yoint bank account vit' couple t'ousand dollars in. Mike, honestly you don't believe Cliff kill himself?"

He thought it over. "Have you taken any medicine?"

"Last night the doc gave me couple pink pills and he tol' me to take couple more today—but I don't. You know I don't t'ink much of doctors."

"I don't want to tell you what I think about Cliff's death if you're full of medicine or if you're going to be. You might talk to somebody about what I tell you. It might mean my life too." It was her business, he told himself silently.

After a stupefied pause, Lilly slowly asked: "Please tell me all about it, Mike. Who'd kill Cliff? Who'd kill you? Those few crazy kids in the Society, they don' like Cliff ever, but they wouldn't kill him. You tell me what it's all about, Mike. Even if somebody tear the eyes out of my head I don't talk."

He pulled his chair to the bedside and lowered his voice. "Yesterday Cliff and I thought we found something fishy about one of the A.S.F.S.F. blueprints. I thought it meant that a foreign country was using the Society to build it a rocket ship. Maybe with Friml or MacIlheny or both fronting, and nobody else in on it. We went to the A.E.C. Security office downtown and saw that man Anheier. He brushed us off—didn't believe a word of it. Last night Cliff got killed and it looked like suicide. But it could have been murder by anybody who could have sneaked into the washroom when he was there—and that's anybody off the street and practically anybody who was at the meeting.

"I don't know how—whoever did it—got wise to his visit to Security or why nobody's taken a shot at me that I know of. Maybe spies keep a twenty-four-hour watch on the Security office to see who visits it. Maybe Cliff's visit was the signal for his death. Maybe I wasn't identified because I'm new in town.

"But none of that matters right now. What matters is that Anheier wouldn't let me tell the police about my idea. He tried to convince me that I was a paranoid. When that didn't work, he threatened to ruin me for life and jail me for perjury if I talk, now or ever."

"You not gonna tell the police, Mike?"

"No. I'm afraid of the smear and—it probably wouldn't do any good. The A.E.C. would make countercharges and any foreign agents would escape in the fuss. I told Anheier the hell with him, I'd nail them alone."

"No," she said, pale-faced. "Not alone, Mike. Vit' me."

"Thanks, Lilly," he said softly, and she was crying at last.

"Don' mind me," she said. "T'anks for coming to see me and now you please go. I cry better by myself..."

He left in silence. She was with him—it felt better. The morning with MacIlheny and Friml, every question a step on a tightrope over the abyss, had told on him.

Amy Stuart laid down a magazine and got up from a blocky chair. "How is she, Dr. Novak?"

"I'm afraid I made her cry."

"It's good for a woman to cry at a time like this. Have you a car?"

"No; I came in a taxi. If I could phone for one—"

"You're downtown, aren't you? I'll drive you; I have some shopping."

Her car was a two-seater English sports job. It looked like a toy in the garage between the big Lincoln and a suburban wagon.

As they went winding through the scrubbed-clean roads he broke the silence. "To me it's just an interesting job, you know. I'm not a Prince Henry like MacIlheny is and maybe Cliff was. Or—what was her name? The girl who raised sand at the meeting. The one you stepped on."

"Gingrich?" Amy Stuart said dispassionately. "She's not particularly interested in space flight and she's a bloody fool besides. If Gingrich and her friends had their way, there'd be a full-dress membership vote by secret ballot on where to put each rivet in the *Prototype*."

160

The little two-seater rolled past the police sentry box and Amy Stuart waved pleasantly to the two policemen. They saluted with broad smiles and Novak abandoned himself to bitter thoughts for a moment.

"Jeffersonians, they think they are," the girl brooded. "But wouldn't Jefferson be the first man to admit that things have changed since his day? That there's a need for something beyond sheer self-regulating agrarian democracy?" The question was put with an intensity that startled him. It was overlaid with a portentous air that made him think of nothing so much as a doctor's oral, where your career is made or unmade by a few score words spoken in a minute or two. What was she driving at?

"People are always accusing engineers of not thinking about social problems," he said carefully. "In my case, I'm afraid they're right. I've been a busy man for a long time. But I wonder—are you by any chance flirting with fascism or Communism?"

"No," she said scornfully, and fell silent.

It was some minutes before she spoke again. "You were in A.E.C. Did you ever read anything by Daniel Holland? He's a friend of father's. And mine."

There was something he could talk about. "I didn't know he wrote, but your friend runs a hell of a silly organization. You know what my field is. Believe me or not but I swear I was transferred out of it and into a highly specialized branch of mathematical physics. I was absolutely helpless, I was absolutely unable to get back to my own work. Finally I—I had to resign."

She said patiently: "That's exactly the sort of thing Holland fights. In his books he analyzed the warped growth of modern public administration under the influence of the Jeffersonian and Jacksonian mistrust of professionals. He calls it the 'cincinnatus complex.'"

He recognized the allusion and felt pleased about it. Cincinnatus was the Roman citizen who left his plowing to lead the army to victory and then returned to his plow, turning down glory and rewards. "Interesting concept," he said. "What does he suggest?"

The girl frowned. "If you'd thought about it, you'd know that's damn-all he could suggest. His books were only analytical and exploratory, and he nearly got booted out of public service for daring to raise the problem—challenging the whole structure of bureaucracy. He thought he could do more good in than out, so he stopped publishing. But he'd stepped on some toes. In *Red Tape Empires* he cited a case from the Nevada civil service. The Senator from Nevada on the joint A.E.C. Committee badgered him from then on. Wonderful irony. He was a master of all the parliamentary tricks that were originally supposed to carry out the majority will without infringing on minority rights."

He was worried about Lilly and getting shot and future long, precarious talks with MacIlheny. "I suppose," he said absently, "you're bound to have a rotten apple in every barrel."

Amy Stuart said flatly but emphatically, with her eyes on the road: "You scientists deserve exactly what you got." And she said nothing more until she dropped him off at his hotel and proceeded to her shopping. Novak had a queasy, unreal feeling that he'd just failed his doctor's oral.

CHAPTER TEN

THE HIGH-TEMPERATURE lab was built, and its equipment installed by the able construction firm that had done the field layout. During this time Novak worked on the manhole problem, and licked it. Studebaker *had* ungreased its titanic boring mill and for a price had cheerfully put a super-finish on the manhole and its seating. In an agony of nervousness for the two priceless chunks of metal, Novak had clocked their slow progress by freight car across the country from South Bend to Barstow.

It was one of those moments when Lilly Clifton or Amy Stuart was helpfully by his side, and this time it happened to be Amy. They stood outside the machine-shop prefab, squinting into the glare of the *Prototype's* steel skin, and at an intenser, bluer glare that was being juggled by a hooded welder on the gantry-crane platform, twenty feet up. The manhole cover and seating assembly were being beadlessly welded into the gap in the ninth tier of plates. It was a moment of emotional importance. *Proto* externally was an unbroken whole.

Novak's pulse pounded at the thought, while the matter-of-fact welder up there drew his hell-hot point of flame like an artist's brush along the gleaming metal. The engineer couldn't be matter-of-fact about it any more. He had plunged into the top-brass job at the Barstow field determined to give a realistic imitation of a space hound, and had become one.

There was no reason not to. In theory, he told himself, he was waiting for a break but one never came. There were no further irregularities beyond the four on which he had committed himself: money, secrecy, the "J. MacI." drawings, and the death of Clifton.

MacIlheny never offered any surprises. He was an insurance man and a space-flight crank. He had cloudy industrial contributors in his pocket and he used them as a club to run the Society his way. His way was to get *Proto* built as a symbol and rallying point for those who demanded a frontal smash by the Government into the space-flight problem instead of the rudimentary, uncoordinated, and unimaginative efforts that were all the United States could show, for whatever reason.

Friml continued to be—Friml. Bloodless, righteous, dollar-honest, hired-hand, party-of-the-second-partish Friml. A reader of the fine print, a dweller in the Y.M.C.A., a martyr to constipation, a wearer of small-figured neckties which he tied in small, hard knots.

The engineer members of the A.S.F.S.F. continued to be hobbyists, hard to tell one from the other, showing up on weekends, often with the wife and kid, for an hour or so of good shoptalk and connoisseurs' appreciation of *Proto* as the big, handsome jigsaw puzzle that she was—to them.

The A.S.F.S.F. youngsters continued to be hagridden kids escaping from humdrum jobs, unhappy families, or simply the private hell of adolescence by actually helping to pay for and work on the dream over *Proto*. Some day it would carry them on wings of flame to adventurous stars where they'd all be broad-shouldered males six feet tall or slim luscious girls with naturally curly hair. They worked like dogs for the new engineer in charge and didn't even ask for a dog's pat on the head; all they wanted was to be near enough to *Proto* to dream. They fought ferociously with words on occasion over this detail or that, and Novak eventually realized that their quarrels symbolized a fiercer squabble they hoped was coming over the passenger list of man's first moon ship.

Novak stood comfortably midway between the engineers and the kids—he hoped. *Proto* was big medicine. The dream of flight, which has filled the nightlives of countless neurotics since, probably, the Eolithic era, had been no dream since the balloons of Montgolfier. This new wish fulfillment of space flight had been for fifty years standard equipment on your brilliant but dreamy youngster. It soaked into you from earliest childhood that some day—not quite in your time, but some day—man would reach the planets and then the stars. Being around *Proto*, putting your hands on her, tinkering with her equipment, smelling her hot metal in the desert sun, hearing her plates sing as they contracted in the desert-night chill, did something to you, and to the "some day" reservation about space flight. Novak had become a true believer, and with each passing week wondered more feverishly what in hell's name he was doing: building a moon ship for China? Running up dummy? Or just honest engineering? Each week he told himself more feverishly: one week more; just get the manhole licked, or the silicone gaskets, or the boron carbides.

The blue, hard twinkle of the welding torch twenty feet up snapped off; the welder shoved back his hood and waved genially. The platform of the gantry crane descended.

"That does it," Novak said hazily to Amy. He lit a cigarette. "You want to push the button?"

"If it doesn't work, don't blame me," she said. There was a six-volt line run from the machine shop into *Proto's* sewer-pipe stern and up through the king post to feed the electric systems. She snapped the control for the manhole motor to open, and they stared up again. The dark disk against the shiny steel plate developed a mirror-bright streak of microfinish bearing surface along one edge. Noiselessly and very slowly the wire-fine streak grew to a new moon; the manhole slowly stood out in profile and halted, a grotesque ear protruding from the ship.

"Okay, Amy. Close it." She snapped the switch to *Shut*, and very slowly the disk swung back and made *Proto* an unbroken whole again. The welder stepped from the gantry platform and asked: "She's all right, Mr. Novak?"

"Fine, Sam. Fine. Was there any trouble fitting the lug into the receptacle?"

"Nope. Only one way to do it, so I did it. It surely is a fine piece of machinery. I used to work at the Bullard Works in Hartford and they didn't make their custom-built machine tools any prettier than your—thing. Confidentially, Mr. Novak, is—"

He held up his hand protestingly. "It's a full-scale mockup for structural study and publicity purposes. Does that answer the question, Sam?"

The welder grinned. "You people are really gonna try it, aren't you? Just don't count on me for a passenger is all I ask. It's pretty, but it won't work."

As they walked to Novak's refractory lab, Amy said: "I worry about everything Cliff installed, like the manhole motor, until it's tested. I know that verdict, 'while of unsound mind' and so on is just legal mumbo jumbo, but...why should the manhole have opened that slowly? It was like a movie, milking it for suspense."

He glanced at her. "Perfectly good reasons. It runs on a worm gear—low speed, power to spare. The motor has to open it against the molecular cohesion of the biggest gauge-block seal ever machined. In space or on the Moon the motor would get an assist from atmospheric pressure in the storeroom, pushing against zero pressure outside."

She laughed. "Of course. I suppose I was being jittery. And there's sometimes melodramatic suspense in real life, too, I suppose."

He cleared his throat. "I've got Lilly in there aging a new boron-carbide series. Want to watch? You can learn enough in a few hours to take some routine off my neck. The volunteer kids are fine and dandy, but they mostly have jobs and school hours. What I need is a few more people like you and Lilly that don't have to watch the clock."

"It must be very handy," she agreed abstractedly. "But you'll have to excuse me. I'm due back in town."

Novak stared after her, wondering what was biting the girl. And he went on into the lab.

It was the dream layout he had sketched not too long ago, turned real by the funds of the A.S.F.S.F. Lilly was in the cooling department clocking temperature drops on six crucibles that contained boron carbides in various proportions. She was looking flushed and happy as she sidled down the bench on which the crucibles were ranged, jotting down the time from the lab clock and temperatures from the thermocouple pyrometers plugged into each sample. Her blond hair was loose on her creamy neck and shoulders; she wore shorts and a blouse that were appropriate to the heat of the refractories lab but intensely distracting. She turned and smiled, and Novak was distracted to the point of wondering whether she was wearing a brassiere. He rather doubted it.

"What are the temperatures now?" he asked.

She read off efficiently: "Seventy-two, seventy-four, seventy-eight, seventy-eight point five, seventy-eight point five, seventy-nine."

The leveling was unexpected good news. "Interesting. Are you afraid to handle hot stuff?"

"Naw!" she said with a grin. "Yust not vit my bare hands."

"Okay; we'll let you use tongs. I want you to take the lid off each crucible as I indicate. I'll slap the ingot in the hydraulic press, crush it, and give you the dial reading. Then I'll put it in the furnace. After all the ingots are crushed and in the furnace I'll turn on the heat and watch through the peephole. When they melt I'll call out the number to you and you note the temperature from the furnace thermocouple. Got it?"

"I t'ink so, Mike."

It went smoothly. The ingots were transferred safely, they crushed under satisfactorily high pressure, and the furnace dashed red and then white in less than five minutes. Staring through the blue glass peephole at the six piles of glowing dust, waiting for them to shimmer, coalesce, and run into liquid, was hypnotically soothing—except that he could sense Lilly at his side, with her eyes on the thermocouple pyrometer and her full hips near him, giving him thoughts that he found alarming.

He stared at the cones of glowing dust and thought bitterly: *I don't want to get any more mixed up in this than I am now.* One of the glowing piles shimmered and looked mirror-like. Abruptly it shrank from a heap of dust into a cluster of little globes like an ornamental pile of Civil War cannon balls and an instant later slumped into a puddle.

"Number five!" he snapped.

"Got it, Mike," she said, and her thigh touched him.

This thing's been coming on for a couple of weeks. I'll be damned if I don't think she's giving me the business. She ought to be ashamed. But what a shape on her. Amy wouldn't pull a stunt like this. He felt a little regretful and hastily damped down on that train of thought. "Number three!"

"Got it."

Minutes later he was at his desk with the figures, and she was an interested spectator. He explained laboriously: "The trick is to reduce your unknowns to a manageable number. We have mixing point of the original solution, rate of cooling, final temperature, and melting point. You call them T1, dT/dt—that's derivative of temperature with respect to time—T2 and T3. Do you follow it so far?"

She leaned over his shoulder and began: "I don't see—"

He found out that she wasn't wearing a brassiere. "The hell with it," he said, and kissed her. She responded electrically, and in her candid way indicated that she meant business. The faint voice of Novak's conscience became inaudible at that point, and the business might have been transacted then and there if the lab door hadn't opened.

Hastily she pulled away from him and tucked in her blouse. "You go see what is, Mike," she ordered breathlessly.

"Fine thing," he growled, and slapped her almost viciously on the rump.

"I know how you feel, boy," she grinned.

"Oh—no—you—don't." He cleared his throat and stalked out from the small private office into the lab. One of the machine-shop kids was waiting. The boy wanted to know whether he should use hot-roll or cold-roll steel for the threaded studs of the acceleration couches; the drawings just said "mild steel." Novak said restrainedly that he didn't think it made any difference, and stood waiting for him to leave.

When he got back to the private office Lilly was putting her face on. She said hastily: "No, Mike. Keep the hands off me for a minute while I tell you. This is no place. You wanna come to my house tonight, we do this t'ing right."

"I'll be there," he said a little thoughtfully. Conscience was making a very slight comeback. He hadn't been to the Clifton house since the day of the murder. But the lady was willing, the husband was six feet under, and it concerned nobody else.

"Good boy. You go back to work now."

He watched her drive from the field in the big maroon Rolls and tried to buckle down. He got nothing done for the rest of the afternoon. He tried first to set up matrix equations to relate the characteristics of the six boron carbides and committed howler after howler. He decided he'd better layoff the math until he was feeling more placid. In the machine shop he took over from an uncertain volunteer who was having trouble threading the acceleration-couch studs. Novak, with a single twitch of the lathe's cross-feed wheel, made scrap out of the job.

It wasn't his day. Among the condolences of the machine-shop gang he declared work over and bummed a ride back to Los Angeles in one of the kids' jalopies.

He bolted a meal in the hotel dining room and went upstairs to shower and shave. There was a minor crisis when he found out he didn't have a belt. Normally he was a suspenders man, but he had a dismal picture of himself struggling with the suspender loops at a tender moment, maybe getting his foot caught in them…he shuddered, and sent a bellboy down to the lobby haberdasher's shop to get him a belt. When he put it on he didn't like the feel of it around his middle, and he missed the feel of the suspenders over his shoulders. But first things first.

Not until he was dressed and down in the lobby did he realize that he didn't remember the Clifton address—if he had ever heard it. Cahunga, Cahuenga Canyon, something like that, and he could probably find the house from a taxi window. He went to the phone book to look up Clifton, and found nothing under August. There were three A. Cliftons with middle initials, but none of them lived on anything that sounded like Cahunga, Cahuenga, or whatever it was. He tried Information and got the standard Los Angeles answer—unlisted number. A girl waiting outside the half-opened door of the phone booth turned red and walked away after overhearing part of his comments on that.

Now what the devil did you do? He recalled suddenly that Friml was good on addresses, just the way you'd expect his card-file type to be. He looked up the Downtown Y.M.C.A. and was connected with Friml's room.

"This is Novak, Friml. I hate to bother you after hours, but I wonder if you can give me Clifton's address. I, um, need it for some reports and he isn't in the phone book."

The secretary-treasurer's precise voice said: "Just one moment, Mr. Novak. I have it in a memorandum book. Please hold the line."

Novak held on for some time and then Friml gave him the address and—unsolicited—the phone number. He jotted them down and said: "Thanks. Sorry to be such a nuisance."

Friml said with a martyred air: "Not at all. I'm not good at remembering numbers myself." There was a plain implication of: "So why the hell don't you keep a memorandum book like good little me?"

Mildly surprised at the admission, Novak thanked him again and hung up. Now for a taxi. Walking up the street to a stand where he could climb in without having to tip a doorman, he wondered how he'd got the notion that Friml kept his address book in his head. Probably just the type of guy he was made you think so. Probably he did nothing to discourage you from thinking so. Probably there was a lot of bluff behind any of these ice-water types...

And then he stopped still in the street, realizing what had made him think Friml was a walking address book. He'd asked once for the Wilson Stuart address, and the secretary-treasurer had rolled it out absently as if it were no great feat to recall offhand where a rank-and-filer of the Society lived. He started walking again, slower and slower.

There was something very wrong. Friml had memorized the Wilson Stuart address, presumably of negligible importance to him. All he could possibly have to do with the Wilson Stuart address was to send a bill for annual dues, meeting notices, the club bulletin—no not even that. All those items were addressographed. Friml had not memorized the August Clifton address or phone number, although presumably he'd be constantly dropping notes and making calls to him for engineering data. If he didn't know the Clifton number and address offhand he was decidedly no good at numbers, as he admitted.

Novak walked slowly past the cab rank and crossed the street. Stepping up to the curb, his right heel caught in the unfamiliar sag of his trouser cuff, and he thought: damn that belt.

It was, clearly, the first break in the Clifton killing. Friml wasn't what he seemed to be. Clearly there was a link of some sort between the secretary-treasurer and Amelia Earhart Stuart—or her father. Now how did you exploit a thing like this? Raid Friml's Y.M.C.A. room looking for the Papers? Tell that fathead Anheier about it and have him laugh in your face? Confront Wilson Stuart with it and have him conk out with a heart attack—or throw you in jail for trespassing? Try to bluff the facts out of Amy?

Friml has even visited the Clifton bungalow—*feller who broke the big mirror and my Svedish glass pitcher and cat'ode-ray tube. That was Friml, Mike. He gets pretty bad.* It had been a gag—maybe. Nothing strange about a Friml swilling his liquor like a pig and breaking things now and then. And talking...

He raised his arm for a passing taxi.

"Downtown Y.M.C.A.," he told the driver.

CHAPTER ELEVEN

HE CALLED UP from the lobby. "Friml? Novak again. I'm downstairs. I'm at a loose end and I wonder whether you'd care to join me for a drink or two some place. Maybe we can have a general bull session about the Society. I've been working like a dog and I need some unstringing."

The voice said grudgingly: "Well...come on up, Dr. Novak. I had some work for this evening, but..."

Friml had a two-room suite, medium-sized and antiseptically clean. He seemed proud of his place. He showed Novak his desk: "Some people tell you it's a sign of inefficiency to take your work home with you. I don't believe that for a minute. You, for instance—I can tell that you don't leave your job behind when you leave the field."

"I don't think any really conscientious person would," Novak agreed with gravity, and Friml glowed dimly at the implied compliment.

"You're right about—unstringing," said the secretary-treasurer. "I'm not a *drinker*, of course. I'll be with you in a minute." He went into the bathroom and Novak heard the lock turn.

He stood undecided over the desk and then, feeling that it was a childish thing to do, tried its drawers. They opened. In the shallow center drawer where pencils, rulers, paper clips, and blotters are kept, Friml kept pencils, rulers, paper clips, and blotters. In the top left drawer were letterheads, carbon paper, second sheets, and onionskin in a rack. In the second left-hand drawer were card-file boxes and a corduroy-bound ledger with red leather corners and spine. In the bottom drawer were books with brown wrapping paper covers on them, the kind school children use on textbooks.

Before he heard water roaring in the bathroom there was time to lift out three books and look at their title pages: *The Homosexual in America, History of Male Prostitution, Impotence in the Male.*

The poor bastard. What a way to be.

Friml appeared, looking almost cheerful. "There's a quiet little place on Figueroa Street," he said. "The pianist does request numbers. He's pretty good."

"Fine," said the engineer depressed.

The place on Figueroa Street wasn't a fairy joint, as Novak had half expected it would be. They sat at a table and had a couple drinks apiece while the pianist played blues. Novak knew vaguely that it was a big blues-revival year. The engineer made conversation about his membership report for the next meeting. "I don't know just what the members expect, because Clifton spoke off the cuff and there aren't any transcripts."

Friml said relaxedly: "Just give 'em the high spots. About fifteen minutes. And don't go by what Clifton did. Some times he used to just get up and joke. Other times he used to be 'way over their heads with math and electronics."

"That sounds like him. I was wondering about visual aids. Do you think I ought to have some easel cards made up? I think the whole trouble is, I don't know whether the membership report is just a formality or whether they really pay attention. If it's just a noise I'm supposed to make so everybody will feel he's getting his money's worth from the Ph.D., then I won't bother with the cards. If they really listen and learn, I ought to have them."

"You ought to just suit yourself, Novak," Friml said rather expansively. "They like you and that's the main thing. How'd you like *my* job, with everybody calling you a son of a bitch?" He took a deep swallow from his drink. He was having blended rye and ginger ale, the drink of a man who doesn't like to taste his liquor.

Novak excused himself and went to the phone booth. He called Lilly Clifton.

"Mike?" she asked. "Ain't you gonna come 'round tonight like you said?"

"Later, I think," he told her. "Listen, Lilly. I think I've found out something about the death of—of your husband." It was an awkward thing to say.

"So? Tell me." Her voice was unexpectedly grim.

It didn't sound like much in the telling, but she was impressed. "You got somet'ing," she said. "See if you can bring him around here later. I t'ink he goes for me."

He told her about Friml's books. She said dryly: "I see. I guess maybe he was a liddle bit queer for Cliff. It drived him nuts the time he was out here, the way Cliff played around vit' me affectionate. Every time Cliff gimme a feel or somet'ing, Friml took a bigger drink. I guess I was flatt'ring myself. You bring him anyway if you can."

He said he'd try, and went back to the table. Friml was a drink ahead of him by then, and said: "No more for me, Mike," when Novak tried to order. He sounded as though he could be talked into it. The pianist, a little black man at a little black piano on a platform behind the bar, was playing a slow, rippling vamp between numbers. "Coffee Blues!" Friml yelled unexpectedly at him, and Novak started.

The vamp rippled into a dragging blues, and Friml listened bleakly with his chin propped in his hand. He signaled their waiter after a few bars and drank his shot of blended rye without mixing or chasing it. "Great number," he said. *"I like my coffee—sweet, black, and hot...I like my coffee—sweet, black and, hot...won't let no body fool...with my coffee pot...* I always like that number, Mike. You like it?"

"Sure. Great number."

Friml beamed. *"Some folks like—their coffee tan and strong...* You ever know any colored girls, Mike?"

"There were a few from Chicago in my classes at Urbana."

"Good-looking?" Friml wouldn't meet his eye; he was turning over in his hands the pack of matches from the table ashtray.

"Some of them yes, some of them no."

Friml gulped his drink. "Could I borrow a cigarette?" he asked. Novak tapped one out of his pack and held the match for the accountant. Friml got his cigarette wet, but didn't cough. From behind a cloud of smoke asked: "Did any of the white fellows at the university go around with the colored girls?"

"Maybe some in Liberal Arts College. None that I remember in Engineering."

"I bet," Friml said broodingly, "I bet a fellow could really let himself go with a colored girl. But if a fellow's trying to build up a good solid record and get some place it wouldn't look good if it got out, would it?"

Novak let him have it. "It wouldn't make much difference if a fellow was just fooling away his time on one bush-league job after another."

Friml quivered and stubbed out his cigarette, bursting the paper. "I really ought to be getting out of here," he said. "One more and then let's beat it, okay?"

"Okay." He signaled and told the waiter: "Double shots." And inquiringly to Friml: "All right, isn't it?"

The secretary-treasurer nodded glumly. "Guess so. 'scuse me." He got to his feet and headed for the men's room. He was weaving. Novak thoughtfully poured his own double shot into Friml's ginger ale.

A sad little man, he thought, who didn't have any fun. Maybe a sad little man who had slunk out of the auditorium of Slovak Sokol Hall during the movie and put a bullet through Clifton's head for an obscure reason that had to do with the Stuarts.

Friml came drifting back across the floor and plopped into his chair. "Don't do this often," he said clearly and gulped his double shot, chasing it with the ginger ale. He put a half-dollar on the table with a click and said: "Let's go. Been a very pleasant evening. I like that piano man."

The cool night air did it. He sagged foolishly against Novak and a cruising taxi instantly drew up. The engineer loaded him into it. "You can't go to the Y in this shape," he said. "How about some coffee some place? I have an invitation to Mrs. Clifton's. You can get some coffee there and take a nap."

Friml nodded vaguely and then his head slumped on his chest. Novak gave the cabby the Clifton address and rolled down the windows to let a breeze through.

Friml muttered during the ride, but nothing intelligible.

Novak and the cabby got Friml to the small front porch of the Clifton bungalow, and Novak and Lilly got him inside and onto a couch. The engineer noticed uncomfortably that she was wearing the strapless, almost topless, black dinner dress she'd had on the night Cliff died. He wondered, with a faint and surprising touch of anger, if she thought it would excite him because of that. The bungalow inside had been cleared of its crazy welter of junk, and proved to be ordinary without it. One lingering touch: on spread newspapers stood a sketch box and an easel with a half-finished oil portrait of Lilly, full face and somber with green.

She caught his glance. "I make that. Somet'ing to do." She looked down at Friml and asked cheerfully: "How you feeling, boy? You want a drink?"

Incredibly, he sat up and blinked. "Yeah," he said. "Hell with the job."

"The yob will keep," she said, and poured him two fingers from a tall bottle of cognac that stood on a coffee table. He tossed it down in one gulp.

"Don't do this often," he said sardonically. "Not good for the c'reer. The ol' man wouldn't like it."

Wilson Stuart. It had to be. Fighting a tremor in his voice, Novak said: "It's a shame to see a trained man like you tied up with a crackpot outfit like the Society."

"That so?" asked Friml belligerently. "'m doing a better job than anybody thinks. And they all call me a son of a bitch for it. So do you. But *I'm* the guy that sees he gets dollar for dollar. I mean dollar's value for a dollar spent." Friml looked cunning. "I got a c'reer, all right. You may not think so, but I'm gonna be com'troller of a certain big aircraft company one of these days. Not at liberty to tell you which. How's *that* for a c'reer? I'm only twenny-six, but I'm *steady.* 'at's what counts." He fell back on the couch, his eyes still open and glassy, with a little smile on his lips. "Where's 'at drink?" he muttered.

Lilly poured another and put it by his hand. "Here y'are, feller," she said. He didn't move or change expression. She jerked her head at Novak and he followed her to the bedroom.

"What you t'ink?" she asked in a whisper.

"Wilson Stuart and Western Air," he said flatly. "They are the famous 'industrial backers.' Friml is Stuart's man in the A.S.F.S.F. to watch Stuart's money. Stuart gives orders to MacIlheny and Friml's right there to see that they get carried out."

She raised her eyebrows. "Old Stuart don't hire such punks, Mike. Cliff told me."

"He seems to have been hired right out of his graduating class for the sake of secrecy," Novak said. "And he must look like a fireball on paper. Straight A's, no doubt. He's a screwed-up kid, but the pressure has to be right before you realize it." He told her about "Coffee Blues."

She snorted. "I guess once his mama catched him in the bat'room and beat his ears off."

"Maybe he should be factored by a biomat'ematicist," he said, straight-faced.

She flicked him on the jaw with her fingertips. "Don' tease me," she said crossly. "I'm t'rough vit' them. All they want is you money.

You so smart, tell me what old Stuart wants vit' a moon ship and where he got atomic fuel for it."

"There's no answer," he said. "It's got to be a government working through him. What countries does he sell big orders to? What small countries with atomic energy programs and dense populations? I guess that narrows the field down a little. And it makes the thing harder than ever to swallow. Wilson Stuart of Western Air a foreign agent." He thought of what Anheier would say to that, and almost laughed. The thing was now completely beyond the realm of credibility. And it was in their laps.

They went silently back into the living room. The brandy glass was empty again and Friml's eyes were closed at last. He was completely out.

"Mike," she said, "I guess you better leave him here."

"But what about—"

"You a sveet boy, but some other time. This yerk depresses me."

She gave him a cool goodnight kiss, and he hiked down the road to a shopping street and taxi stand, reflecting that he might as well have worn suspenders after all.

CHAPTER TWELVE

NOVAK SAW, with a pang, that Lilly was not on the field. He asked casually around whether she had phoned or left word with anybody. She hadn't. After last night's fiasco with the drunken secretary-treasurer, he supposed, she felt shy...

Amy Stuart was there, reporting for assignment, and he savored the mild irony of the situation. Her father, board chairman of Western Air, was funneling money into the A.S.F.S.F and dictating its policies. And his daughter was reporting for assignment to a hired hand of the Stuart funds. He toyed for a moment with the notion of assigning her to make the lunch sandwiches and dismissed it as silly. She had training and keen intelligence that he needed for *Proto*, whatever *Proto's* destiny was to be.

"Help me in the refractories lab?" he asked.

She said a little woodenly: "I thought that was Lilly's job."

"She didn't show up today. You're not afraid of hot stuff, are you?"

"Hot-radioactive or hot-centigrade?"

He laughed with an effort. She was very boldly playing dumb. "Hot-centigrade. Two thousand degrees of it and up. Tongs, gauntlets, masks, and aprons are furnished. But some people get trembly anyway and drop things."

"I won't," she said. "Not if Lilly didn't."

He taught her routine for an hour and then set her to compounding six more boron carbides by rote. "Call me if there's any doubt at all about a procedure," he said. "And I hope you have a conscience. If you make a mistake, start all over again. A cover-up of a mistake at this stage would introduce a hidden variable in my paper work and wreck everything I'm doing from now on."

"You don't have to impress me with a wild exaggeration like that, Mike. I know my way around a chemistry lab."

The arrogance of the amateur was suddenly too much for him. *"Get out,"* he said. "Right now. I'll get by somehow without you."

She stared at him, openmouthed, and her face became very red. And she left without a word.

Novak strode to the compounding area. His hands deftly did their work with the great precision balance while his mind raged at her insolent assurance. He was letting the beam of the balance down onto the agate knife-edge fulcrum for the sixteenth time when she spoke behind him: "Mike."

His hand, slowly turning a knurled bronze knob, did not twitch. "Minute," he growled, and continued to turn the knob until he felt the contact and the long pointer began to oscillate on the scale. He turned and asked her: "What is it?"

"What the devil do you think it is?" she flared. "I'm sorry got you sore and in the future I'll keep my mouth shut. Is that satisfactory?"

He studied her indignant face. "Do you still think I was trying to impress you with a wild exaggeration?"

She set her mouth grimly and was silent for a long moment. Then she stubbornly said: "Yes."

Novak sighed. "Come with me," he said, and took her into the small private office. He pulled out yesterday's work sheets and asked: "Know any math?"

"Up to differential calculus," she said cautiously.

That was a little better than he had expected. If she could follow him all the way it would be better for her work—far better than her taking him on faith.

In a concentrated one-hour session he told her about the method of least squares and how it would predictably cut his research time in half, about matrix equations and how they would pin down the properties of the boron carbides about n-dimensional geometry and how it would help him build a theory of boron carbides, about the virtues of convergent series and the vices of divergent series, and about the way sloppy work at this stage would riddle the theory end of it with divergent series.

"Also," he concluded, "you made me mad as hell."

Laughter broke suddenly through her solemn absorption. "I'm convinced," she said. "Will you trust me to carry on?"

"With all my heart," he grinned. "Call me when the batches are ready for solution."

Cheerfully he tackled yesterday's data and speedily set up the equations that had defied him yesterday.

Amy Stuart called him and he guided her through the rest of the program on the six new carbides. She was a neat fast worker who inked her notes in engineer's lettering. She wasn't jittery about handling "hot-centigrade" material. A spy? A handy one to have around. Lilly didn't have her cool sureness of touch.

They worked through the morning, finishing the batch, had sandwiches, and ran another batch in the afternoon. She left at five with the machine-shop gang and Novak put a third batch through himself. He wrote his weekly cumulative report during the four hours it sat aging. The report included a request for Friml to reserve sufficient time with I.B.M.'s EBIC in New York to integrate 132 partial differential equations, sample enclosed, and to post bond on their estimate at $100 per hour, the commercial rate. With this out of the way he ran tests on the third batch and phoned Barstow for a cab. The gate guard's farewell was awed. Night hitches were unusual.

Novak had dinner in the desert town while waiting for the Los Angeles bus. He asked at his hotel's desk whether there had been any calls. There had been no calls. Phone her? No, by God! He wanted to be alone tonight and think through his math.

In ten days of dawn-to-dusk labor, he had his 132 partial differential equations. The acceleration couches got finished and installed. He ordered the enigmatic "fuel tanks" and left the fabrication to the vendor, a big Buena Vista machine shop. He was no aero-engineer; all he felt competent to do was give them the drawings and specify that the tanks must arrive disassembled enough pass through *Proto's* open end for final assembly in place.

Amy continued to be his right bower; Lilly did not reappear at the field. She phoned him once and he phoned her. Astonishingly, they were on a we-must-get-together-some-time basis. He asked about Friml and Lilly said vaguely: "He's not such a bad kid, Mike. I t'ink you don't do him yustice." Novak wondered fleetingly whether Friml was wearing a belt or suspenders these days, and realized that he didn't care a great deal. Amy Stuart asked after Lilly regularly, and he never had anything to tell her.

On a Friday afternoon he zipped a leather briefcase around twenty-two ledger sheets on which were lettered in Amy's best engineer style the 132 equations that EBIC would chew into.

"Drive me to town?" he said to her. "I'd like to get to the office before they close up."

"With—the Papers," she said melodramatically, and they laughed. It came to him with a faint shock that it should be no laughing matter, but for the moment he couldn't persuade himself that there was anything sinister about this pretty girl with the sure, cool hands. The shared research, a common drain on them in progress and a mutual triumph at its end, was too big a thing to be spoiled by suspicion—for the moment. But depression stole over him on the desert road to Los Angeles, as he rode by Amy's side in the little English sportster.

She dropped him in front of the run-down building at 4:30.

He hadn't seen Friml since the secretary-treasurer's brannigan had broken up his plans for an evening. Without a blush, Friml laced into him. He seemed to be trying out a new manner for size: bullying instead of nagging; Friml the Perfect Master instead of Friml the Perfect Servant. "I'm *very* glad to see you again, Dr. Novak. I've tried several times to advise you that you should report regularly, at least once a week, in person, or by telephone if unavoidable."

Nuts. Let him have his fun. "Been pretty busy." He tossed the briefcase on Friml's desk. "This is the stuff to send I.B.M. When's our reservation?"

"That's just what I wanted to see you about. Your request—it was fantastic. Who—*who*—is this Mr. Ebic whom you wish to call in as a consultant at *one hundred dollars an hour?*" His voice was a sort of low, horrified shriek.

Novak stared at him in amazement. "Didn't you check to see what it was if you had doubts?"

"Certainly not. It's insane on the face of it. Just what do you think you're up to?"

"Somebody's been feeding you raw meat, Friml. And I think I know who." Friml looked smug for a moment. "EBIC is I.B.M.'s Electronic-Binary-Integrating-Calculator. Get it? It's the only major electronic calculator available to the private citizen or firm, thanks to I.B.M.'s generosity and sense of public relations."

The secretary-treasurer said petulantly: "You might have made your request clear, Novak."

"Doctor Novak to you," said the engineer, suddenly very sick of the new Friml. It was such a stinking, messy thing to run into after such a beautiful spell of research work. "Now just get me lined up for a crack at EBIC. It's I.B.M., New York. One hundred and thirty-two partial differential equations. Just get it done and stay out of my hair until then."

He walked out of the office, boiling, and picked up a pint of bourbon at a drugstore before he went to his hotel. Swear to God, he thought, this deal's as lousy as A.E.C. and you don't get a pension either.

There were several slips in his pigeonhole at the hotel mail desk. They all said to call Miss Wynekoop at such and such a number as soon as he could, please. He had never heard of Miss Wynekoop, and the phone number didn't ring any bells. He took off his shoes when he got to his room, had a drink of the bourbon, and called the number.

A woman's brightly noncommittal voice said: "Hello?"

"This is Michael Novak. Miss Wynekoop?"

"Oh, Dr. Novak. I wonder if I might see you this evening about employment?"

"I'm not hiring."

She laughed. "I meant employment for you. I represent a firm which is adding to its technical and executive staff."

"I have a job. And a one-year contract with options."

"The contract would be our legal department's worry," she said cheerfully. "And if you meet our firm's standards, I think you'd hesitate to turn down our offer. The pay is very, very good." Then she was crisp and businesslike. "Are you free this evening? I can be at your hotel in fifteen minutes."

"All right," he said. "Why not? I suppose from the way you're putting all this that you're not going to tell me the name of your firm?"

"Well, we do prefer to keep such things quiet," she apologized. "There's speculation and wasted time and broken hearts for the people who think they're going to get it and don't. I'm sure you understand. I'll see you very soon, Dr. Novak." She hung up and he stood for a moment at the phone, undecided. More funny business? Wait and see.

He put his shoes on again, grunting, and chain-smoked until Miss Wynekoop knocked on our door. She was tall, thirty-ish and engaging in a lantern-jawed way. "Dr. Novak. I could tell you were a scientist. They have a look—it was very good of you to let me see you on a moment's notice like this. But I hesitated to contact you through the A.S.F.S.F. In a way I suppose we're trying to steal you from them. Of course our legal people would buyout your contract with them so they'd suffer no financial loss in retraining a man to take your place."

"Sit down, please," he said. "What are these standards your firm wants me to meet?"

She settled herself comfortably. "Personality, for one thing. Our technical people have looked over your record and decided that you're the man for the job if you're available—and if you'll fit in. Our department head—you'd recognize the name, but of course I can't tell you yet—our department head would like me to check on some phases of your career. We're interested, for example, in the events that led up to your separation from A.E.C.

"Oh, are you?" he asked grimly. "As far as anybody is concerned, I resigned without notice after a short, hot discussion with Dr. Hurlbut, the director of the Argonne National Lab."

She giggled. "I'll say. You socked him."

"Well, what about it? If you people thought that means I'm incurably bad-tempered you wouldn't be here interviewing me now. You'd be trying the next guy on the list."

Miss Wynekoop became serious again. "You're right. Naturally we don't want a man who's going to fly off the handle over a trivial difference of opinion. But we certainly wouldn't hold it against you if you had actually been pushed to the breaking point by intolerable conditions. It could happen to anybody. If you will, I'd like you to tell me what brought the disagreement about."

The thing was sounding more legitimate by the minute—and is there anybody who doesn't like to tell his grievance? "Fair question, Miss Wynekoop," he said. "What brought it about was months of being assigned to a hopelessly wrong job and being stymied every time I tried to get back to my proper work. That's not just my subjective opinion; it's not a gripe but a fact. I'm a ceramics engineer. But they put me into nuclear physics theory and wouldn't let me out. Hurlbut apparently didn't bother to acquaint himself with the facts. He insulted me viciously in public. He accused me of logrolling and incompetence. So I let him have it."

She nodded. "What are the details?"

"Details. What details?"

"Things like, when were you transferred and by whose authority. Your relationship with your superiors generally."

"Well, last August, about mid-month, my transfer order came through without warning or explanation. It was signed by the director of the Office of Organization and Personnel—one of the Washington big shots. And don't ask me about my relationship with him; I didn't have any. He was too high up. My orders before that had always been cut by my working directors."

She looked understanding. "I see. And the working directors: did they ride you? Keep you short of supplies? Stick you on the night-side? That kind of thing?"

Night-side. He had known reporters, and that was newspaper talk. They said without thinking: day-side, night-side, city-side, sport-side. *"Smear us Novak,"* Anheier had grimly said, *"and we'll smear you back."* He tried not to panic. "No," he said evenly. "There never was anything like that."

"What was your relationship with, say, Daniel Holland?"

Novak didn't have to fake a bewildered look. "Why, I had nothing at all to do with anybody on his level," he said slowly. "Maybe there's been a mistake. Do you have it clear that I was just a Grade 18? I wasn't in the chain of command. I was just hired help, why should I have anything to do with the general manager?"

She pressed: "But we understand that your transfer order was put through by the director of the Office of Organization and Personnel on the direct suggestion of Mr. Holland."

He shook his head. "Couldn't be. You've been misinformed. Holland wouldn't have known me from Adam's off ox."

Miss Wynekoop smiled briefly and said: "We were pretty sure of our facts. There's another matter. Your A.E.C. Personnel Form Medical 11305 was altered by some means or other last September. Were you retested by the psychologists before that happened?"

"What the deuce is my Personnel Form Medical whatever-it-was?"

"'Personality card' is what they call it unofficially."

Oh. Personality cards he knew about; they were an A.E.C. joke. You took a battery of tests during employment processing and a psychologist evaluated the results and filled out the card with attention to such things as "attitudes," "anxieties," "responses," and other items supposed to give your working director an idea of how to handle you. Your personality card went everywhere with you and it was never, never altered. It was a very peculiar question and it was becoming a very peculiar interview. "Yes," Novak lied. "They ran me through the works again at N.E.P.A. It was some psychologist's brilliant idea of a controlled experiment."

That rocked Miss Wynekoop back on her heels. She smiled with an effort and said, rising: "Thanks very much for your co-operation, Dr. Novak. I'll call you early next week. Thanks *very* much."

When he saw the elevator door at the end of the corridor close on her, Novak called Information. He asked: "Do you have Directory Service in this city? What I mean is, I have a phone number and I want the name and address of the subscriber."

"Yes, sir," said Information. "Just dial the exchange of the number and then dial 4882." Same routine as Chicago.

Directory Service said Miss Wynekoop's phone was an unlisted number and that was that. He called Miss Wynekoop's number again and a man with a pleasant voice answered, saying: "Howard here."

"Let me talk to the editor, Howard," Novak said.

There was a long pause and then: "Who is this, please?"

Novak hung up. "Editor" had meant something to Howard—or maybe Howard just wasn't a quick thinker.

Novak had last seen Anheier, agent in charge for the Los Angeles Regional A.E.C. Security and Intelligence Office, at the inquest on Clifton. Novak had woodenly recited his facts while Anheier's calm eyes were on him, with their threat of instant and total ruin if he voiced his suspicion that Clifton had been murdered in some shadowy atomic intrigue. The verdict had been suicide...

The engineer hesitated a long minute and called the Security Office in the Federal Building. "Mr. Anheier, please," he said. "This is Dr. Michael Novak."

A man said: "Mr. Anheier's gone home, sir. I'll give you his home phone if it's important, or take a message."

Novak said: "It's important," and got Anheier's home phone number.

The agent in charge was as placid as ever. "Good to hear from you, Dr. Novak. What can I—"

Novak cut him off. "Shut up. I just want to tell you something. You were afraid of my ideas getting into the papers. You said you'd smear me if I did anything to publicize them. I want you to know that the newspapers are coming to me." He proceeded to tell Anheier what had been said, as close to verbatim as he could. At the end of the recital he said: "Any questions?"

"Can you describe this woman?"

He did.

Anheier said: "It sounds like somebody who hit town today. I'm going into the Federal Building office now. Will you come down and look at some pictures? Maybe we can identify this Wynekoop."

"Why should I?"

Anheier said grimly: "I want your co-operation, Novak. I want to be sure you aren't leaking your story to the papers and trying to avoid retaliation in kind. The more co-operation we get out of you, the less likely that theory will seem. I'll be waiting for you."

Novak hung up the phone and swore. He drank again from the bottle of bourbon and took a taxi to the Federal Building.

There was a long wait in the dimmed hall for the single after-hours elevator. When its door rolled open on the eighth floor, Novak saw that the Security office glass door was the only one on the floor still lit from inside. Twenty-four hours a day, he had heard, with the teletype net always up.

He gave his name to the lone teletype operator doubling at night as receptionist.

"Mr. Anheier's in his office," said the operator. "You see it there?"

Novak went in. The tall, calm man greeted him and handed him a single eight-by-ten glossy print.

"That's her," he said without hesitation. "A reporter?"

Anheier was rocking gently in his swivel chair. "An ex-reporter," he said. "She's Mary Tyrrel. Senator Bob Hoyt's secretary."

Novak blinked uncomprehendingly. "I don't see what I can do about it," he said, shrugging, and turned to leave.

"Novak," Anheier said. "I can't let you out of here."

There was a gun in his hand, pointed at the engineer.

"Don't you know who killed Clifton?" Anheier asked. "I killed Clifton."

CHAPTER THIRTEEN

NIGHT OF A BUREAUCRAT.

The bachelor apartment of Daniel Holland was four rooms in an oldish Washington apartment house. After six years in residence, Holland barely knew his way around it. The place had been restrainedly decorated in Swedish modern by the wife of a friend in the days when he'd had time for friends. There had been no changes in it since. His nightly track led from the front door to the desk, and after some hours from the desk to the dressing closet and then the bed. His track in the morning was from the bed to the bathroom to the dressing closet to the front door.

Holland was there in his second hour of paperwork at the desk when his telephone rang. It meant a wrong number or—trouble. His eyes slid to the packed traveling bag he always kept beside the door; he picked up the phone and gave its number in a monotone.

"This is Anheier in L.A., chief. Let's scramble."

Holland pushed the scrambler button on the phone's base and asked: "Do you hear me all right?"

"I hear you, chief. Are you ready for bad news?"

The general manager felt a curious relief at the words; the moment had arrived and would soon be past. No more night sweats... "Let me have it."

"Hoyt's got the personnel angle. Tyrrel's been grilling Novak. The questions showed that she had just about all of it on ice."

"What does Novak know?"

"Too much. I have him here." The Security man's voice became embarrassed. "I have a gun on him, chief. I've told him I shot Clifton to let him know I mean business. And we can't leave him wandering around. Hoyt would latch onto him, give a sugar-tit, listen to all he knows and then—we're done."

"I don't doubt your judgment, Anheier," Holland said heavily. "Put him in storage somewhere. I'll fly out to the coast. I've got to talk to him myself."

"You can't fly, chief. It'd be noticed."

"Too much has been noticed. It's a question of time now. Now we must ram it through and hope we're not too late. Good-by." He hung up before Anheier could protest, and went to get his hat and coat.

Novak listened to the Los Angeles end of the conversation, watching the gun in Anheier's big, steady hand. It never wavered.

The Security man put his odd-looking telephone back into his desk drawer. "Get up," he said. "You won't be killed if you don't make any foolish moves." He draped a light raincoat over the gun hand. If you looked only casually it would strike you as nothing more than a somewhat odd way to carry a raincoat.

"Walk," Anheier told him.

In a fog, Novak walked. It couldn't be happening, and it was. Anheier guided him through the office. "Back late tomorrow, Charles." Yell for help? Break and run? Charles was an unknown, but the big black gun under the coat was a known quantity. Before the thing could be evaluated they were in the corridor. Anheier walked him down the lonesome stairs of the office building, sadly lit by night bulbs, one to a landing. Swell place for a murder. So was the parking lot back of the building.

"I know you drive," Anheier said. "Here." He handed him car keys. "That one."

Use your head, Novak told himself. He'll make you drive to a canyon and then you'll get it without a chance in the world of witnesses. Yell here, and at least somebody will know—

But the big gun robbed him of his reason. He got in and started the car. Anheier was beside him and the gun's muzzle was in his ribs, not painfully.

The Security man gave him laconic traffic directions. "Left. Left again. Right. Straight ahead." Aside from that, he would not talk.

After an hour the city had been left behind and they were among rolling, wooded hills. With dreamlike recognition he stopped on order at the police sentry box that guarded the wealthy from intrusion by kidnappers, peddlers, and thieves. The gun drilled into his ribs as he stopped the car, painfully now. Anheier rolled down his window and passed a card to the cop in the handsomely tailored uniform.

Respectfully: "Thank you, Mr. Anheier. Whom are you calling on?" The best was none too good for the rich. They even had cops who said "Whom."

"Mr. Stuart's residence. They'll know my name." Of course. The gun drilled in.

"Yes, sir," said the flunky-cop. "If you'll wait just a moment, sir." The other man in the booth murmured respectfully into his wall phone; he had his hand casually on an elegant repeating shotgun as he listened. He threw them a nod and smile.

"Let's go, Novak," Anheier said.

The gun relaxed little when the booth was behind them. "You're all in it," Novak said at last, bitterly.

Anheier didn't answer. When they reached the Stuart place he guided Novak up the driveway and into the carport. Lights in the rangy house glowed, and somebody strode out to meet them. Grady, the Stuart chauffeur. "Get out, Novak." For the first time, the gun was down.

"Grady," Anheier said, "keep an eye on Dr. Novak here. We don't want him to leave the grounds or use the phone or anything like that." He stowed the gun in a shoulder holster. "Well, let's get into the house, shall we?"

The old man was waiting for them in his wheelchair. "What the hell's going on, Anheier? You can't turn this place into an office."

"Sorry," said the Security man briefly. "It can't be helped. The chief's coming out to see Novak. He's found out too much. We can't leave him wandering around."

Wilson Stuart glared at Novak. "My daughter thinks you're intelligent," he said. "I told her she was crazy. Anheier, when's all this going to happen?"

"I don't know. Overnight. He said he'd fly. I tried to talk him out of it."

"Grady," the old man said, "put him in a bedroom and lock the door. I'll have Dr. Morris mix something to give him a good night's sleep."

Incongruously the chauffeur said: "This way, sir."

The bedroom was the same one Lilly had been put up in. Its solid door closed like the door of a tomb. Novak dashed to the long, low window and found it thoroughly sealed to the wall. The place was air-conditioned. Of course he could smash it with a table lamp and jump. And be brought down by a flying tackle or a bullet.

Grady was back in five minutes with a yellow capsule in a pillbox. "Dr. Morris sent this for you, Dr. Novak," he said. "Dr. Morris said it would help you rest." Grady stood by expectantly as Novak studied the capsule. After a moment he said pointedly: "There's water and a glass in the bathroom, sir."

Put on a scene? Refuse to take their nassy ole medicine? He cringed at what would certainly happen. These terrifyingly competent people would stick him with a hypodermic or—worse—have their muscle man hold him while the capsule was put in his mouth and washed down. He went silently to the bathroom and Grady watched him swallow.

"Good night, Dr. Novak," the chauffeur said, closing the door solidly and softly.

The stuff worked fast. In five minutes Novak was sprawled in the bed. He had meant to lie down for a minute or two, but drifted off. His sleep was dreamless, except that once he fancied somebody had told him softly that she was sorry, and touched his lips.

A man was standing beside the bed when he awoke. The man, middle-aged and a little fleshy, was neither tall nor short. His face was a strange one, a palimpsest. A scholar, Novak fuzzily thought— definitely a pure-research man. And then over it, like a film, slipped a look so different that the first judgment became inexplicable. He was a boss-man—top boss-man.

"I'm Daniel Holland," he said to Novak. "I've brought you some coffee. They told me you shouldn't be hungry after the sleeping capsule. You aren't, are you?"

"No, I'm not. Daniel Holland. A.E.C.? You're—"

The top-boss face grinned a hard grin. "I'm in this too, Novak."

What was there to do? Novak took the coffee cup from the bedside table and sipped mechanically. "Are you people going to kill me?" he asked. The coffee was helping to put him together.

"No," said Holland. He pulled up a chair and sat. "We're going to work you pretty hard, though."

Novak laughed contemptuously. "You will not," he said. "You can make me or anybody do a lot of things, but not that. I guess just a few clouts in the jaw would make me say anything you wanted me to. Those Russian confessions. The American police third degree. If you started to really hurt me I suppose I'd implicate anybody you wanted. Friends, good friends, anybody. You can do a lot of things to a man, but you can't make him do sustained brainwork if he doesn't want to.

And I don't want to. Not for Pakistan, Argentina, the Chinese, or whoever you represent."

"The United States of America?" asked Holland.

"You must think I'm a fool," Novak told him.

"I'm working for the United States," said Holland. "God help me, but it's the only way left. I was hemmed in with this and that—" There was appeal in his voice. He was a man asking for absolution.

"I'll tell it from the beginning, Novak," he said, under control again.

"In 1951 a study was made by A.E.C. of fission produce, from the Hanford plutonium-producing reactors. Properties of one particular isotope were found to be remarkable. This isotope, dissolved in water and subjected to neutron flux of a certain intensity, decomposes with great release of energy. It is stable except under the proper degree of neutron bombardment. Its level of radioactivity is low. Its half-life is measured in scores of years. It is easy to isolate and is reasonably abundant. Since it is a by-product, its cost is exactly nothing."

"How much energy?" asked Novak, guardedly.

"Enough to flash the solvent water into hydrogen and oxygen by thermolysis," Holland said. "You've seen the drawings for *Prototype*'s fuel tanks, as we called them…"

Anheier came into the room and Novak barely noticed him. His engineer's mind could see the blueprint unrolled before him again. The upper tank containing the isotope-water solution…the lower tank containing a small heavy-water "fishbowl" reactor for the neutron source…the dead-end control systems completed, installed, one metering the fuel solution past the neutron spray of the reactor, the other controlling flux level by damper rods run in and out on servomechanisms…the fuel solution droplets flashing into hell's own flame and roaring from the throat with exhaust velocity unobtainable by merely chemical reaction…

Holland was talking again, slowly. "It was just numbers on paper, among thousands of other numbers on paper. It lay for years in the files until one of the high-ranking A.E.C. technical people stumbled on it, understood its implications and came to me. His exact words were: 'Holland, this is space flight.'"

"It is," Novak breathed. His voice became hoarse. "And you sold it…"

"*I saved it.* I saved it from the red-tape empire builders, the obscurantists, the mystagogues, the spies. If I had set it up as an A.E.C. project, the following things would have happened. First, we would have lost security. Every nation in the world would shortly have known the space-flight problem had an answer, and then what the answer was. Second, we would have been beaten to the Moon by another nation. This is because our personnel policy forbids us to hire the best men we can find merely because they're the best. Ability ranks very low in the category of criteria by which we judge A.E.C. personnel. They must be conservative. They must be politically apathetic. They must have no living close-relatives abroad. And so on. As bad as the personnel situation, interacting with and reinforcing it, is the fact of A.E.C.'s bigness and the fact of its public ownership. They mean accounting, chains of command, personnel-flow charts—the jungle in which third-raters flourish. Get in the A.E.C., build yourself a powerful clique and don't worry about the work; you don't really have to do any."

The words were fierce; his tone was dispassionate. Throughout his denunciation he wore the pure-research man's face, lecturing coolly on phenomena which he had studied, isolated, linked, analyzed endlessly. If any emotion was betrayed it was, incongruously, the residual affection of a pure-research man for his subject. When the pathologist calls it a beautiful carcinoma he is being neither ironical nor callous.

"As you know," Holland lectured quietly, "the nation that gets to the Moon first has the Moon. The lawyers will be arguing about it for the next century, but the nation that plants the first moon base need not pay any attention to their arguments. I wanted that nation to be the United States, which I've served to the best of my ability for most of my life.

"I became a conspirator.

"I determined to have a moon ship built under non-Government auspices and, quite frankly, to rob the Government to pay for it. I have a long reputation as a dollar-honest, good-government man, which I counted on to help me get away with quite outrageous plundering of the Treasury.

"A study convinced me that complete assembly of a moon ship by a large, responsible corporation could not be kept secret. I found the idea of isolated parts manufactured by small, scattered outfits and then a rush assembly was impractical. A moon ship is a precision instrument of huge size. One subassembly under par would wreck the project. I admit I was toying with the idea of setting up a movie company and building the moon ship as, ostensibly, a set for a science-fiction film, when the A.S.F.S.F. came to my attention.

"Psychologically it seems to have been perfect. You deserve great credit, Dr. Novak, for stubbornly sticking to the evidence and logic that told you *Prototype* is a moon ship and not a dummy. You are the only one who has. Many people have seen the same things you did and refused to believe it because of the sheer implausibility of the situation.

"Hoping that this would be the case, I contacted my old friend Wilson Stuart. He and his company have been the pipeline for millions of Government dollars poured into the A.S.F.S.F. I've callously diverted thousands of A.E.C. man-hours into solving A.S.F.S.F. problems. I had you transferred within the A.E.C. and had your personality card altered so that Hurlbut would goad you into resigning—since the moon ship needed a full-time man with your skills."

"You dared—" choked Novak, stung with rage.

"I dared," Holland said matter-of-factly. "This country has its faults, but of all the nations in the world I judge it as least disqualified to operate a moon base. It's the power of life and death over every nation on the face of the earth, and some one nation has got to accept that power."

Suddenly his voice blazed with passion and the words came like a torrent. "What was I to do? Go ahead and do it the wrong way? Go to the commissioners, who'd go to the congressmen, who'd go to their good friends on the newspapers? Our secrecy would have been wiped out in twelve hours! Set up a Government project staffed with simon-pure but third-rate scientists? Watch the thing grow and grow until there were twenty deskmen for every man who got his hands dirty on the real work—and all the deskmen fighting like wild beasts for the glory of signing memos? Was I to spare your career and let those A-bomb racks on the Moon go by default to the Argentines or Chinese? Man, what do you think I am?"

"A killer," Novak said dully. "Your man Anheier murdered my friend Clinton."

Anheier's voice was cold. "Executed," he said. "You were there when I warned him, Novak. The penalty for espionage is death. I told him so and he smiled at me to tell me that I wouldn't dare. I told him: 'The penalty is death.' And he went to his home and telephoned his contact, Mr. Boris Chodorov of Amtorg, that he'd have something for him in a day or two. God almighty, Novak, be reasonable. Should I have written Clifton a letter? I told him: 'Import-export used to be a favorite, but it was too obvious.' So he smiled at me and went home to call his contact. He had something juicy, something out of the general run-of-the-mill industrial-preparedness information he collected for the Soviets.

"*He* may have thought he was just augmenting his income, that it wasn't *really* espionage, that the United States hasn't got the guts to hit back anyway—" His voice trailed off. "I killed him," he said.

"Clifton a spy," Novak said stupidly. He began to laugh. "And Lilly?"

"Just a stupid woman," Anheier said. "We monitored the Cliftons for a long time, and nothing ever emanated from her."

Novak couldn't stop laughing. "You're quite wrong," he said. A hundred little things slipped suddenly into place. "There is no doubt in my mind that Lilly was the brains of the outfit. I can see now that Lilly was leading me by the nose for weeks, getting every scrap of information I possessed. And when she got just one chance she landed Friml and is now milking him."

Anheier had gone white. "How much does Friml know?" asked Holland.

The Security man said: "Friml knows he's employed by Wilson Stuart. And he can guess at a lot of the rest. The way there's always enough material on hand when we order it from a jobber—even gray-market stuff like copper and steel. Our work. And he knows there are calls to and from Washington that have a connection. Between his brains and Mrs. Clifton's, I think we'd better assume that secrecy is gone." He looked and sounded sick.

"Novak," the general manager asked softly, "are you in this too?"

Novak knew what he meant. "Yes," he said. "It looks like the right side of the fence to me."

Holland said: "I'm glad…how close to finished is the moon ship?" He was the boss-man again.

"Is the fuel solution ready and waiting?"

"It is. Waiting for word from me. I've also oiled the ways for the diversion of a fish-bowl reactor for your neutron source. It's going to go astray on its way to Cal Tech from Los Alamos."

"EBIC's got to work out my math and I've got to fabricate the liner and vane. At the same time, the ship could be stocked with water, food, and pressure dome. At the same time the dead-ended circuits can be finished. Do you have the food, water, air tanks and lockers?"

"Yes. Give me a figure!" Holland snapped.

Novak choked on it, terrifyingly aware that no man ever before had borne such tidings as he spoke in the bedroom of a rich man's house in Beverly Hills. "It could take off in two weeks," he said. Here we are at last, Novak thought. Time to close the old ledger on man. Add it up, credit and debit, and carry your balance forward to the first page of the next ledger...

"And now," said Holland grimly, "we ought to go and see some people. They'd both be at her house?"

Novak knew what he meant, and nodded. "I suppose so. It's Saturday."

He led the way to the garage. Amy Stuart's little sports car was at home.

"Mr. Holland," Novak said, "there's going to be a hell of a smash when this comes out, isn't there?"

"We hope not," the general manager said shortly. "We have some plans of our own if they try to jail me for fraud and Anheier for murder and the rest of the crew for whatever they can think of."

"Why should Amy be mixed up in this?"

"We need her," Holland snapped. His manner ruled out further questions. They got into Anheier's car and the Security man drove them to the house in Cahuenga Canyon.

CHAPTER FOURTEEN

LILLY MET THEM at the door in a housecoat. "Hallo, Mike," she said. "Who're these people? Oh, you' Anheier, ain't you?"

"My name is Daniel Holland, Mrs. Clifton," the general manager said. She didn't move a muscle. "Do you mind if I come in?"

"I t'ink I do," she said slowly. "Mike, what is all this?"

Novak looked at Holland, who nodded. "Espionage," he said.

She laughed tremulously and told him: "You cra-a-azy!"

"Lilly, you once asked me to find out who killed Cliff. I found out. It was Anheier. Cliff was a spy."

Her expression didn't change as she said: "Cliff was a damn bad spy. Come on in. I got somet'ing to tell you too."

They filed into the living room. "Where's Friml?" Novak asked. She jerked her thumb carelessly toward the bedroom door.

"He's a lot smarter than any of you t'ought," she said, making a business out of lighting a cigarette. "He telled me what he saw and figgered out, and I did some figgering too. You' a very smart man, Mr. Holland. But what I got to tell you is I got this stuff to a friend of mine already. If he don't hear from me by a certain time, he sends it on to the newspaper. How you like that, killer?" She blew a plume of smoke at Anheier. The large, calm man said: "That means you've got it to your employers by now."

"Does it?" she asked, grinning. "It don't matter. All I got to do is sic the papers on you, and you' democra-a-atic country does the rest for us like always. I don't know you' rocket fuel yet. Prob'ly wouldn't know what to do vit' it if Friml brought me a bottleful; I don't know science. But it don't matter; I don't worry. The papers and the Congress raise hell vit' you and lead us right to the rocket fuel so our people that do know science can move in and figger it out."

Stirred by a sudden, inappropriate curiosity, Novak couldn't help asking: "Are you a Communist? Your husband reported to an Amtorg man."

She was disgusted. "Communist, hell! I'm a European."

"I don't see what that—"

"Listen, Mike," she said flatly. "Before you' friends kill me or t'row me in yail or whatever they gonna do. You fatbelly people over here don' begin to know how we t'ink you all a bunch of monkeys vit' the atom bombs and movies and at'letes and radio comics and two-ton Sunday newspapers and fake schools where the kids don' work. Well, what you guys going to do vit' me? Shoot me? Prison? Drop an atom bomb? Solve everyt'ing? Go ahead. I been raped by Yerman soldiers and sedooced vit' Hershey bars by American soldiers. I had the typhus and lost my hair. I walked seventy-five kilometers on a loaf of sawdust bread for a yob that wasn't there after all. I speak t'ree languages and understand t'ree more a liddle and you people call me dumb because I got a accent. You people that don' even know how to stand quiet in line for a bus or kinema and t'ink you can run the world.

194

I been lied at and promised to by the stupid Americans. Vote for me and end you' troubles. I been lied at and promised to by the crazy Russians. Nah, vote for *me* and end you' troubles.

"*Sheisdrek.* So I voted for me-myself and now go ahead and drop you' damn atom bomb on the dumb squarehead. Solve everyt'ing, hey boys? *Sheisdrek.*"

She sprawled in the chair, a tight grin on her face, and deliberately hoisted the skirt of her housecoat to her thighs. "Any of you guys got a Hershey bar?" she demanded sardonically, and batted her eyes at them. "The condemned European's la-a-ast request is for a Hershey bar so she can die happy."

Friml was standing there with his thinnish hair tousled, glasses a little crooked on his face, wrapped in a maroon bathrobe. His skinny, hairy legs shook with a fine tremor.

"Hallo, sugar," she said to him with poisonous sweetness. "These yentleman and I was discussing life." She turned to them and lectured elaborately: "You know what happen in Europe when out came you' Kinsey report? This will kill you. All the dumb squareheads and the dumb dagoes and the dumb frogs and krauts said we knew it all the time. American men are half pa-a-ansy and the rest they learn out of a marriage book on how to *zigzig.*" She looked at Friml and laughed.

"P-p-pull your skirt down, Lilly," Friml said in a weak, hoarse voice.

"Go find you 'self a nice boy, sugar," she said carelessly. "Maybe you make him happy, because you sure as hell don'—" Friml's head bobbed as though he'd been slapped. Moving like an old man, not looking at anything, he went to the bathroom and then to the bedroom and closed the door.

"Like the yoke!" giggled Lilly half-hysterically. "He'll do it too; he's a manly liddle feller!"

"I think—" said Novak starting to his feet. He went to the bedroom door with hurried strides and knocked. "Friml! I want to—to talk to you for a minute!"

The answer was a horrible, low, roaring noise.

The door was locked; Novak lunged against it with his shoulder repeatedly, not feeling the pain and not loosening the door. Anheier pulled him back and yelled at him: "Cut that out! I'll get the window from outside." He rushed from the house, scooping up a light, toylike poker from the brass stand beside the fireplace.

Holland said at his side: "Steady. We'll be able to help him in a minute." They heard smashing glass and Novak wanted to run out and look through the window. "Steady," Holland said.

Anheier opened the door. "Get milk from the kitchen," he snapped at Novak. The engineer got a brief glimpse of dark red blood. He ran for the kitchen and brought a carton of milk.

While Holland phoned for a doctor, Novak and Anheier tried to pour the milk into Friml. It wouldn't go down. The thrashing thing on the floor, its bony frame and pallid skin pitifully exposed by the flapping, coarse robe, wasn't vomiting. They would get a mouthful of milk into it, and then the milk would dribble out again as it choked and roared. Friml had drunk almost two ounces of tincture of iodine. The sickening, roaring noises had a certain regularity. Novak thought he was trying to say he hadn't known it would hurt so much.

By the time the doctor arrived, they realized that Lilly was gone.

"God, Anheier," Novak said white-faced. "She planned it. A diversion while she made her getaway. She pushed the buttons on him and—is it possible?"

"Yes," the Security man said without emotion. "I fell down badly all around on that one."

"Damn it, be human!" Novak yelled at him.

"He's human," Holland said. "I've known him longer than you have, and I assure you he's human. Don't pester him; he feels very badly."

Novak subsided.

An ambulance with police pulled up to the house as the doctor was pumping morphine into Friml's arm. The frightful noises ebbed, and when Novak could look again Friml was spread laxly on the floor.

"I don't suppose—" Novak said, and trailed off.

"Relation?" the doctor asked. He shook his head. "He'll linger a few hours and then die. I can see you did everything you could, but there was nothing to be done. He seared his glottis almost shut."

"Joel Friml," Novak told the sergeant, and spelled it. It was good to be doing something—anything. "He lives at the Y in downtown L.A. This place is the home of Mrs. August Clifton—widow. He was spending the night here. My friends and I came to visit. Mrs. Clifton seems to have run out in a fit of nerves." He gave his name, and slowly recognition dawned on the sergeant's face.

"This is, uh, kind of funny," the cop told him. "My brother-in-law's in that rocket club so I happen to remember—it was her husband, wasn't it? And wasn't there an Anslinger—"

"Anheier," said the Security man. "I'm Anheier."

"Funnier and funnier," said the sergeant. "Doc, could I see you for a—"

The doctor had been listening, and cut him off. "Not necessary," he said. "This is suicide. The man drank it like a shot of whisky—threw it right straight down. (Was he a drinker, by the way? "Yes." "Thought so.) There aren't any smears on the lips or face and only a slight burning in the mouth, which means he didn't try to retain it. He drank it himself, in a synchronized toss and gulp."

The sergeant looked disappointed, but brightened up to ask: "And who's this gentleman?"

Holland took out a green card from his wallet and showed it to the sergeant. Novak craned a little and saw that it was a sealed, low-number White House pass. "Uh," said the sergeant, coming to something like attention, "I can't see your name, sir. Your finger—"

"My finger stays where it is, sergeant," said Holland. "Unless, of course, you *insist*—?" He was all boss.

"No, no, no, not at all, sir. That's quite all right. Thank you." The sergeant almost backed away as from royalty and began to snarl at his detail of two patrolmen for not having the meat loaded yet.

They rushed into action and the sergeant said to nobody in particular and very casually: "Think I'd better phone this in to headquarters." Novak wasn't surprised when he heard the sergeant say into the phone, louder than he had intended: "Gimme the city desk, please." Novak moved away. The thing had to come out sooner or later, and the tipster-cop was earning a little side money honestly.

After completing his call, the sergeant came up beaming.

"That wraps it up except for Mrs. Clifton," he said. "She took her car? What kind?"

"Big maroon Rolls Royce," Novak said. "I'm not sure of the year—maybe early thirties."

"Well, that don't matter. A Rolls is a Rolls; we'll be seeing her very soon, I think."

Novak didn't say what he thought about that. He didn't think any of them would be seeing Lilly again. He thought she would vanish

197

back into the underworld from which she had appeared as a momentary, frightening reminder that much of the world is not rich, self-satisfied, supremely fortunate America.

In Anheier's car on the road back to the Wilson Stuart place, the Security man asked tentatively: "What do you think, chief?"

"I think she's going to release everything she's got to the newspapers. First, as she said, it means we'll lose secrecy. Second, it would be the most effective form of sabotage she could practice on our efforts. The Bennet papers have been digging into my dirty work of the past year for circulation-building and for Hoyt, whom they hope to put in the presidency. The campaign should open in a couple of days, when they get Lilly's stuff as the final link.

"I've got to get to Washington and contract a diplomatic illness for the first time in my life. Something that'll keep me bedridden but able to run things through my deputy by phone. Something that'll win a little sympathy and make a few people say hold your horses until he's able to answer the charges, I can stall that way for a couple of weeks—no more. Then we've got to present Mr. and Mrs. America with a *fait accompli*. Novak!"

"Yessir!" snapped Novak, surprising himself greatly.

"Set up a *real* guard system at the moon ship. If you need any action out of Mr. MacIlheny, contact Mr. Stuart, who will give him your orders. MacIlheny—up to now—doesn't know anything about the setup beyond Stuart. Your directive is: *build us that moon ship. Fast.*"

"Yes, sir."

"And another thing. You're going to be busy, but I have some chores for you nevertheless. Your haircut is all wrong. Go to a really good barber who does theatrical people. Go to your dentist and have your teeth cleaned. Have yourself a couple of good suits made, and good shoes and good shirts. Put yourself in the hands of a first-rate tailor. It's on the expense account and I'm quite serious about it. I only wish there were time for..."

"How's that, sir?" Novak couldn't believe he had heard it right.

"Dancing lessons," snapped Holland. "You move across a room with all the grace of a steam thresher moving across a Montana wheatfield. And Novak."

"Yes?" said the engineer stiffly.

"It's going to be rough for a while and they may drag us down yet. Me in jail, you in jail, Anheier in the gas chamber. Stuart fired by his board—if I know the old boy he wouldn't last a month if they took Western away from him. You're going to be working for your own neck—and a lot of other necks. So work like hell. Hoyt and Bennet play for keeps. This a bus stop? Let Novak out, Anheier. You go on downtown and let's see production."

Novak stood on the corner, lonely, unhappy, and shaken, and waited for his downtown bus.

His appetite, numbed by last night's sedative, came on with a rush during the ride. After getting off, he briskly headed for a business-district cafeteria, and by reflex picked up a newspaper. He didn't go into the cafeteria. He stood in the street, reading.

DEATH STRIKES AT 2ND ROCKET-CLUB CHIEF: POISONED ON VISIT TO 1ST VICTIM'S WIDOW

POST *Special Correspondent*

Violent death struck late today at a leader of the American Society for Space Flight, nationwide rocket club, for the second time in less than a month. The first victim was club engineer August Clifton, who committed suicide by shooting in a room next door to a meeting of the club going full blast. Today club secretary-treasurer Joel Friml, 26, was found writhing in pain on the floor of a Cahuenga Canyon bungalow owned by Clifton's attractive blond widow Lilly, 35. Both bodies were discovered by club engineer Michael Novak. A further bizarre note lies in the fact that on both occasions A.E.C. Security agent J. W. Anheier was on the scene within seconds of the discovery.

Police Sergeant Herman Alper said Novak and Anheier paid a morning visit to Mrs. Clifton's home and chatted with her and Friml, who had arrived earlier. Friml disappeared into the bedroom, alarming the other guests. They broke into the bedroom by smashing a window and found Friml in convulsions, clutching a two-ounce bottle of a medicine meant for external use. They called a doctor and tried to give milk as an antidote, but according to the physician the victim's throat had been so damaged that it was a hopeless try.

Friml was taken by ambulance under sedative to Our Lady of Sonora hospital, where no hope was given for his recovery. In the confusion Mrs. Clifton fled the house, apparently in a state of shock, and had not returned by the time the ambulance left.

Friends could hazard no guess as to the reason for the tragedy. Friml himself, ironically, had just completed auditing the rocket club's books in a vain search for discrepancies that might have explained the Clifton suicide.

It was bad. Worse was coming.

CHAPTER FIFTEEN

NOVAK MOVED OUT to the field, bag and baggage, that night and worked himself into a pleasant state of exhaustion. He woke on his camp cot at nine to the put-put of an arriving jalopy. It was a kid named Nearing. He made a beeline for Novak, washing up in a lab sink.

"Hi, Dr. Novak." He was uncomfortable.

"Morning. Ready for business?"

"I guess so. There's something I wanted to ask you about. It's a lot of nonsense, of course. My brother's in the C.B.S. newsroom in L.A., and he was kidding me this morning. He just got in from the night shift and he said there was a rumor about *Proto*. It came in on some warm-up chatter on their teletype."

Already? "What did he have to say?"

"Well, the A.S.F.S.F. was—'linked' is the word, I guess—with some big-time Washington scandal that's going to break. Here." He poked a wad of paper at Novak. "I thought he was making it up. He doesn't believe in space flight and he's a real joker, but he showed me this. He tore it off their teletype."

Novak unfolded the wad into a long sheet of cheap paper, torn off at the top and bottom.

Blue nose and a purple goatee.
Ha ha that's a good one. U know one abt bishop of birmingham???
Sure who dont. O gosh three am and three hours to go
Look who's bitching. Here its six am and six hours to go. Wish i'd learned a trade or stayed in the navy.
What u do in navy???
Teletype opr. Cant get away from dam ptrs seems as if.
Min fone
Who was it???
Eleanor roosevelt asking for a date u nosy bastrd

Ha ha ogod wotta slo nite. Any nuz ur side???
Not yet. First cast half hour. Nuzman came in with rumor abt some ur local screwballs to wit los angeles space flite club.
Hey hey. Nuzriter here got kid brother in club. Wot he say???
Said strictly phony outfit with wa tieup top adminxx
Administration got it finally figures.
Govt money goes to club and club kix back to govt officials. Sweet racket huh.
More???
No more. Min i ask. Says got it fm bennet nuz svc man.
No more.
Tnx. Coffee now.
Welcm. Dont spill it.
Ha ha u r a wit or maybe i am only half rite.

Nearing said as Novak looked up from the paper: "Of course Charlie may have punched it out himself on a dead printer just to worry me." He laughed uncomfortably. "Oh, hell. It's just a rumor about a rumor. But I don't like them tossing *Proto's* name around. She's a good girl." His eye sought the moon ship, gleaming in the morning sun.

"Yes," Novak said. "Look, Nearing. I'm tightening up the guard schedule and I'm going to be very busy. I'd like to turn the job of handling the guard detail over to you. I'll put you on salary, say fifty a week, if you'll do it."

"Fifty? Why sure, Dr. Novak. That's about what I'm getting at the shoe store, but the hell with it. When do I start and what do I do?"

"Start now. I want two guards on duty at all times. Not under twenty-one, either. At night I want one guard at the gate and one patrolling the fence. I want strict identification of all strangers at the gate. I want newspapermen kept out. I want you to find out what kind of no-trespassing signs we're legally required to post and how many—and then post twice as many. I want you to get the huskiest youngsters you can for guards and give them night sticks." He hesitated. "And buy us two shotguns and some shells."

The boy looked at Novak and then at the *Prototype* and then at Novak again. "If you think it's necessary," he said quietly. "What kind of shells—bird shot?"

"Buckshot, Nearing. They're after her."

"Buckshot it is, Dr. Novak," the shoe clerk said grimly. He worked all morning in the machine shop, turning wooden core patterns for the throat liner on the big lathe. Laminated together and rasped smooth, they would be the first step in the actual fabrication of the throat liner. Half a dozen youngsters showed up, and he put them to work routing out the jacket patterns. Some of the engineer-members showed up around noon on their Sunday visits and tried to shop-talk with him. He wouldn't shop-talk.

At three in the afternoon Amy Stuart was saying to him firmly: "Turn that machine off and have something to eat. Nearing told me you didn't even have breakfast. I've got coffee, bologna on white, cheese on rye—"

"Why, thanks," he said, surprised. He turned off the power and began to eat at a workbench.

"Sorry they pulled rough stuff on you," she said.

"Rough?" he snorted. "That wasn't rough. Rough is what's, coming up." Between bites of sandwich he told her about the teletype chatter.

"It's starting," she said.

The next day the dam broke.

Reporters were storming the gate by mid-morning. In due course a television relay truck arrived and from outside the fence peered at them with telephoto lenses.

"Find out what it's all about, Nearing," Novak said, looking up from his pattern making.

Nearing came back with a sheaf of papers. "They talked me into saying I'd bring you written questions."

"Throw 'em away. Fill me in in twenty seconds or less so I can get back to work."

"Well, Senator Hoyt's going to make a speech in the Senate today and he's wired advance copies all over hell. And it's been distributed by the news agencies, of course. It's like the rumor. He's going to denounce Daniel Holland, the A.E.C. general manager. He says Holland is robbing the Treasury blind by payment to the A.S.F.S.F. and Western Air, and getting kickbacks. He says Holland's incompetence has left the U.S. in the rear of the atomic weapons parade. Is my time up?"

"Yes. Thanks. Try to get rid of them. If you can't, just make sure none of them get in here."

There were days when he had to go into town. Sometimes people pointed him out. Sometimes people jostled him and he gave them a weary stare and they either laughed nervously or scowled at him, enemy of his country that he was. He was too tired to care deeply. He was working simultaneously on the math, the controls, installation of the tanks, and the setup for forming the liner and vane.

One day he fainted while walking from the machine shop to the refractories lab. He came to on his cot and found Amy Stuart and her father's Dr. Morris in attendance.

"Where did you come from?" he asked dimly.

Dr. Morris growled: "Never mind where I came from. You ought to be ashamed of yourself, Novak. Playing the fool at your age! I'm telling you here and now that you are going to stay in bed for forty-eight hours and you are not going to use the time to catch up on your paper work either. You are going to sleep, eat, read magazines—*not* including the *Journal of Metallurgical Chemistry* and things on that order—and nothing else."

"Make it twenty-four hours, will you?" said Novak.

"All right," Dr. Morris agreed promptly and Novak saw Amy Stuart grin.

Novak went to sleep for twelve hours. He woke up at eleven p.m., and Amy Stuart brought him some soup.

"Thanks," he said. "I was thinking—would you get me just the top sheet from my desk? It won't be *work.* Just a little calculation on heat of forming. Really, I'd find it relaxing."

"*No,*" she said.

"All right," he said testily. "Did the doctor say you had to keep a twenty-four-hour guard on me?"

"He did not," she told him, offended. "Please excuse me. There are some magazines and newspapers on the table." She swept out and he wanted to call after her, but...

He got out of the cot and prowled nervously around the room. One of the papers on the table was the Los Angeles paper of the Bennet chain. It was a shrieking banner headline...

HOYT DARES "ILL" HOLLAND TO SHOW MD PROOF!

Novak swore a little and climbed back into the cot to read the paper.

The front-page first-column story was all about Hoyt daring "ill" Holland to show M.D. proof. Phrases like "since Teapot Dome" and "under fire" were liberally used. Also on the front page a prominent officer of a veterans' organization was quoted as daring "ill" Holland to show M.D. proof. So were a strident and aging blond movie actress, a raven-haired, marble-browed touring revivalist, and a lady Novak had never heard of who was identified as Washington's number-one hostess. The rest of the front page was given over to stories from the wire services about children rescuing animals from peril and animals rescuing children from peril.

Novak swore again, a little more strongly, and leafed through the paper. He encountered several pages of department store ads and finally the editorial page and feature page.

The two-column, heavily-leaded editorial said that no reasonable person could any longer ignore the cold facts of the A.E.C-Western Air-rocket-crackpot scandal. Beyond any doubt the People's taxes and the People's fissionable material—irreplaceable fissionable material—was being siphoned into a phony front for the greed of one man.

For Bennet patrons who wanted just the gist of the news, or who didn't read very well, there was the cartoon. It showed a bloated, menacing figure, labeled "Dan Holland," grinning rapturously and ladling coins and bills from a shoebox Treasury Building into his pockets. There was one ladle in each hand, one tagged "Western Aircraft" and the other "Rocket Crackpots." A tiny, rancid, wormy, wrinkled old man was scooting in a wheelchair in circles about the fat boy's ankles, picking up coins Holland carelessly let dribble from the overflowing ladles. That was Wilson Stuart, former test pilot, breaker of speed and altitude records, industrialist whose aircraft plants covered a major sector of America's industrial defense line. Other little figures were whizzing in circles astride July-fourth rockets. They also were grabbing coins. Wild-eyed and shaggy under mortarboard hats, they were the rocket crackpots.

On the opposite page there was something for everybody.

For the women there was a column that wept hot tears because all America's sons, without exception, were doomed to perish miserably on scorching desert sands, in the frozen hell of the Arctic, and in the steamy jungles of the Pacific, all because of Daniel Holland. "How long, a lord, how long?" asked the lady who wrote the column.

For the economist there was a trenchant column headed: "This Is Not Capitalism." The business writer who conducted the column said it wasn't capitalism for Western Air's board of directors to shilly-shally and ask Wilson Stuart exactly where he stood vis-a-vis Daniel Holland and what had happened to certain million-dollar appropriations rammed through under the vague heading of "research." Capitalism, said the business writer, would be for Western Air's board to meet, consider the situation, fire Stuart, and maybe prosecute him. Said the business writer: "The day of the robber barons is past."

For the teen-ager there was a picture of a pretty girl, with enormous breasts and nipples clearly defined under her tight blouse, holding her nose at some wiggly lines emanating from a picture of the Capitol dome. Accompanying text:

"Joy-poppers and main-liners all, really glom onto what Mamaloi's dishing this 24. I don't too often get on the sermon kick because young's fun and you're a long time putrid. But things are happening in the 48 that ain't so great so listen, mate. You wolves know how to handle a geek who glooms a weenie-bake by yacking for a fat-and-40 blues when the devotees know it's tango this year. Light and polite you tell the shite, and if he doesn't dig you, then you settle it the good old American way: five-six of you jump him and send him on his meddy way with loose teeth for a soo-ven-war. That's Democracy. Joy-poppers and mainliners, there are grownups like that. We love and respect Mom and Dad even if they are fuddy-duddy geeks; they can't help it. But what's the deal and hoddya feel about a grownup like Danny-O Holland? And Wheelchair Wilson Stuart? And the crackpot cranks with leaky tanks that play with their rockets on dough from your pockets? Are they ripe for a swipe? Yeah-man, Elder. Are their teeth too tight? Ain't that man right! Sound off in that yeah-man corner, brethren and cistern! You ain't cackin', McCracken! So let's give a think to this stink for we, the youths of America today, are the adults of America tomorrow."

For those who vicariously live among the great there was the Washington column. "Local jewelers report a sharp, unseasonal drop in sales. Insiders attribute it to panic among the ranks of Dan (Heads-I-Win-Tails-You-Lose) Holland and his Little Dutch Boys over the fearless expose of his machinations by crusading Senator (Fighting

Bob) Hoyt. Similar reports in the trade from the West Coast, where Wilson (Wheel-Chair) Stuart and the oh-so-visionary-but-where's-the-dough pseudo-scientists of the A.S.F.S.F hang out. Meanwhile Danny Boy remains holed up in his swank ten-foam penthouse apartment claiming illness. Building employees say however that not one of his many callers during the past week has carried the little black bag that is the mark of the doctor!... What man-about-Washington has bought an airline ticket and has his passport visaed to Paraguay, a country where officials are notorious for their lack of co-operation in extradition proceedings—if their palms are properly greased?"

For lovers of verse there was a quatrain by one of the country's best-loved kindly humorists. His whimsical lines ran:

> *They say Dan Holland will nevermore*
> *Go anywhere near a hardware store.*
> *He'll make a detour by train or boat*
> *Because he knows he should cut his throat.*

Novak smiled sourly at that one, and heard a great tooting of horns. It went on, and on, and on, and on. Incredulously he clocked it for three solid minutes and then couldn't take any more. He pulled on his pants and strode from the pre-fab into a glare of headlights. There were jalopies, dozens of them, outside the fence, all mooring.

Nearing ran to him. "You ought to be in bed, Dr. Novak!" he shouted. "That doctor told us not to let you—"

"Never mind that! What's going on?" yelled Novak, towing Nearing to the gate. The two guards were there—husky kids, blinking in the headlights. They'd been having trouble filling the guard roster, Novak knew. Members were dropping away faster every day.

"Kids from L.A.!" Nearing shouted in his ear. "Came to razz us!"

A rhythmical chant of "O-pen *up!*" began to be heard from the cars over the horns.

Novak bawled at them: "Beat it or we'll fire on you!" He was sure some of them heard it, because they laughed. One improbably blond boy in a jalopy took it personally and butted his car into the rocket field's strong and expensive peripheral fence. It held under one car's cautious assault, but began to give when another tanker joined the blond.

"All right, Eddie!" Novak shouted to the elder of the gate guards. "Take your shotgun and fire over their heads." Eddie nodded dumbly and reached into the sentry box for his gun. He took it out in slow motion and then froze.

Novak could understand, even if he couldn't sympathize. The glaring headlights, the bellowing horns, the methodical butting of the two mastodons, the numbers of them, and their ferocity, "Here," he said, "gimme the goddam thing." He was too sore to be scared; he didn't have time to fool around. The shotgun boomed twice and the youth of America shrieked and wheeled their cars around and fled.

He handed back the shotgun and told Eddie: "Don't be scared, son." He went to the phone in the machine shop and found it was working tonight. People had been cutting the ground line lately.

He got the Stuart home. "Grady? This is Dr. Novak. I want Mr. Stuart right away and please don't tell me it's late and he's not a well man. I know all that. Do what you can for me, will you?"

"I'll try, Dr. Novak."

It was a long, long wait and then the old man's querulous voice said: "God almighty, Novak. You gone crazy? What do you want at this time of night?"

Novak told him what had happened. "If I'm any judge," he said, "we're going to be knee-deep in process servers, sheriff's deputies, and God-knows-what-else by tomorrow morning because I fired over their heads. I want you to dig me up a real, high-class lawyer *and fly him out here tonight.*"

After a moment the old man said: "You were quite right to call me. I'll bully somebody into it. How're you doing?"

"I can't kick. And thanks." He hung up and stood irresolutely for a moment. The night was shot by now—he'd had a good, long rest anyway—

He headed for the refractories lab and worked on the heat of composition. He cracked it at six a.m. and immediately started to compound the big batch of materials that would fuse into the actual throat-liner parts and steering vane. It was a grateful change of pace after working in grams to get going on big stuff. He had it done by ten-thirty and got some coffee.

The lawyer had arrived: a hard-boiled, lantern-jawed San Francisco Italian named DiPietro. "Don't worry," he grimly told Novak. "If necessary, I'll lure them onto the property and plug 'em with my own gun for trespassing. Leave it in my hands."

Novak did, and put in an eighteen-hour stretch on fabricating pieces of the throat liner. Sometime during the day Amy brought him some boxes. He mumbled politely and put them somewhere.

With his joints cracking, he shambled across the field, not noticing that his first automatic gesture on stepping out of the shop into the floodlit area was to measure the *Prototype* with his eye in a kind of salute.

"How'd it go?" he asked DiPietro.

"One dozen assorted," said the lawyer. "They didn't know their law and even if they did I could have bluffed them. The prize was a little piece of jailbait with her daddy and shyster. Your shotgun caused her to miscarry; they were willing to settle out of court for twenty thousand dollars. I told them our bookkeeper will send his bill for five hundred dollars' worth of medical service as soon as he can get around to it."

"More tomorrow?"

"I'll stick around. The word's spread by now, but there may be a couple of die-hards."

Novak said: "Use your judgment. Believe I can do some work on the servos before I hit the sack."

The lawyer looked at him speculatively, but didn't say anything.

CHAPTER SIXTEEN

A MORNING came that was like all other mornings except that there was nothing left to do. Novak wandered disconsolately through the field, poking at details, and Amy came up to him.

"Mike, can I talk to you?"

"Sure," he said, surprised. Was he the kind of guy people asked that kind of question?

"How are the clothes?"

"Clothes?"

"Oh, you didn't even look. Those boxes. I've been shopping for you. I could see you'd never have time for it yourself. You don't mind?"

There it was again. "Look," he said, "have I been snapping people's heads off?"

"Yes," she said in a small voice. "You didn't know that, did you? Do you know you have a week-old beard on you?"

He felt it in wonder.

"I've never seen anything like it," she said. "The things you've accomplished. Maybe nobody ever saw anything like it. It's finished now, isn't it?"

"So it is," he said. "I didn't think—just installing the last liner segment and hooking on the vane. Mechanical oper—

"God, we've done it!" He leaned against one of *Proto's* delta fins, shaking uncontrollably.

"Come on, Mike," she said, taking his arm. She led him to his camp cot and he plunged into sleep.

She was still there when he woke, and brought his coffee and toast. He luxuriated in the little service and then asked abashedly: "Was I pretty bad?"

"You were obsessed. You were barely human for ten days."

"Holland!" he said suddenly, sitting full up. "Did anybody—"

"I've notified him. Everything's going according to plan. Except—you won't be on the moon ship."

"What are you talking about, Amy?"

She smiled brightly. "The counter-campaign. The battle for the public being waged by those cynical, manipulating, wonderful old bastards, Holland and my father. Didn't you guess what my part in it was? I'm a pretty girl, Mike, and pretty girls can sell anything in America. I'm going to be the pilot—hah! pilot!—of the first moon ship. So gallant, so noble, and such a good figure. I'm going to smile nicely and male America will decide that as long as it can't go to bed with me, the least it can do is cheer me on to the Moon."

She was crying. "And then I showed I was my father's daughter. The cynical Miss Stuart said we have a fireworks display in the takeoff, we have conflict and heroism, we have glamour, what we need is some nice refined sex. Let's get that dumb engineer Novak to come along. A loving young couple making the first trip to the Moon. Pretty girl, handsome man—you *are* handsome without that beard, Mike." She was crying too hard to go on. He mechanically patted her shoulder.

Her sobs abated. "Go on," he said.

"Nothing to go on about. I told 'em I wouldn't let you go. I love you too much."

His arm tightened around her. "That's all right," he said. "I love you too much to let you go without me."

She turned her tear-stained face to him. "You're not going to get noble with *me*—" she began. "Ouch! Mike, the beard!"

"I'll shave," he said, getting up and striding to the lab sink.

"Don't cut yourself, Mike," she called after him. "But—please hurry!"

There was one crazy, explosive week.

There was something in it for everybody. It was a public relations man's dream of heaven.

Were you a businessman? "By God, you have to give the old boy credit! Slickest thing I ever heard of—right under the damn Reds' noses, stuck right out there in the desert and they didn't realize that a rocket ship was a rocket ship! And there's a lot of sense in what Holland had to say about red tape. Makes you stop and wonder—the armed services fooling around for twenty years and not getting to first base, but here this private club smacks out a four-bagger first time at bat. Illegal? Illegal? Now mister, be sensible. Don't get me wrong; I'm not any admirer of the late F.D.R., but he did get us the atom bomb even if he did practically hand it to the Reds right after. But my point is, F.D.R. didn't go to Congress with a presidential message that we were going to try to make an atomic bomb. He just quietly diverted the money and made one. Some things you have to do by the book; others you just plain can't. For my money, Dan Holland's a *statesman.*"

Were you a girl? "Oh, that dreamy man Mike! It just chills me when I think of him flying all the way to the Moon, but it's kind of wonderful, too. Did you ever notice the way he's got kind of a dimple but not quite on the left when he smiles?"

Were you a man? "Amy's got real looks and class. Brains, too, they tell me, and God knows, she's got guts. The kind of girl you'd want to *marry,* if you know what I mean. He's a lucky guy."

Were you old folks? "Such a lovely couple. I don't know why more young people aren't like that nowadays. You can see how much they're in love, the way they look at each other. And the idea of them going to the Moon! I certainly never thought I'd see it in my time, though of course I knew that some day... Perhaps their rocket ship won't work. No, that's absurd. Of course it'll work. They look so nice when they smile at each other!"

Were you young folks? "I can't get over it. Just a pair of ordinary Americans like you and me, a couple of good-looking kids that don't give a damn and they're going to shoot off to the Moon. I saw them in the parade and they aren't any different from you and me. I can't get over it."

Were you a newspaper publisher? "Baby, this is *it!* The perfect cure for that tired feeling in the circulation department. I want *Star-Banner-Bugle-and Times-News* to get Mike-and-Amy conscious and stay that way. Pictures, pictures, pictures. Biographies, interviews with roommates, day-by-day coverage, our best woman for Amy and our best man for Mike. The hell with the cost; the country's on a Mike-and-Amy binge. And why shouldn't it be? A couple of nice young kids and they're going to do the biggest thing since the discovery of fire. A landmark in the history of the human race! And confidentially, this is what a lot of boys have been waiting for with Bennet. Naturally only a dirty Red rag would attack a fellow-publisher, but I don't see any ethical duty to keep me from sawing off a limb Bennet crawled out on all by himself. He's mouse-trapped. To keep his hard core of moron readership he's got to keep pretending that *Proto's* still a fake and Holland's still a crook and only taper off slowly. I'm almost sorry for the dirty old man, but he made his bed."

Were you a congressman? "Hmm. Very irregular. In a *strict* sense illegal. Congress controls the money. Damn uppity agencies and commissions. Career men. Mike and Amy. Wonder if I could get a picture with them for my new campaign picture. Hmm."

On the fourth day of the crazy week they were in Washington, in Holland's office.

"How's it going?" he demanded.

"I don't know how MacArthur stood it at his age," Amy muttered.

There was a new addition to Holland's collection of memorabilia on the wall behind his desk: a matted and framed front page from the New York *Times.*

HOLLAND BREAKS SILENCE, CALLS ASFSF NO FRONT
SAYS CLUB HAS MOON SHIP READY TO MAKE TRIP
WILSON STUART DAUGHTER, ENGINEER TO PILOT

The agitation of the *Times* was clearly betrayed in the awkwardly rhyming second line.

"Air Force gentlemen are here, Mr. Holland," said the intercom.

"Send them in, Charlie."

Three standard-brand Air Force colonels, one general and an off-brand captain walked in. The captain looked lost among his senior officers, six-footers all. He was a shrimp.

"Ah, gentlemen. General McGovern, Colonels Ross, Goldthwaite, and Behring. And the man you've been waiting to meet, Captain Dilaccio. Gentlemen, you know Amy and Mike, of course. Be seated."

They sat, and there was an ugly pause. The general exploded, almost with tears in his voice: "*Mister* Holland, for the last time. I will be perfectly frank with you. This is the damn'dest, most unreasonable thing I ever heard of. We have the pilots, we have the navigators, we have the experience, and we ought to have the moon ship!"

Holland said gravely: "No, General. There's no piloting involved. The landing operation simply consists of putting the throat-vane servo on automatic control of the plumb bobs and running in the moderator rods when you hit. The navigation is child's play. True, the target is in motion, but it's big and visible. And you have no experience in moon ships."

"*Mister* Holland—" said the general.

Holland interrupted blandly, "Even if there were logic on your side, is the public deeply interested in logic? I think not. But the public is deeply interested in Amy and Mike. Why, if Amy and Mike were to complain that the Air Force has been less than fair with them—"

His tone was bantering, but McGovern broke in, horrified: "No, no, no, no, Mr. Holland! They aren't going to do anything like that, are they? Are you?"

Holland answered for them, "Of course not, General. They have no reason to do anything like that—do they?"

"Of course not," the general said glumly. "Captain Dilaccio, good luck." He and the colonels shook hands with the puny little captain and filed out.

"Welcome to the space hounds," Novak laughingly told Dilaccio.

The captain said indistinctly: "Pleasure'm sure."

On the flight back to Barstow he didn't say much. They knew he had been chosen because he was (a) a guided-missile specialist, (b) single and with no close relations, (c) small and endowed with a singularly sluggish metabolism. He was slated for the grinding, heartbreaking, soul-chilling job of surviving in a one-man pressure dome until the next trip brought him company and equipment.

On the seventh day of the crazy week, Daniel Holland heard somebody behind him say irritably: "Illegal? Illegal? No more illegal than Roosevelt raking funds and developing the atomic bomb. Should he have gone to Congress with a presidential message about it? It was the only way to do it, that's all."

Holland smiled faintly. It had gone over. The old cliches in their mouths had been replaced by new cliches. The sun blazed into his eyes from the polished shell of the moon ship, but he didn't turn or squint. He was at least a sub-hero today.

He caught site of MacIlheny as the band struck up the sedate, "President's March." MacIlheny was on the platform, as befitted the top man of the A.S.F.S.F., though rather far out on one of the wings. MacIlheny was crying helplessly. He had thought he might be the third man, but he was big-bodied and knew nothing about guided missiles. What good was an insurance man in the Moon?

The President spoke for five minutes limiting himself to one comic literary allusion. ("This purloined letter—stainless steel, thirty-six-feet tall, plainly visible for sixty miles.") Well, *he* was safely assured of his place in history. No matter what miracles of statesmanship in war or peace he performed, as long as he was remembered he would be remembered as President during the first moon flight. The applause was polite for him, and then slowly swelled. Amy and Mike were walking arm in arm down a hollow column of M.P.s, Marines and A.F.P.s. Captain Dilaccio trailed a little behind them. The hollow column led from the shops to the gantry standing beside *Proto*.

Holland felt his old friend's hand grip his wrist. "Getting soft, Wilson?" he muttered out of the corner of his mouth.

The old man wouldn't be kidded. "I didn't know it would be like this," he said hoarsely. Amy's jacket was a bright red patch as the couple mounted the stand and shook hands with the President. Senile tears were running down Wilson Stuart's face. Great day for weeping, Holland thought sullenly. All I did was hand the U.S. the Moon on a silver platter and everybody's sobbing about it.

The old man choked: "Crazy kid. Daniel, what if she doesn't come back?"

There was nothing to say about that. But—"She's waving at you, Wilson!" Holland said sharply. "Wave back!" The old man's hand fluttered feebly. Holland could see that Amy had already turned to speak to the President. God, he thought. They're *hard*.

"Did she see me, Dan?"

"Yes. She threw you a big grin. She's a wonderful kid, Wilson." Glad I never had any. *And* sorry, too, of course. It isn't that easy, ever, is it? Isn't this show ever going to get on the road?

The M.P.s, Marines, and A.F.P.s reformed their lines and began to press back the crowd. Jeeps began to tow the big, wheeled reviewing stand slowly from the moon ship. With heartbreaking beauty of flowing line, Amy swung herself from the platform to the hoist of the gantry crane. Mike stepped lightly across the widening gap and Captain Dilaccio—had the President even spoken to him?—jumped solidly. Mike waved at the craneman and the hoist rose with its three passengers. It stopped twenty-five-feet up, and there was clearly a bit of high-spirited pantomime, Alphonse-and-Gaston stuff, at the man-hole. Amy crawled through first and then she was gone. Then Dilaccio and then Novak, and they all were gone. The manhole cover began to close, theatrically slow.

"Why are we here?" Novak wondered dimly as the crescent of aperture became knifelike, razorlike, and then vanished. What road did I travel from Canarsie to here? Aloud he said: "Preflight check; positions, please." His voice sounded apologetic. They hunkered down under the gothic dome in the sickly light of a six-watt bulb. Like cave people around a magic tree stump they squatted around the king-post top that grew from the metal floor.

"Oxygen-C02 cycle," he said.

That was Dilaccio's. He opened the valve and said, "Check."

"Heater." He turned it on himself and muttered, "Check."

Novak took a deep breath. "Well, next comes fuel metering and damper rods—oh, I forgot. Amy, is the vane servo locked vertical?"

"Check," she said.

"Right. Now, the timers are set for thirty seconds, which is ample for us to get to the couches. But I'd feel easier if you two started now so there won't be any possibility of a tangle."

Amy and Dilaccio stood, cramped under the steep-sloping roof. The captain swung into his couch. Amy touched Mike's hand and climbed to hers. There was a flapping noise of web belting.

"Check."

"All secure," said Dilaccio.

"Very good. *One*—and *two.*" The clicks and the creak of cordage as he swung into his couch seemed very loud.

Time to think at last. Canarsie, Troy, Corning, Steubenville, Urbana, N.E.P.A., Chicago, L. A., Barstow—and now the Moon. He was here because his parents had died, because he had inherited skills and acquired others, because of the leggy tough sophomore from Troy Women's Day, because Holland had dared, because he and Amy were in love, because a Hanford fission product had certain properties, because MacIlheny was MacIlheny—

Acceleration struck noiselessly; they left their sound far behind.

After a spell of pain there was a spell of discomfort. Light brighter than the six-watt bulb suddenly flooded the steeple-shaped room. The aerodynamic nose had popped off, unmasking their single port. You still couldn't pick yourself up. It was like one of those drunks when you think you're clearheaded and are surprised to find you can't move.

She should have spent more time with her father, he thought. Maybe she was afraid it would worry him. Well, he was back there now with the rest of them. Lilly, paying somehow, somewhere, for what she had done. Holland paying somehow for what he had done. MacIlheny paying. Wilson Stuart paying.

"Mike," said Amy's voice.

"All right, Amy. You?"

"I'm all right."

The captain said: "All right here."

A common shyness seemed to hold them all, as though each was afraid of opening the big new ledger with a false or trivial entry.

THE END

If you've enjoyed this book, you will not want to miss these terrific titles...

ARMCHAIR SCI-FI & HORROR DOUBLE NOVELS, $12.95 each

D-31   **A HOAX IN TIME** by Keith Laumer
            INSIDE EARTH by Poul Anderson

D-32   **TERROR STATION** by Dwight V. Swain
            THE WEAPON FROM ETERNITY by Dwight V. Swain

D-33   **THE SHIP FROM INFINITY** by Edmond Hamilton
            TAKEOFF by C. M. Kornbluth

D-34   **THE METAL DOOM** by David H. Keller
            TWELVE TIMES ZERO by Howard Browne

D-35   **HUNTERS OUT OF SPACE** by Joseph Kelleam
            INVASION FROM THE DEEP by Paul W. Fairman,

D-36   **THE BEES OF DEATH** by Robert Moore Williams
            A PLAGUE OF PYTHONS by Frederick Pohl

D-37   **THE LORDS OF QUARMALL** by Fritz Leiber and Harry Fischer
            BEACON TO ELSEWHERE by James H. Schmitz

D-38   **BEYOND PLUTO** by John S. Campbell
            ARTERY OF FIRE by Thomas N. Scortia

D-39   **SPECIAL DELIVERY** by Kris Neville
            NO TIME FOR TOFFEE by Charles F. Meyers

D-40   **JUNGLE IN THE SKY** by Milton Lesser
            RECALLED TO LIFE by Robert Silverberg

ARMCHAIR SCIENCE FICTION CLASSICS, $12.95 each

C-10   **MARS IS MY DESTINATION**
            by Frank Belknap Long

C-11   **SPACE PLAGUE**
            by George O. Smith

C-12   **SO SHALL YE REAP**
            by Rog Phillips

ARMCHAIR SCI- FI & HORROR GEMS SERIES, $12.95 each

G-3   **SCIENCE FICTION GEMS, Vol. Two**
           James Blish and others

G-4   **HORROR GEMS, Vol. Two**
           Joseph Payne Brennan and others

Made in United States
Orlando, FL
27 January 2025

57867713R10136

4-22